Urban Dragon

Volume 2

by

JW Troemner

First Edition November 2016

Cover design by Deranged Doctor Designs

ISBN 978-1-945182-01-3

For Andrew, who gave me hope,

for Tane, who gave Arkay her chair,

and for the woman with knitting needles on the edge of the

circle

Table of Contents

Book 4:

Potnia Theron

Adam

From the outside, the Chicago headquarters of the Order of Saint Michael of the Sun didn't look much different than any of the other office buildings in the area. It was perfectly hidden— a single tree in a forest. The marble-floored lobby maintained the illusion, but careful eyes could spot runes and sigils worked into the polished mosaic on the walls.

The constant noise of urban traffic softened to a faint buzz as I stepped inside. The regular door at the side entrance was only for show, sealed as tightly as the bullet-resistant glass lining the first floor. Any attackers would have to go through the revolving door, and that meant they'd have to enter in ones and twos— easy pickings for the receptionist and security.

I nodded at the woman at the desk and crossed the lobby with my head held high, all too aware of the cameras that took in my every move. I'd handled my situation to the best of my ability. I had nothing to hide. If I projected confidence, then the Synod would understand that. They would support the decisions I made.

I reached the elevator and swiped my badge against the RFID reader.

Nothing happened. The light remained red. The elevator doors remained shut.

I pushed the 'UP' button, just in case.

Still nothing.

I tried again, faster this time. Then slower. Then in a different order.

Still no change.

Alright. Just a minor setback. I marched to the receptionist's desk, and the woman there surveyed me with a carefully composed neutrality.

"My name is Adam Preston. ID number A83-9119." The receptionist turned her attention to her computer. Her expression didn't change. "I have an appointment at eleven-thirty."

"Adam Preston." Her gaze returned to me, as sphinxine as before.

It's one of the security measures, I told myself. Forcing a time delay like this could frighten an impostor into revealing themselves. It would give security ample chance to prepare a counter attack.

Or it could be the incompetence of a bored receptionist. One or the other.

"Yes?" she asked.

For the love of all that's holy... "Could you please let me up?"

She reached under her desk and tapped out an intricate pattern on a hidden keypad. Across the lobby, the central elevator finally swept open. "Go ahead."

I maintained my dignity long enough for the elevator doors to shut behind me, and then I dug my phone out of my pocket. 11:26. Assuming there were no more issues, I could still make it in time. But the delay unnerved me. My badge should have given me access to the elevator. Not to the highest floors, of course, but I should at least have managed to get inside.

Maybe I'd damaged the RFID somehow. I had gotten in a fist fight with a river dragon not too long ago, so maybe there'd been an electrical surge I hadn't noticed. Or maybe this building required enough security that even badge-wearing members couldn't get inside without special clearance.

Or maybe they'd revoked my access already.

I swallowed and straightened, checking my composure in the mirrored walls.

On the twenty-third floor, the elevator opened into a claustrophobic hallway with a ceiling so low I could touch it. More defensive runes formed a border along the top of the wall and at the edges of the thick carpet underfoot. The rest of the wall space was taken up by brass memorial plates. They were only a few inches wide, but there were so many the walls blazed with fiery hues all the way to the end of the hall. Each plate was inscribed with a name and a date, starting sometime in the fifteenth century and steadily advancing to the modern day, and each one represented a death. A soldier of the Order who had fallen in the fight against the beasts of the world lurking in the shadows.

This was our calling. To stand between monsters and mankind.

A Polynesian woman glanced at me from behind yet another desk, but thankfully she seemed more interested in helping me than the previous receptionist. She shooed me through another set of doors and into a larger, more spacious room.

On the far wall stood a mural of the archangel Michael, a golden sun radiating like a halo behind his head. Pinned under one foot was the first dragon, from whom all others traced their ancestry: Satan himself.

Floor-to-ceiling windows offered an impressive view of the city, stained sepia by the tinted glass. Six people sat at a long table. They watched me with imperial stares as I took my seat across from them. They were cast almost into silhouette by the bright light from outside, but I recognized a few by shape: Mara Kovak, a retired field agent and my handler, who watched me so intently she might have been trying to think secret messages directly into my head; Emmanuel Gage, the Grand Master under whom I served, a stern man with hawkish eyes; and a severe woman with a curtain of silver hair beneath an embroidered shawl. I had only ever seen her in photographs, but my stomach dropped at the sight of her. Archduchess Gianna Stavros. A member of the High Council.

That's the moment when it finally sank in: I was in trouble.

I tried to read their expressions as Gage presented me to the Synod and read aloud my charges, but their shadowed faces gave away nothing. Finally Gage ceded the floor to me, and I stood before them.

"Fourteen months ago, I was called to investigate a rash of demonic activity in Santa Fe. I ascertained recent construction activity liberated a minor demon that had previously been imprisoned in an old chapel's walls, and it subsequently targeted a local priest. He fled, and in June I was finally able to corner him and the demon in an abandoned factory in Indianapolis. There I found the demon already in active conflict with a female Japanese river dragon and a human woman by the name of Rosario Hernandez. Upon further investigation, I was able to surmise that neither was affiliated with the Hoarde, or any other major monstrous organization."

"How did you reach that conclusion?" asked Gage.

"I didn't have a chance to speak to the dragon—"

"Obviously," said Gage.

I tried not to be disheartened by yet another interruption. "Rosario Hernandez struck me as inexperienced. She very obviously had no knowledge of monsters beyond the purely practical. The finer details of exorcism seemed to be completely beyond her understanding, and she hadn't conducted any sort of investigation into the matter. All evidence indicates that she and her dragon just barged onto the scene and expected to be able to handle it."

"Which, according to your report, she did." Archduchess Stavros folded her long, spindly hands in front of her. Deep scars crossed the protruding veins— trophies of a long and storied career on the field.

I didn't get the chance to reply before Gage spoke again. "You could have killed the dragon while it was possessed. You didn't."

"I couldn't," I corrected quickly. "I included in my report that it destroyed my weapons and ammunition shortly after it killed the priest." Nobody made any attempt to point out my lie. Hopefully that meant they hadn't fact checked that particular detail when they scoured the rest of my report. "The only firearm I had left was of an insufficient caliber to take down a creature of that size."

"Even after the exorcism?"

I'd practiced this. "After the exorcism, the dragon was still visibly feral."

"And you left it alive," said Gage. "In the middle of a densely populated urban area. Do you have any idea the amount of damage control that would have been necessary if it had manifested in front of civilians?"

Of course I did. That was the point. "I believed attacking it in that condition would have pushed it into a full rampage, which would have escalated the threat of discovery from possible to unavoidable, with massive casualties. In its current state, it wasn't hurting anyone," I said before I could stop myself, and then quickly amended. "I mean that literally. After the exorcism, it laid down beside Hernandez and refused to move until paramedics arrived. Its reactions to my approach after that point were still consistent with a feral dragon, but subdued. Its stance was clearly defensive, rather than aggressive, to the point that the paramedics noted nothing unusual or inhuman about its nature."

Archduchess Stavros hummed with interest. "And is that when you formed your theory regarding Hernandez?"

"It only confirmed what I already believed to be true. The demon had previously identified her as such."

"Demons lie," she said.

I shook my head. "With all due respect, Your Grace, I don't believe it was lying about Hernandez. She rebuked a demon without tokens or training. She successfully commanded a possessed dragon to give us the demon's name, and completely obliterated the demon in the process. She persuaded a ghoul to be her landlady. She held weekly dinner parties for one of the largest and most diverse known gatherings of monsters in the region, outside of known monstrous organizations. There is no doubt in my mind that Rosario Hernandez was a Potnia Theron."

The revelation should have been stunning. Others like her had been suspected over the years, but the last confirmed Potnia Theron had died in the eighteen hundreds. Finding such a rare and valuable specimen could make a career.

"*Was*," Gage said. "Before you shot her."

And shooting her could end it.

I looked down. "That was an accident, Sir."

"It says here that you requisitioned funds to cover Hernandez' hospital bills after the incident in June," Gage continued.

"She was unwilling to go to a hospital otherwise," I said. "And if you look further, you'll see that I used the opportunity to procure samples which prove my theory—"

"Support, not prove," Gage corrected.

"Ahem. Yes. *Support* my theory that a Potnia Theron is human. Which, of course, could potentially have far-reaching—"

"You aren't here to argue your theories," Gage said sharply. "You're here to defend your behavior during the past six months."

I bristled. Did he have to keep interrupting me? "Yes, Sir."

"I recall you were given permission to pursue further investigation into the Hernandez girl," said Archduchess Stavros. "Yet you refused to bring her in for further testing."

"She had a notable distrust of organized authority," I said. "She'd already fled the scene of one similar incident. I believed that bringing in other agents might spook her into disappearing again, or that she would use her dragon to force a violent confrontation. I believed that regardless of immediate outcome, her value as an asset would be diminished as a result. My hope was to persuade her to see reason and join our side. And I believe she was close to taking that position."

"Before you shot her," Gage said.

I clenched my teeth. "Yes, Sir."

The Archduchess extended one hand. "Continue your report, Preston."

"Yes, Your Grace." I tried to keep my breathing level. "In the report, you'll find that assisting Hernandez with her healthcare gave me an opening to continue my investigation. Hernandez was under the impression that I was, in her words, a supernatural social worker, and I encouraged the belief. While I performed in that capacity, she was willing to divulge personal information about herself and the dragon, as well as ancillary detail about the other monsters with which she kept regular company."

She hadn't just been willing to talk to me, she'd been eager. To Arkay and Father Gabriel, she had projected the unruffled calm of authority. To the ever-increasing number of monsters who visited her home, she had played the perfect neophyte, open-minded and free of judgment. Only to me could she express her biases and anxieties. Only to me could she ask her most secret questions— the ones that began with "I know this is none of my business, but…" and ended with the kind of relief known only to sinners after confession.

She'd respected me. She'd trusted me.

So much so that those had been her last words.

Archduchess Stavros broke me out of my thoughts. "Explain your dealings with Emilio Paternoster."

"He was a smalltime crook with ambitions of consolidating the local drug market into a criminal empire. He attempted to take over a local…" I glanced at Archduchess Stavros. "…gentleman's club… to be his first money laundering operation. It also happened to be the establishment at which the dragon was employed."

Gage raised a hawkish eyebrow. "As security?"

"As an…" I cleared my throat. "Entertainer."

The Archduchess gave another interested hum. "You left that out of the report."

"I believed the detail to be irrelevant," I said quickly, trying to keep the red off my face. The Archduchess was the highest authority on the continent. How the hell was I supposed to explain to her that the dragon I'd been hunting moonlighted as a stripper? "Upon hearing about the incident, I approached Paternoster and advised him on the best way to pursue a confrontation."

"You encouraged a civilian to get in a fight with a dragon?" asked another member of the council— a slight man with sharp eyes and a copper complexion.

My handler finally spoke up in my defense. "These weren't innocent bystanders. Paternoster was an aspiring mobster who employed junkies and street thugs. He and the members of his organization were approved by headquarters as acceptable casualties."

I tried to communicate my gratitude with a glance, but I kept it quick. I didn't want the rest of the Synod to think Mara was showing more support than necessary.

"I've read the report, Kovak," the man said. "I've also read the part where you gave clearance for two ambushes in a residential area, as well as the arson of a civilian building."

"The gentleman's club and its employees were harboring a dragon," said the Archduchess. Her voice took on a dangerous edge. "They were hardly civilian." She fixed me with a long, judicious stare and steepled her fingers. "However, Grandmaster Burns is not without a point. Your recommended tactics are questionable. Explain your reasoning."

"Your Grace, my methods were thoroughly researched, and based on campaigns that successfully brought down dragons in 1953, 1876, 1841, and—"

"I don't want to see your footnotes," she said sharply. "Explain your reasoning."

"Yes, Your Grace." I swallowed and tried to reorganize my thoughts. "I believed the traditional methods for dispatching a dragon to be unsuited to a populated area. The terrain didn't provide sufficient cover, a resulting rampage would have resulted in countless civilian casualties, and the local environmental conditions make it nearly impossible to blame it on natural phenomenon. I orchestrated the first ambush so that the dragon wouldn't perceive its attackers as a sufficient threat to warrant a rampage. The attack would be seen as challenging, exhausting, but not overwhelming."

All the while I'd been on standby with an anti-material rifle in hand and Rosario on the phone, in case I'd miscalculated.

"Before the dragon had a chance to recover from the fight, I advised Paternoster to fortify his own home against an attack and burn down the club. As predicted, the dragon retaliated with a tightly controlled rampage, focused specifically on Paternoster and his men. Meanwhile, I collected Hernandez and brought her to Paternoster's house."

That had been my final gamble, and I'd bet my life on it. If Rosario really wasn't a Potnia Theron, then Arkay would have mowed through us both without a second thought.

Instead, Rosario had halted a dragon's killing spree with a single word.

It was no wonder that people used to believe Potnia Theron to be goddesses. There had been something almost spiritual about the way Rosario had spoken to Arkay. Not with fear, not with the wheedling reassurances of a hostage negotiator, but with the unflinching conviction of a martyr.

Which, as it turned out, hadn't been all that far from the reality.

"At that point I had spent months priming Hernandez to recognize the necessity of putting down a dragon, and she'd been generally receptive. Seeing the result of the rampage should have been enough to cement that idea in her head. I believed that Hernandez could subdue the dragon while I put a bullet in its head— at which point Hernandez would return with me to headquarters for a proper debriefing. I believed that she could be persuaded to join the Order."

Having a Potnia Theron on our side would have changed everything. We could find out the source of her influence over monsters— maybe even extend it to the Order's ground troops. It would be better than a weapon, better than battle armor. It would mean near invincibility against our most vicious enemies.

"But that didn't happen," Gage said.

"I believe that it would have worked," I said quietly. "But Paternoster and his brother blew my cover before I got the chance. The dragon attacked me, and—"

"And you shot Hernandez." Gage ground the words between his teeth. Aside from Mara, he'd been my loudest supporter. My success would have accelerated his career almost as much as it would have mine.

I lowered my eyes. "Yes, Sir."

My failure had damned us both.

Arkay

"Arkay, put the nice doctor down."

The nice doctor's fingernails scratched uselessly against my hands. He kicked, but his toes barely skidded the linoleum tile of the hospital room floor.

"He didn't mean to upset you," Rosario continued from beside him. "There's a protocol he has to follow in these situations. He's just doing his job."

A whimper escaped the doctor's collapsing trachea.

"Come on, Arkay. I taught you better than this. Put him down. Please."

Slowly I peeled my fingers off his throat. He slid down the wall to the floor, choking and gasping for breath.

"There you go," Rosario said. "It would help if you said you were sorry."

I wasn't sorry.

"Now answer his question," she prompted me, sounding absurdly like a kindergarten teacher.

"Rosario Hernandez will not be donating her organs to anyone," I said through clenched teeth. "Because you won't be taking her off life support. Is that clear?"

The doctor stared up at me with bulging eyes. His throat was raw and red. He'd be seeing my fingerprints there for days. "Yes," he rasped. It sounded an awful lot like "please don't kill me." He didn't look at Rosario. He couldn't see her, but I did. She was always in the corner of my eye, tall and soft and exasperated.

Even though she wasn't actually there.

My anger dissolved, taking with it the burst of adrenaline that had kept me on my feet. Weary, I staggered back to my spot in the uncomfortable hospital chair. The real Rosario lay on her side before me, hooked up to the web of IVs and feeding tubes that kept her alive.

That's how I knew the voice wasn't her ghost: she wasn't dead yet. I'd managed to get her to the hospital in time to save her, but not before blood loss had irreparably damaged her brain. Ischaemic hypoxia, the doctors called it. A persistent vegetative state.

The doctor fled the room, and the world went fuzzy at the edges, growing dimmer and hazier around the focal point of Rosario's face. Gingerly I stroked her long, dark hair, careful not to pull it. I didn't want to hurt her.

Not again.

Not ever again.

Adam

The bar was small, tucked into a space that might have been an alley and decorated in imitation of an old-fashioned speakeasy. I hunched over the counter, running my finger in endless circles over the rim of the glass. I needed another whiskey, but the bartender was busy. A businessman was having a nervous breakdown in the back corner, despite the comforting words from the muscular woman beside him. If he kept drinking at that pace, he'd probably die of alcohol poisoning before the drink had a chance to properly soothe his nerves.

I considered saying something, but returned to tracing circles around the edge of my glass. Not my problem. Besides, the receptionist outside the interrogation room had given me paperwork to fill out before I left.

I stared at the page until the first words came into focus.

Name: Adam Preston

DOB: Sept. 3, 1994

ID No.: A83-9119

Rank: ________

My pen hesitated over the blank line. What was my rank anymore? Had it changed without my knowing, like my building access?

Would it be presumptuous to put my old rank on the line? Would a question mark make them think I wasn't taking this seriously? Would leaving it blank suggest that I just didn't care?

I tapped the pen against the page, leaving a stippled pattern on the edge of the paper. Dammit, that was definitely going to look bad. I'd need to get another. Unless I didn't have access to that floor anymore?

With the paper already ruined, I let my pen roam over the page, connecting letters together with sharp, straight lines that turned into nonsensical geometric patterns. As I fidgeted, the lines grew thicker and duller, coming together to form a crude silhouette of a long desk lined with dark, judicial shapes. My pen traced the shapes over and over again. With each pass they grew bigger, until they stretched out to cover the paper.

My thoughts were interrupted by the rhythmic tap of a cane, and my handler settled onto the stool beside me. She was broad-shouldered and toned, with long brown hair pulled into a ponytail rather than cut regulation short. It was a luxury she could afford, now that she wasn't directly on the field anymore.

Mara glanced at the page in front of me. "Is that what you've been doing to our paperwork all this time?"

"No." I flipped the page over, covering the texture on the back of the page with my hand. "I was just letting off steam."

"And here I thought that was what the drink was for." She set her cane against the bar. "You got room for one more?"

"Depends," I said. "Did that go as badly as I think it did?"

As my handler, Mara's reputation had been butchered in the same stroke as my own, but I'd been holding out hope for her sake. After all, she hadn't made the fatal mistake the way I had, and she'd never had any real political presence to tarnish. Her time on the field had ended when she'd been subdued by a soucouyant in San Fernando. She'd managed to bring the monster down, but not before it had peeled the skin off her left leg. It wasn't a story she talked about, but that hadn't stopped it from spreading through the Order's ranks in hushed whispers. What she lacked in authority, she made up for with sheer respect.

Hopefully she could still use that to her advantage.

She raised her hand to flag down some service. "Can I get a Jack Daniels over here?"

"Make that two." I raised my empty glass for emphasis.

The bartender finally begrudged us our drinks, and he went back to comforting the businessman.

"That bad?" I asked.

Mara took a swig and grimaced. "The good news is that the Archduchess likes your theory. She's putting in orders to collect tissue samples from the hospital where Hernandez is being kept. Within a couple of weeks, we should know for sure if she's actually human."

"Here's to small victories." I raised my glass, and she gave me a halfhearted toast.

People like Rosario Hernandez had always been on the verge of legend, which made it difficult to sift truth from fantasy. The term Potnia Theron had only really come into use in the late fourteenth century. Before that point, people with similar abilities had gone by other names— virgin, if they were young and beautiful; saint, if they were revered; witch, if they weren't. Alleged reports went back for thousands of years, but we still didn't know exactly what they were or how they functioned.

I'd read up on the existing theories: that they could entrance monsters through direct eye contact like poludnica, or that they had a siren's hypnotic voice, or a succubus' weaponized pheromones. All of those theories began with the assumption that Potnia Theron were a variety of monster themselves, but I had met Rosario. I'd spoken to her. She'd wrestled a demonically-possessed dragon to save me, and she'd done it without any special abilities. All she'd had was her own gumption and a need to do the right thing.

So I'd put forward a theory of my own. If Potnia Theron were human, then maybe their hold over monsters was far less concrete than we'd come to believe. Maybe they were ordinary people who had— for whatever reason— decided to befriend maneating monsters, and managed to earn loyalty in return.

The theory had problems, of course. The kind of loyalty Potnia Theron commanded was beyond what most monsters were capable of feeling, for one. But I was a soldier, not an anthropologist. It wasn't my job to sit around and think about these things.

Mara tapped on the counter with her cane to reclaim the bartender's attention. "Two more!" She signaled with her remaining fingers, then returned her attention to me. "So there's a problem."

"Of course there is," I said.

"The Archduchess thinks that if you're right and Hernandez just has a magnetic personality, then it'll work on more than monsters."

"Meaning what?"

"Meaning there was a second witness at that mobster's house, and the Archduchess has been questioning him day and night. According to him, you had a good dozen chances to take down the dragon. You didn't."

I tried to put down my glass, but almost knocked it over instead. "I would have endangered civilian—"

"Not the way he tells it," she said. "It's not just that, either. You were given expressed permission to bring Hernandez in for further examination. You didn't do that, either."

"I didn't want—"

"Don't try to justify it, Adam. You were concerned for her mental and emotional wellbeing, and you made that your first priority."

"What's wrong with that?" I asked, feeling uneasy.

"You were on assignment. You were dealing with a *dragon*, for God's sake. That calls for speed and precision, and you hesitated on multiple occasions. The problem isn't that some mobster blew your cover, the problem is you let it get to the point where he could. You were standing right behind the fucking dragon, and you could have pulled the trigger. You didn't. Not until the last possible second."

"I was trying to cultivate an asset," I stammered.

"So you've told me," she said. "So you've kept telling me as long as we've been on this assignment." She drained her glass with another grimace. "But I can't help but wonder: was she your asset, or were you hers?"

"No." The word slipped out as a reflex, more than as an answer. The accusation— the *insinuation*— "No! I'm a good soldier. I'm loyal—"

"I know," Mara said. "God help me, I know. I want to believe you're on our side. But now the question's in the air, and the rest of the Synod isn't so sure."

"Then let me prove it." My knuckles were white around my glass. The Order was everything to me. It had been as long as I could remember. Its compounds had been my home. Its ranks my family. "Have them test me. Whatever it is they want, I'll do it."

"I know," she said.

"Mara, please—" She raised a hand, and I fell silent.

"I've already said my piece."

I choked back a breath.

"The Synod is giving you a chance to finish this assignment. Properly."

"I can do that," I said hastily. "Of course I can. I'd want nothing more—"

"You don't understand," she said. "There won't be any second chances. There won't be another opportunity to regroup. You're going to kill this dragon, or you're going to die trying."

Arkay

A new scent cut between the astringent antiseptic of the hospital and the subdued notes of Rosario's body. Roses. Beneath that, lavender lotion and almond milk and the odd inhuman scent of ghoul.

I looked up, and it took my eyes a moment to adjust to the light. "Danielle."

"Hey, Arkay." She set a vase of burgundy roses on the bedside table and offered me a thin smile. She was beautiful, all cinnamon and mahogany, with a slender neck and large, haunting eyes. She never looked quite the same two days in a row— like all ghouls, she slowly took on the qualities of the last people she'd eaten— but the subtle shifts in her appearance only made her more striking. Maybe working as a coroner meant she got to choose from the prettiest corpses for her meals.

Or maybe I thought of her as beautiful because Rosario had decided she was.

"Is everything okay?" Danielle asked gently. "Security's circling again."

"I think I strangled a doctor," I said.

"You think? You mean you don't know?"

"He wanted to take her off her tubes."

Danielle's face fell. "Arkay..."

"It's okay," I said. "I fixed it. They won't be taking her anywhere."

A silence fell between us.

Danielle traced her fingers across the palm of Rosario's hand. She was answered with the slight twitch of a thumb. Hope flickered in Danielle's eyes.

"It's a reflex," I said, answering the unspoken question. "She's not really waking up."

I'd called the nurses the first time Rosario had moved in response to touch, and they'd explained the automatic responses to me. It still took a couple more frantic attacks on the call button before it sank in, though.

Danielle bit her lip. "Arkay, how long has it been since you've slept?"

I didn't answer.

"Those are the same clothes I brought you when you got out of the ICU," she said. "Have you been home since then?"

"I need to be here."

"It's okay," she said. "They'll call you if there's any change." She laid her hand on my shoulder. The sudden warmth reminded me just how cold they kept this room most of the time. I wanted to lean into her hand and bask in that warmth.

Instead, I pulled away from her touch. "The nurses aren't doing their jobs right. They're supposed to turn her every two to three hours. They're always late."

"Maybe they want to give you some privacy," Danielle offered. It was a nice thought, but too generous. More likely they were scared of me, and kept putting off their duties as long as they could get away with it.

Lots of people were scared of me. More than I'd realized.

Rosario had been one of them.

"Hey. Arkay. Look at me." Danielle leaned into my field of view and reeled in my wandering thoughts. "If Rosa were awake right now, she'd tell you to take care of yourself. She'd say you should go home right now and get some sleep and some real food in you. Because she loves you, Arkay. She wouldn't want you to keep doing this to yourself."

"She's not wrong," said the apparition in the corner of my eye.

"I know what she wants," I said. "But she needs me here. In case Adam comes back."

"Oh. You don't mean..." Her voice became small. Hesitant. "Has he come here? Since..." She bit her lip, searching for the right words.

"No," I said quietly. If he had come back, they would still be scrubbing his gray matter off the ceiling.

So far, the only ones who had come had been the police. They kept wanting to know what happened at the house, instead of focusing on the important details: Adam had shot

Rosa, and he was still out there somewhere. It had been a frustrating few hours that ended in a hastily aborted investigation. Infuriating. But I'd kept calm. I didn't snarl or bare my teeth or punch through any walls.

I kept still. I behaved myself. Because Rosa wanted me to.

I laid my head on Rosa's lap, but Danielle tugged me upright again.

"Rosa's going to be alright," she said gently. "They're going to take good care of her here, okay? So how about we get you to a more comfortable bed."

"I'm fine here," I grumbled, but I let her shepherd me out of the room.

I was tired of fighting.

Adam

Rather than setting up and fortifying a new base of operations, the entire six-man team moved into my existing setup, in the office floors above an abandoned department store. Five new cots and a pile of regulation duffel bags joined my own, clustering in the opposite end of the open space that had once been a break room, far away from the flashbangs and EMP bombs that had been plastered into the walls in case of a breach. Mara had been moved in to oversee the entire operation. Supervising her was a lean man named Weiss, who reported our actions directly to the Synod. In addition, we'd gained an aspiring commander named Caitlin Burke, and Tyrone Green, an ex-undercover operative who'd suffered a string of failures too major to be ignored, but as of yet too minor to get him killed. The last member of our team was a fierce-eyed woman named Monica Sharp, a police detective who'd lost her badge after a confrontation with Arkay about a year back. The fact that she'd survived the encounter at all spoke to her talent, but that was all the more reason to keep her off the team. Casualties were guaranteed on the field, but the death toll climbed notoriously high on dragon hunts. Positions like ours were reserved for the ambitious and the expendable.

I had been the former; now I was the latter.

The manager's office had been outfitted with half a dozen computer screens, each of them linked to the surveillance cameras I'd installed around town. Half the cameras covered the house Rosario had been living in for the past year; the rest of the cameras watched the exits of her girlfriend's home, the bar where the two of them worked, and the burnt-out husk of a strip club.

I tapped at the last screens. "The dragon won't be returning to this location anytime soon. We're better off moving these cameras to the hospital. Do we know what room they've got Hernandez in?"

Burke and Green exchanged uneasy glances. They didn't want to be seen cooperating with an accused traitor, even if I was officially on probation. Weiss fixed me with an unchanging stare.

Was this how it was going to be from now on? Could I not even offer helpful input without scrutiny?

"Where did they put Hernandez?" Mara asked, rescuing me from my humiliation.

"Room 2305, in the ICU," said Sharp. "They've beefed up security in that wing, though. That may make setting up cameras a challenge."

"We'll put it on the to-do list," Mara said. "Burke, Green, I want you to get out there and take down the cameras from the strip club. Adam, what's your say on the bar? Do we need to take those down, too?"

"Not yet. Ar— the dragon spent enough time there socializing. That might not change now that Hernandez is out of the picture. I recommend keeping them up until a new pattern of behavior is established."

"All right, let's get moving. Adam, Sharp, you two stay on watch. I want to know the minute the dragon comes back into our sights."

Arkay

After we left the hospital, Danielle took a brief detour to her house to pick up a tuna casserole she'd made me. It was a nice gesture. I thought about thanking her. But for the rest of the ride I only stared at the foil covering the dish. Rosa had never made casseroles before, if you didn't count enchiladas, but I'd heard about them. They were the kind of thing people gave to somebody who was grieving.

The car stopped. I only realized it when Danielle walked around to my side and took the casserole off my lap.

When I opened the door, the house was unchanged. There were no white shrouds over the furniture. No sad musician had painted the doors black. It hadn't even stood unoccupied long enough to gather more than the usual layer of dust. It looked normal, like Rosario had spent the night at her girlfriend's house, rather than at the hospital.

Danielle disappeared into the kitchen with the casserole, and I heard a brief clatter and the beeping of a microwave before she returned.

"Sorry I had to nuke it," she said, setting a plate of steaming casserole on the table. "But I figured you'd want to sleep sooner rather than later."

"That's fine. I'll eat it when I get up."

Danielle leaned in, her expression crumpled in concern. "Arkay, when's the last time you ate?"

I didn't have an answer for her. It could have been that morning, or three days ago. Time got kind of funny inside a hospital room.

She pulled up a chair for me. "Come on. Just have a little, and then I'll get out of your hair."

I sighed and sat in front of her, pointedly dragging a forkful of colorless mush into my mouth. I could taste the fish, the cream, the butter, the spray of Mrs. Dash. The components were all there— and most of them animal proteins that Danielle couldn't actually eat, being a ghoul— but the flavors felt like words in a language I couldn't read.

I had to remind myself how to swallow.

Something in the back of my head remembered exactly how long it had been since I'd last stopped at the hospital's vending machine, and it urged me to take more. But what I'd eaten settled uncomfortably in my stomach. I felt nauseous.

"So," she said, grasping at straws. "You said his name was Adam?"

"Adam Smith, he said."

She frowned. "It's a pretty common name."

"Probably fake," I agreed.

He'd specifically asked Rosario and Father Gabriel not to mention him and his organization to their friends. He'd said it had to do with confidentiality.

Fuck confidentiality.

"He said he was part of the Order of Saint Michael of the Sun." The mouthful of words came out in a single putrid mass, like puss from an infection. "Ever heard of them?"

Danielle's face lost its color.

"I'll take that as a yes."

"They're… they're not nice people," she said, checking over her shoulder as if we could be overheard in an empty house. "God, Arkay. If I'd known—"

"Who are they?" I asked.

"They call themselves monster hunters."

"Like demons?" It made sense. We'd met Adam when he was hunting a demon, after all.

"And anything else that fits their definition," she said. "Nonhumans used to be a lot more common than we are now. There was a time when we were everywhere, but then the Order showed up, and people started dying. They killed off the obvious ones first— the manticores and the minotaurs, the naga and the oni. Anything that couldn't hide. Because of them, a lot of races are completely extinct at this point, or damn close to it. The only ones who ever stood a chance are the people like you and me— the ones who could pass for human well enough to get lost in a crowd. And that still doesn't stop them from murdering us by the dozen."

I slouched deeper into my chair. "He seemed like a decent enough guy."

"I guess some monsters really can blend in with regular people," she said. I pushed my plate away, and she frowned. "Arkay, you need to eat more than that."

I shook my head. "I'll finish it later."

She looked… disappointed? Concerned, maybe. I was too tired to puzzle out the expression on her face. "You've had two bites."

"You're exaggerating. It's more like…" I glanced down. The glob of casserole hadn't changed size. I'd definitely eaten some of it, though. The sticky mess clung to the inside of my mouth. "Like I said. I'll finish it later. I just want to sleep."

It seemed like a straightforward hint, but it still took Danielle two hugs and five or six reassurances before she finally let the door shut behind her.

I was alone.

I padded into Rosario's room and climbed into her bed, wrapping the quilt around me. It smelled like her— like her sweat, her shampoo, and the splashes of beer that always found their way onto her shirts at work. I buried my face in the pillow and inhaled, over and over again. Maybe if I did it long enough, I could burn the scent into my memory.

A large figure sat on the edge of the bed, though the mattress didn't dip with added weight.

"You're not really here," I told Rosario.

"No, I'm not."

I raised my head from the pillow. "Am I going crazy?"

"Some people would call it growing a conscience," she said. "You didn't kill that doctor. You could have."

Fuck that. "You're a hallucination. You're what happens when people under too much stress go too long without sleeping."

She smiled. "Guess you're not going crazy, then."

"It's not mutually exclusive," I said with an indignant sniff. But I curled toward the hallucination, and it laid a weightless hand on my hip.

My eyelids felt heavy, but I kept watching the vision. Over and over again I mentally traced the contours of Rosario's face, her body, her gentle smile. I had to remember them. I had to.

"That's my girl," she said, leaning forward to kiss my forehead. "Get some rest."

Absently I reached for her hand, but I felt nothing. "Will you go away if I sleep?"

"Of course, Arkay." Her smile turned sad. "I always do."

Adam

"Mara, we've got eyes on the dragon."

"What's its location?" she asked from the other side of the phone, her voice fuzzy and distant from interference.

"In the house," I said. "And she's not in good shape. I'm seeing obvious signs of stress. Definite evidence of exhaustion, possible starvation and dehydration." What the hell went on in these hospitals?

"It," Mara corrected. "It's a dragon, not a person. Don't forget that, Adam."

I glanced up. Weiss hadn't been in the room to observe my slip. Sharp sat a few feet away from me, but she had heavy headphones over her ears and an icy scowl on her face.

"Keep me updated," Mara said. The call ended, and we resumed our silence.

I'd always hated surveillance. Sitting still for endless stretches of time, snacking on bad food that did more to stifle my boredom than it did to satisfy any other need, wheedling Mara for stories that she had no inclination to share.

Then I'd met a Potnia Theron and her dragon.

Rosario's patterns had been fairly mundane. She had a steady job as a waitress, a loving girlfriend, Mass on Sundays. And, of course, a weekly monster convention that seemed to serve no higher purpose than an ordinary dinner party.

And then there was Arkay. Arkay, who spent at least one night of every week engaged in a back-alley brawl. Whose day job involved gyrating around a pole while eager customers pinned money to her ass. Who regularly went home with her favorite coworkers, dancer and support staff alike, many of whom neglected to shut their bedroom windows. I'd had to pay careful attention— one of her partners could have been another monster, and that would need to be included in my report. The rest of what I'd learned didn't need to be passed on to anybody.

All of that changed since the incident. Stress had turned her celibate. She paced like a caged tiger, but aside from a few isolated outbursts, her violence was contained. Controlled.

And with very few exceptions, hellishly boring. There had been a possibility of whiling away the dull hours with decent conversation, but aside from Mara, the rest of the team barely spoke to me. They watched me the way they might watch a bomb with a faulty detonator— wary, and from a safe distance.

Only Mara engaged me in regular conversation, but most of what she said involved orders, and the demands of a field assignment kept her constantly out of reach.

Meanwhile I was left to smother under the silence.

Finally, a break in the monotony. In front of the rows of screens, Sharp yanked the headphones off her head.

"Have you got something?" I asked, mostly out of reflex.

She didn't take her eyes off the screen. In her fury, she'd forgotten to ignore me. "I know that woman."

I frowned, leaning closer. "She's a ghoul. Danielle Johnson. She was pretty close with Hernandez and the dragon."

"I bet she was," Sharp said. "She was involved with the necromancer incident last November." Her glare deepened. "She murdered three cops and got away with it. One of them was a friend of mine."

Weiss returned to the room and settled in his chair. The hairs on the back of my neck prickled as his gaze burned into the back of my head.

"That ghoul is already on our list," I said carefully. "But right now the dragon is our priority."

Arkay

I wanted to sleep. I did.

After more than a week of micronaps, I craved the kind of deep, intensive rest that can only come from curling up on a comfortable mattress.

But when I laid my head down, all I could see were looming shadows. My attempts at sleep were interrupted by tossing and turning. No matter how I arranged myself on the pillows, the mattress always felt too flat. No matter how many blankets I crawled under, I never felt warm, and there was nobody else to cling to.

Come morning, I tried going back to the hospital, only to find the security in my way. Turns out assaulting a doctor on hospital grounds didn't go over all that well with the rest of the staff.

I'd considered marching right past them and shredding anyone who got in my way. I could do it, too. But Rosa wouldn't want that, so I let them escort me off the premises. When the police pulled up to ask why I'd been staring at the hospital doors for the past seven hours, I didn't snap at them. I didn't demand to know where they'd been when Rosario got shot. I didn't slash their tires with my bare hands.

They're only doing their jobs, Rosa would have said. *They're only trying to keep me safe.*

So I grudgingly accepted the offered ride back to the house, and I stayed there.

Night happened. So did day. Beyond that, time stopped making much of an impression. The club had burnt down, so I didn't have a job to come back to. I had a house to sleep in, so there was no need to keep moving to avoid the police clearing me out.

Danielle came by a few times, but I kept our conversations short. Every exchanged word frayed my nerves. I wanted to beat the living shit out of someone, and I didn't care who. I wanted to make them bleed. I wanted to make them pay.

Rosa wouldn't want that.

Rosa wasn't here right now.

Which just made me want to take it out on someone even more.

I paced the house. I went to the gym and swam laps until my limbs burned more than the chlorine in my still-healing wounds. I changed my bandages until the house first aid kit ran out of supplies. I scrolled endlessly through every single social media page I could find. I binge-watched shows with plots I couldn't remember once I turned my attention away from the screen. I microwaved portions of Danielle's tuna casserole until it went too stale and dry to classify as food anymore.

But mostly I curled up on my chair, wrapped in Rosario's blankets, and waited for my phone to ring.

Sooner or later there had to be a change.

Sooner or later, Rosario had to wake up.

Adam

"I don't see why we're wasting our time here," Burke grated after almost a week of surveillance. "The dragon's weak and wounded. We've got a golden opportunity to strike, and we're letting it go to waste."

Somebody had skipped their background reading. I opened my mouth to tell her off, but Sharp beat me to it.

"When a dragon is hurt is when it's most dangerous," she said. "I've seen this one go from half-dead to homicide in less than a second. And she's got a history of pulling wounded gazelle gambits. We'd be playing right into her hands."

"It," Green corrected.

"Doesn't change the fact that there's only one of it and six of us," Burke said. "If we surround it and lay down enough suppressing fire—"

"Then you're only going to provoke a rampage," I said. I'd seen her rip through twenty armed men like they were nothing. We had training they didn't, but that would only tip the scales so far during a direct confrontation. "I've already tried an ambush. It doesn't work."

"Try sedating it, then?" Burke suggested.

Sharp shook her head. "The only thing I've seen that kept her contained was Hernandez, and she's out of the picture."

"The dragon's an it," Green corrected again. "Not a she." On the screen behind him, the dragon paced irritably across the living room floor.

"If Hernandez is this dragon's off switch, then why not use her?" Burke argued. "We're already prepped to have her transferred to HQ. We can arrange to bring her here before they take her to Chicago. Use her as a human shield."

The thought chilled me. Rosario had kept company with all sorts of monsters, but beyond that one sin, she was still a human being— and more than that, she tried to be a good person. As long as I'd known her, she'd never been anything but decent, and merciful, and kind. The idea of parading her body in front of her best friend, of making it into a weapon, turned my stomach.

And that was nothing compared to what they'd do to her at the regional headquarters. I only knew a few details of the standard procedure for new specimens of undocumented racial profile, mostly because I tried to avoid being in the room when it was talked about. Collecting comprehensive tissue samples had always been a priority— blood, brain, bone, various organs and secretions.

All of which were typically retrieved during a vivisection.

"You're forgetting something," I said, trying to contain my disgust. "Hernandez is on life support, and none of us is qualified to stabilize her condition. If she dies on us, then we don't just lose our shield against the dragon. We'll be provoking an uninhibited rampage. There's a chance she'll raze half the city before she's done."

A pair of glasses caught the light. Weiss had turned his attention to me. He narrowed his eyes.

Damn it all to hell.

"Right now the dragon's inactive," I said, more careful of my words. "And as long as it is, we still have a chance to come up with a plan. Hopefully one that isn't guaranteed to backfire."

"Because you're the expert in that," Burke said dryly. "Somebody remind me why we're taking advice from the guy who botched the last job?"

On the screen, Arkay had stopped pacing to stand rigid, as tense as a predator who'd picked up a scent. For a bizarre moment, I wondered if she'd somehow overheard our conversation. Instead she pounced on the cell phone on the coffee table and yanked it off its charger. She picked up pacing again, but some of the tension had left her shoulders.

A call from a friend, perhaps.

She flopped into her armchair and some of that tension returned. More than tension.

I leaned in to get a better look.

Arkay

"Father Gabriel and I were talking, and we got to thinking," Danielle said. "We haven't had one of those potluck dinners in a while."

My legs folded, and I let the big pink armchair catch me. "Danielle, I'm not in much of a partying mood right now."

"I know," she said quickly. "I know. I don't mean as a party. Not exactly. But I think it might be good to get people in the house again. You know, get back to something like normal."

"Normal is overrated." I put the phone on speaker and tossed it onto the coffee table.

"Don't start on that. You know what I mean." Danielle's voice softened. She was probably biting her lip. "Arkay, I know what Rosa meant to you. I can't imagine how hard this must be for you right now. But you don't have to do this alone. And being around people, around friends, that's going to help you heal."

I scowled at the phone. I didn't want to heal. What I wanted was Rosa.

"Too fucking bad," said a voice that probably wasn't real. I squeezed my eyes shut to avoid looking behind me. How long had it been since I'd last slept? "You're a big girl, Arkay. You know better. Isolating yourself isn't going to wake me up any faster."

I dragged my hand over my eyes. I didn't want to see anyone. Not the hallucination, not Danielle, not a house full of people who usually only came by to eat food and make small talk. I didn't want to listen to people talking about Rosa like she was already dead. I didn't want to start thinking about her as gone.

She was in the hospital. People came back from the hospital all the time.

"You're in denial," Rosario's voice said. "It's one of the stages."

I rocked back and forth. I wanted to snap at her, but I couldn't yell at Rosa. Besides, she wasn't really there. I wanted to punch something. To throw something.

Denial was one of the stages of grief, but grief meant loss, and loss meant someone wasn't coming back.

"Arkay, look at what you're doing to yourself. You can't keep going on like this. Something has to change."

Damn straight, something had to change. Rosa needed to wake up already, and then everything would be okay again.

"Bargaining," she said. "And it doesn't work that way. When I wake up is my business. Until I do, getting your ass in gear is your business. Don't you dare make me your excuse for not getting help."

I didn't need help.

"Bullshit."

I glared at the hallucination. Stupid, demanding figment of my imagination. It wasn't even real.

"Maybe I'm not," she said. "But I'm still talking more sense than you have in weeks."

"Arkay?" Danielle asked gingerly, her voice made fuzzy by the speakers. "Are you still there?"

"I'm here," I said. The hallucination swam under my gaze, but I didn't take my eyes off it.

"Will you at least think about it?" she asked.

I grabbed the phone and took it off speaker, pulling it to my ear. "You know what? I changed my mind. Bring them over. Let's do this."

Adam

Legend spoke of a dragon that once plagued the city of Tarascon, somewhere in France. It was a formidable beast, and vicious. Hunters and champions rose up to slay it, and they were butchered like cattle. Armies were crushed by its rampage.

It was, by all means, invincible.

At least, until a woman arrived at the mouth of its cave. She came unarmored and unarmed, speaking softly and singing hymns, and she charmed the dragon that had slaughtered hundreds.

When she returned to Tarascon, the dragon followed with all the devotion of a trained hound. For her sake, it became utterly harmless. It didn't lift a claw to attack the people of the city— not even when they closed in to butcher it like the animal it was.

The people of Tarascon called the woman a saint for the things she'd done; the Order called her Potnia Theron.

There were other ways to kill a dragon, especially in the era of modern warfare, but even with anti-materiel rounds, they were notoriously slow to die. I had hoped that Rosario would subdue Arkay long enough for me to land a killing shot, the way the saint of Tarascon had with her dragon. Without Rosario, though, Arkay was as dangerous as ever.

At least, so I'd thought.

"Look at that," I said, tapping the screen.

Despite the stigma of my presence, the rest of the team pulled in closer to see.

"Green, what's she talking about?" Mara demanded.

Green pulled the headphones close against one ear. "Throwing a party?"

"It doesn't matter what they're talking about," I said. "Look at her face. The way she's sitting. She's angry. Hostile."

"What about it?" Burke asked.

"Exactly," I said. "She's not doing anything about it. With this degree of agitation, you'd expect her to be yelling. I wouldn't be surprised to see her throw the phone. But look at her."

Arkay covered her eyes, but we still got a clear view of her gnashing teeth.

Sharp watched her intently. "She's showing restraint."

"She's being careful," I agreed. Apparently some of Rosario's philosophies had made an impression on Arkay.

"Whoever's on the other end of that conversation is someone she doesn't want to lash out at."

Green glanced at Mara. "The dragon's talking to Danielle Johnson."

Sharp's eyes narrowed. It looked like we might bag our cop killer after all.

I sat back. "I think our human shield is a ghoul."

Arkay

When I finally rallied the will to look at myself in the mirror, I cringed. My skin was sallow and clung awkwardly to my bones. My hair was shaggy and limp with oil. The circles under my eyes could have passed for bruises.

Rosa wouldn't stand for this.

"Good," I told my reflection. "Let her wake up and fix it if she's got a problem with it."

It didn't sound nearly as good once I said it aloud.

I could stage hunger strikes, I could refuse to sleep and bathe and leave the house, but that wouldn't make an iota of difference if Rosa wasn't awake to feel guilty about it. All my ranting and raging wouldn't do a damn thing to wake her up.

"And if I do wake up, what then?" the hallucination asked.

"When, not if," I said.

"What happens then?" it persisted. "Do I go back to taking care of you the way I have been?"

"No, you're going to focus on getting better." I peeled my clothes off and stormed into the shower. "And you're going to get better, and things are going to be okay again. I'm going to take care of us both. See?" I scrubbed shampoo into my hair for emphasis.

"And who's going to clean things up when you get yourself into another gang war?" she persisted.

"I won't," I said. "I'm one of the good guys."

She stared me down. "Not the way I remember it."

"I did what I had to do," I said, turning on the faucet. "It's part of the business. Watch a movie sometime."

The hallucination didn't reply. The rush of cold water had woken me up enough to drive it back into the farthest corners of my mind.

Good riddance.

Adam

The plan was set, the preliminaries prepared, and we only had to wait for the opportune moment.

Until then, we returned to our usual arrangement, watching Arkay in five-hour shifts. I got the impression my midnight-to-five slot was intended as a punishment, but it didn't feel like one. Thanks to her work at the club, Arkay always kept unusual hours, and recent events hadn't exactly stabilized her sleeping patterns. Usually around this time, she'd be curled up in that godawful chair of hers, wrapped in a blanket that could probably use a wash and staring idly at an old crime drama.

Only tonight she didn't.

She emerged from the bathroom, still damp from a long-overdue shower, and marched resolutely up the stairs to her room.

She hadn't bothered to put clothes on first.

Of course not. Why would she? She was alone, the curtains were drawn, and she clearly had no idea that I'd installed cameras throughout the house. Which made this a practical, reasonable behavior, and not noteworthy in the slightest.

I wrote it down anyway: *2:38 AM — took a shower.*

I'd spent three months watching her. I'd seen her at every angle and contorted into every possible pose, I'd even bought a lap dance from her while she'd worked in the club, and I still couldn't get over how *human* she looked. Only her scars gave any hint that she was one of the most evil and dangerous creatures on the planet. She had no cleverly hidden scales, no extra vertebrae, no sharpened teeth, no slit-pupiled eyes.

No matter how hard I looked, no matter how thoroughly I knew better, I could only see a person.

She crossed from screen to screen as she climbed the stairs and disappeared into her room. Not to sleep, though. She dressed warmly, in a hoodie and sweats and fuzzy socks, and ventured into the cold night.

2:49 AM - left the house.

I pulled up the feeds from her local haunts and stepped into the kitchen to hunt down something to eat. There was no telling how long it would take her to get back into view of one of the cameras; until then, I might as well do something productive with my time.

Not long after I returned to my post, I found her in the back parking lot of the bar where Rosario had been a waitress.

3:13 AM - arrived at Gene's.

It was a minor relief to be able to write that. There'd been some push to remove the camera from the bar. Arkay hadn't come back here since the incident— but then, she hadn't gone much of anywhere, except to swim herself into exhaustion at the gym.

For a long while she just stared at the building, apparently deep in thought, until the door opened and another waitress stepped outside.

Arkay startled; Kindra, Rosario's girlfriend, did the same. I hadn't bothered to check up on the other woman before now. She looked like she'd been getting about as much sleep as Arkay, and she'd gained a few pounds since the last time I'd seen her. Dark roots showed beneath her bleached braids.

I adjusted the volume on the headset until the wind in the leaves became a dull roar.

"Kindra," Arkay said. "Hey."

"Hey." Kindra pulled a cigarette from her purse and fidgeted with her lighter, making an obvious effort not to look at Arkay.

"It's been a while."

"Yeah. I haven't seen you since the hospital." Finally the tip of the cigarette lit, and Kindra took a drag. "Did something happen?"

"No," Arkay said quickly. "No, there's been no change. Either that, or the guy at the reception desk has stopped taking my calls."

"Oh." I couldn't tell if Kindra's shoulders sagged with relief or disappointment. A long silence passed between them.

"What about you?" Arkay asked, burying her hands in her pockets. "How are you holding up?"

"Kind of a complicated question, don't you think?" The cigarette glowed as Kindra took another long pull. "I'm coping. You?"

"Anything I can do?" Arkay asked.

"No. Maybe. I don't know." The cigarette burned to the filter, and Kindra threw it onto the parking lot. "Honestly, I don't know anything anymore. One minute she was fine, and then…" She ground the cigarette into the pavement. "Only it wasn't like that, really. She was anxious for a while. Even before she got that phone call. It's like she was waiting for something horrible to happen. And then it did, and I—" She blinked. Her mascara had started to run. "I don't even know what happened to her. Fuck, I barely knew anything about her. And I was okay with that. I thought she'd tell me eventually, you know? When she was ready. I thought—" She fell silent, except for the click of her labret piercing between her teeth. When she spoke again, her voice shook. "She's gone, and I don't even know why."

Arkay pulled her into a hug, albeit one as halting and awkward as their small talk had been.

I glanced at my notes. I should have been writing this down. It was important to mark the people that Arkay interacted with and the things they talked about. If Kindra kept asking questions, then the Order needed to know about it. If she was human and useful, then she could be recruited. If not, then she would need to be eliminated.

Bar was already closed. She left.

It was hardly the biggest omission I'd made recently; I'd told a similar lie to keep Father Gabriel Mendoza out of my reports. They were white lies. Innocent.

Kindra had already lost her girlfriend. I didn't need to add to her suffering.

Besides, the dragon would be dead soon enough.

Arkay

I balanced a single spark in my hand. It danced across my fingertips, crossing over the candlewick between them until it glowed with a gentle flame. Father Gabriel continued the soft chant of his prayer, signing the words as he spoke them. My candle joined his on a blanket of aluminum foil. Beside me, Danielle lit a candle of her own, then passed her long-necked lighter to a wendigo named Valerie, who passed it on to a ghoul named Samson, and on and on.

It was a candlelight vigil, not a funeral. Danielle had been very specific about that when she'd arranged the event, even though a sudden thunderstorm had forced the event indoors. Not a single person wore black, though I noticed a heavy concentration of the soft browns and greens Rosario preferred. The low tones of soft rock were drowned out by the murmurs of voices joining Father Gabriel in prayer.

I stood back as the candles filled the dining room table, then the end tables, the kitchen counters. Every inch of available space had been turned over to them, and they still threatened to spill out onto the floor. It was good, so long as we didn't run out of foil. Rosario was popular. She was loved.

I loved her.

People hugged, some in comfort, some in greeting, some purely in affection. Some people cried. Elsewhere in the house, I heard the faint crinkle of more foil, and caught a whiff of chocolate chip cookies. Other voices rose up over the sounds of prayers, telling the story of when somebody had tried to teach Rosario the Single Ladies dance and we'd had to replace the microwave. Elsewhere someone recounted a disaster known only as The Stromboli Incident. An encantado named Javier suggested everyone heading out for sushi later. He stepped to the living room window, raising his hand to count the cars parked in front of the house.

The glass shattered. Javier spun in a bizarre pirouette, dousing those nearest him in a thick red splatter before he crumpled to the ground.

Somebody screamed and rushed away. Another person dove at him, trying to resuscitate him. Apparently they hadn't noticed the massive hole in his chest.

Rain poured through the broken window.

There was a sound like a dog's bark, followed by two fresh gouts of blood. An enormous bullet had carved right through one woman's arm and embedded itself in the man behind her.

"Get away from the windows!" Danielle shouted, her voice lost to the screams. A burly were-hyena charged for the door. He barely pulled it open before another gunshot burst his skull.

"This way! Out the back!" I grabbed Danielle by the arm and started dragging her through the crowd. If the others had any sense, they'd follow the first person who looked like she knew what she was doing. "Come on, this way!"

A few caught on and started running toward the back door. A teenage Hulder scrambled onto the kitchen counter and tried to pry open the window. Another gunshot threw her backward onto the linoleum, and she lay twitching for a few moments before she fell still.

More gunshots barked behind us in a steady rhythm. One thundered as it blasted a crater through a brick wall.

Danielle pushed through the crowd. "Arkay! The back—"

Another bullet buried itself in the refrigerator.

Danielle pulled back. "We're trapped."

I looked wildly between her and the rest of the crowd. More than two dozen people had come here tonight. The shooters could pick us off one at a time, easy. Or they could wait for us to choke: the wail of a smoke detector joined the shouts. The air nearest the ceiling turned murky and thick with the reek of melting plastic and burning hair.

"Danielle, I'm gonna need you to start throwing shit." I dug a sauté pan out of the cabinet and pushed it into her hands. "As much as you can. Don't stop until you hear from me. Got it?"

I didn't wait for a reply. We didn't have time.

I crept to the door. Sheathed my skin in thick scales. Wrapped my hand around the doorknob.

"Wait!" Danielle hissed. "What am I throwing this at?"

I blinked. How did she not know? Rosario always knew.

"Out the window," I said, pointing with both hands. And fuck it all, she'd probably need help with the timing, too. "On three. One. Two." How had I ever survived without Rosa? "Three!"

I yanked open the door and lunged into the storm just as the pan flew at the kitchen window. It didn't go all the way through— the long handle caught on the windowsill and the whole thing tumbled back into the sink with a clumsy, noisy clatter.

It wasn't perfect, but it was loud and unexpected, and that made it distracting. Two gunshots thundered up ahead of me. Both went wide.

While the Order goons adjusted their aim, I leaped sharply to the right, away from the cascade of kitchenwares. I rolled to my feet beside a bright-eyed blond woman. She turned, but not before I grabbed the gun out of her hand. The still-hot barrel of the gun scorched my palm, but I twisted it out of her grip and stepped into her, bending to throw her over my shoulders.

I didn't get a chance.

"Burke!" a man shouted.

A barrage of gunshots knocked me into the mud, but they didn't pierce my scales. Those bullets that didn't strike the blond woman's body armor had been slowed down by the unprotected flesh of her throat and underarm.

A tall black man stepped into the light, an enormous golden handgun in his grip, a look of horror on his face. He pulled the trigger. Nothing happened.

"Shit!" He grabbed at his belt, and I threw the woman's body off my own. A spent magazine hit the ground. Another was slammed into the grip of the handgun. I gathered both feet underneath me and sprang at him, almost slipping in the mud.

The gun fired somewhere to the left of my head. The roar was deafening. Agonizing. But I had momentum on my side, and momentum didn't care about pain.

I slammed into him hard enough to knock him down. But while he went sprawling, I dug my claws into his shoulders and my teeth into his throat. A moment of concentration, and his entire body surged with electricity. A second magazine emptied in a flurry of gunshots as his hand seized around the trigger.

I pried it out of his hand afterward, just in case, and hurled it into the dark.

A plate soared through the kitchen window like a Frisbee and shattered against my hand.

I hissed in pain.

Right. Escape plans.

I rushed to the open door. "Out this way!" I shouted. "Everybody out! Split up and stay away from the main road. Don't let them see you!" I pushed my way back inside, past the rush of people moving the opposite way. "Out the back! Get out the back door!"

Between the barrage of brick-shattering gunshots, my shouted instructions, and the current of bodies, most of the crowd got the idea to scram. But one caught my attention.

Either Father Gabriel hadn't noticed the rush to escape, or he didn't care. He was on his knees beside a fallen patasola, trying desperately to apply a tourniquet to the mangled stump of her arm. She clung to him with the other hand, her eyes wide, her skin unnaturally pale. She switched frantically between English and Spanish, but I could understand her pleas just fine: *please, dear God, please don't leave me.*

"I'm not kidding, Gabe!" I snarled, more for my benefit than his. I pounced on the patasola, scooping her up with both arms and jerking my head for Father Gabriel to follow me. "Come on, we've gotta go!" He hurried to his feet, and together we ran for the door.

We got as far as the hallway.

Flames licked the ceiling. Thunder roared outside. An anti-tank round took out the last splinter of the load-bearing wall.

The house creaked. Groaned. Leaned.

And finally it came down on top of us.

Adam

The monsters scattered into the night, taking shelter in the fury of the storm. Sharp and I chased after them, but there were too many. We only managed to bring down three or four before the rest disappeared. We could keep chasing them, but this was a residential area. Even if we managed to avoid taking civilian casualties, gunfire would attract unnecessary attention.

"Where are Burke and Green?" Sharp asked, peering after the stragglers. "They should be here by now."

"I'll go look for them," I said. "You go back to Mara. Make sure she's got backup."

Mara had Weiss watching her back, but he was administrative personnel— useless in a fight, especially against a dragon. Still, she had the best vantage point of all of us, holed up in the attic of the rundown house across the street with an M107 Barrett. Arkay would have to climb two stories to get to her, and hopefully that would give Mara a chance to sink enough rounds into her to bring her down.

A dragon might bleed out, but not before taking down a full city block. But now, the people who got in the way weren't people at all, but monsters. And more importantly, they were her friends. Arkay would try to hold back a rampage. She'd try to protect them. And meanwhile, Mara would have that much more time to put a .50 caliber bullet between her eyes.

Since the beginning of the ambush, I'd been listening hard. The radio buzzed with static. Beyond it, I'd heard the roll of thunder, the crack of gunfire, the screams of dozens of frightened monsters. Even the crash of a collapsing building.

But not the roar of a dragon.

I hurried toward the back of the wreckage that had once been a house. A pair of bodies lay in the mud. They'd been trampled by the fleeing crowd, their features obscured by darkness and grime, but I could still make out the contours of their body armor.

I switched on my radio. "Mara! Burke and Green are dead."

No response.

I hauled Green onto his back. Something had bitten through his throat, but there was little blood: the flesh around the wounds had been cauterized.

"Mara! Come in! The dragon came around back— she might be heading to you right now. Be on the lookout! Weiss, Sharp— can anybody hear me?"

I turned to take off running, but a flash of lightning illuminated movement in the ruins of the house. A shape dragged itself through the collapsed roof.

A small, familiar shape.

I crept forward. My clothes clung to my skin, cold and waterlogged. My body armor dragged me down with every step.

Arkay was caked in plaster dust and bits of insulation, but I recognized her instantly. She was on her knees, digging through the rubble with her bare hands. Beside her lay the body of a woman in white, the side of her skull caved in by the remains of a brick.

I raised my Desert Eagle and lined up a shot. It wouldn't cause lethal damage when Arkay was at her full size, but right now she looked deceptively human. One solid shot through the skull, and she'd be down.

I exhaled. This was what I'd trained for. What I'd spent months planning for. Finally it would all be over. I could put this behind me and get back to repairing the fragments of my reputation. I could have my life back.

The pile of rubble shifted, and a plaster-covered hand broke out from the debris, grasping weakly at the air. Arkay dug more frantically, exhuming an arm, a shoulder, a head.

My finger stiffened on the trigger.

Only the figure in the wreckage wasn't a monster.

That was Father Gabriel. A priest. A human. A good man.

He shouldn't have been here. This was a gathering of monsters. He didn't belong here.

Arkay embraced him briefly before she resumed digging him out of the wreckage. He coughed, looking at her with the gratitude of a man who'd witnessed miracles.

His eyes fell on the body beside her, and his expression turned to grief.

And then he saw me.

"Arkay, look out!" he shouted, waving his free arm frantically.

She whirled to face me, and her whole frame lowered into a defensive stance. Her lips peeled back in a vicious snarl.

I took aim. I'd get one shot. That was it.

"Arkay, hurry! Get out of here!" Gabriel tried to drag himself out of the rubble, but he fell back with a cry of pain.

Arkay stared at me with an expression of the purest hatred.

Then she sank to her knees between me and the priest, and with a visible effort, she turned her back on me and she resumed excavating him from the rubble.

"Arkay, please, you have to—" He waved a hand for her to run, but she caught him by the wrist and pulled him back behind the shelter of her body.

She kept digging.

She was less than ten feet away from me, almost unmoving. The back of her head was exposed, and with it the vulnerable brainstem.

I could make that shot drunk. It would be quick, too. Painless. A mercy killing, really.

Arkay unearthed the rest of Father Gabriel's body, as stained with blood and plaster as her own. One of his legs bent at an unnatural angle. She signed something to him.

He glanced over her shoulder at me, then gave a frantic nod. "I trust you," he said.

She angled herself under him and hefted him onto her shoulders in a fireman's lift, carefully steadying his wounded leg with one arm, and started to the left.

"Wait!" I said abruptly.

She stopped, turning to fix me with a calculating stare. Even that motion drew a groan from Father Gabriel.

"If you head that way, you'll be in view of a sniper nest. Go the other way."

Her expression didn't change. I couldn't even be sure she'd heard me. But when she darted away, she went the other direction, away from Mara's line of sight. Arkay and Father Gabriel vanished behind a curtain of rain, and they were gone.

I stared into the darkness after her. My Desert Eagle still pointed at the spot where she had been.

Footsteps splashed close behind me. When I turned to face them, Sharp already had her firearm trained on me. "You want to explain what the fuck just happened?"

Arkay

Like a complete idiot, I was too busy making my dramatic exit to grab a brick from the giant pile of rubble that had been my house. Instead, I wound up shuffling through half a neighborhood's gardens, looking for a rock and an older-model car to use it on.

Father Gabriel laughed weakly as I eased him into the front seat of an old Impala. "I'm pretty sure I should be advising against grand theft auto."

"Consider me advised," I signed, and I ripped open the panels around the steering column. Right now, the best alternative to stealing the car was walking to the hospital, and he was already pale and panting. I didn't need medical training to know what shock looked like.

More gunshots rang out behind me. In the storm, they almost sounded like thunder.

I clenched my teeth and put on the gas. I'd given the others the chance to escape. There was nothing more I could do for them. Right now, the priority was getting Father Gabriel to safety.

I forced myself to repeat that over and over again, but my claws still scratched patterns into the back of the steering wheel. I wanted to go back. I wanted to chase those fuckers down and run them over. Rip them open.

Father Gabriel was the priority.

They'd destroyed my home. They'd murdered my friends.

Father Gabriel was the priority.

Rosa would never forgive me if I left him to die, even if it was to avenge her.

In fact, that would probably make it worse.

I turned too sharply into the ER entrance. Father Gabriel groaned with pain as his entire body slid to the left.

"Sorry," I muttered, rubbing my fist in a circle across my chest so he could actually understand the sentiment. I'd controlled my anger so far. I could hold it in a little longer.

I pulled the car into park as gently as I could manage and scooped him out of the passenger seat. He was heavy in my arms. A familiar weight.

I didn't bother kicking shut the car door. The adrenaline was wearing off, and in its absence my mind was starting to fuzz with deja vu.

I'd walked this stretch before. I'd almost tripped on that same curb while carrying another body in my arms. The automatic doors hesitated before me, just as they had before.

It looked like they'd already repaired the broken pane from when I'd kicked it in.

The ER was full. A few weary heads turned to watch us enter, but there was no shock or horror on their faces. Never mind that my world had just been blown apart again. They were all here for the same reason. Every person here had just lived their own personal horror story, and every single one of them was tapped dry of fucks to give.

I recognized the nurse who sat at the front desk. She was the same woman who'd taken my information when I brought in Rosario, and she didn't recognize me any more than she had those few weeks ago.

I spoke clearly this time. "My friend needs help. His leg is broken and I think he's in shock."

She looked us over and pushed a clipboard at me. "There's a wheelchair right over there. Take a seat and start filling out these forms, and we'll get someone to see you as soon as possible."

I stared at the clipboard.

Talking was overrated.

The last time I hadn't bothered with the front desk at all. I'd just stormed toward the nearest cluster of nurses and snarled; they seemed to have figured out what I'd meant quickly enough. I considered revisiting that strategy. Instead, I carried Father Gabriel to the line of wheelchairs and eased him into the seat as gently as possible, then brought him the fucking clipboard.

Frustration did nothing to calm my rage. I wanted to rev up the stolen car and charge right back into the fray. I wanted to find the motherfuckers who'd demolished my house and murdered my friends. I wanted blood and carnage.

But Father Gabriel's hands shook too much to hold the pen, so I had to fill out his clipboard. The nurses called out for their next patients verbally, so I had to stay by his side and listen for his name. He needed me, so I stayed. Because he was my friend, and he was Rosario's friend. I wouldn't abandon him.

Adam

Sharp never took me out of her sights— not when she forced me into her car, not when she marched me up the stairs and forced me to sit, not even when Mara and Weiss stormed inside after us. Weiss fixed me with an accusing stare, but Mara dragged him into the privacy of the office, and they resumed what sounded like an ongoing argument.

Mara seemed to have my side, but there was no confidence in her voice.

And then she went entirely quiet.

When they emerged from the office, I caught a glimpse of a web browser in place of one of the video feeds.

"I can explain," I said, the moment I had a chance to get a word in edgewise.

Weiss squared off in front of me. "I don't think that will be necessary. The evidence speaks for itself quite fluently."

"What evidence?" I asked. "Evidence of what?"

"Don't bother, Adam," Mara said wearily. She sat down against the wall, her cane set between her knees like a shield. "We already know."

Of course they knew. Sharp had told them that I'd let Arkay escape. She'd still had a gun to my head when she told them.

"I hesitated," I said. "It was a mistake. It was a shit move, and I don't know why I let it happen, but—"

"I think you know exactly why," Weiss said.

Mara looked away, her jaw tight.

Maybe I did know. Shooting Rosario had taken a bigger toll on me than I'd wanted to believe. The idea of slaughtering another innocent bystander, even one who regularly associated with monsters, left a bad taste in my mouth. Maybe even killing a dragon was too much for me right now. Maybe—

"You mentioned in your report that the dragon worked as an adult entertainer," Weiss said.

I looked up. Where the hell had this come from? "I did. But what—"

"And yet you failed to mention that you employed its services."

The accusation hit me like a punch in the gut. Comprehension bloomed in its wake, and with it, horror. "Wait—"

"On the night of September fifteenth, you withdrew a large quantity of cash from an ATM across the street from the gentleman's club where she worked. Isn't that right?"

"You've got it wrong," I sputtered. "I went to that club as part of my investigation. I brought cash in order to better maintain my cover. It was research."

"And I'm sure you felt the need to conduct a full cavity search." Weiss' lip curled in disgust. "It is well documented that dragons have voracious sexual appetites. Your own reports have indicated as much. I'm sure you wanted your understanding of the matter to be… thorough."

I reddened. "The fuck are you accusing me of?"

"If you must be crass, yes."

I couldn't be hearing this. This couldn't be happening. I rose to my feet and turned to Mara for help. "You can't seriously believe this bullshit."

"Sit down, Preston," he ordered.

Mara shuddered. She looked like she was on the verge of throwing up.

"Mara, you know me," I said. "You've known me for years. You know I wouldn't— I would never! This is…" I searched for the word, but came up empty.

"Circumstantial," Sharp supplied. Her gun was still trained on me. "The evidence is circumstantial. You withdrew more than a hundred dollars cash and walked into a strip club. Perfectly innocent. I'm sure there were dozens of girls there who weren't dragons, and you could've been getting dances from any of them. Funny how you didn't lead with that defense." It sounded more like an accusation than an assist. Another nail in my coffin.

"I'm a soldier, not a lawyer," I snapped. "Arkay is evil. I know that. She killed Burke and Green. She—"

"—is an 'it'," Weiss said, and suddenly I realized my mistake. "Not a person. Not a woman. A dragon. An unholy abomination of the highest order. The spawn of Hell itself. So why do you keep calling it by name?"

"Habit. Just habit." I backpedaled. "I spent months ingratiating myself with Hernandez. Adopting her speech patterns was a necessary part of forming a connection."

"That's what I kept telling myself, too," Mara said quietly. "That it was just a quirk you picked up from the Hernandez girl. But it's not the only thing you picked up from her, is it?"

"Mara," I began.

"Hernandez was under the delusion that monsters are people. And that's all it is, Adam. A delusion. But somehow she got you thinking it, too."

My fingers dug into the armrests. "That's not what happened."

"Then what, Adam? Enlighten me. Explain what I've been seeing these last weeks. Explain why you've consistently kept putting off that thing's execution. Because this wasn't some fluke. You had months to kill the dragon. *Months.* And yet there it is, alive and kicking and butchering our people. You weren't waiting for the opportune moment. You weren't hesitating. You had a shot, and you deliberately refused to take it. And more than that, you helped the dragon escape. Right now it could be God-only-knows-where, doing unspeakable damage to innocent people, and that's on your hands, Adam. That's on you."

I fell back, staring. Stupefied.

"You want to tell me you haven't been fucking a goddamn lizard? That you aren't on this thing's side? You need to prove it to me, Adam, and you need to do it right the hell now, because this is the last chance you've got left."

"I'm not," I said weakly. My mind raced. How was I supposed to convince them of anything if I couldn't convince myself? "I'm a good soldier. I'm loyal."

"I'm sure you are, Adam." Mara rose to her feet and leaned heavily on her cane. "Just not to us." She squeezed her eyes shut. Her fists clenched around the head of her cane. "Go ahead, Weiss. Get on with it."

I stared at her. Horror gaped at the borders of my consciousness, too vast and overwhelming for me to comprehend. "Am... am I being sent in for another Synod?"

"The Synod already reached its decision," she said. "I already told you, Adam. You got one chance, and that was it. It's over. All that's left is the sentencing."

My insides hollowed out. "Mara, please—"

She turned away.

"Stay where you are, Novak," Weiss said. And to me: "On your knees."

"Wait—" He cut off my protest with a sharp gesture, and Mara and Sharp forced me onto the floor.

"Adam Preston." Weiss pronounced every syllable with a corrosive finality. "You have been found guilty of fraternizing with monsters. Of aiding and abetting monsters. Of assisting monsters in the murder of your fellow soldiers—"

"I didn't!"

"—and of intimate contact with the inhuman. You are a failure and a traitor to your people, and a stain upon the Order of Saint Michael of the Sun." His gaze bored into mine. His eyes were like chips of ice. "And the Order will be wiped clean of your corruption. By the power vested in me by the High Synod, I strip you of your name and your rank. May your shame be lost to history."

Damnatio memoriae.

I tried to speak, but my voice caught in my throat. I couldn't make a sound.

I needed to put my thoughts in order. To figure out the right things to say to make them see they were wrong. To make Weiss change his mind. I needed to be eloquent and logical. I needed to be clever. I needed to come up with a better idea than throwing myself at his feet and begging him to forgive me, but that was all that went through my overloaded brain.

He picked up my Desert Eagle and hefted it in his hands. Mara cringed away from me, leaning heavily on her cane.

"Wait," Sharp said. "You didn't say you were going to kill him."

"The sentence must fit the crime." Weiss racked the slide to make sure the chamber was loaded.

Sharp started to argue, and in that moment, she loosened her hold on me. I forced my arms out of her grip and got one leg out from under me, lunging headlong into Weiss. His finger closed on the trigger, but the bullet went wide, striking the ceiling and raining down plaster.

He had combat training, but only the most rudimentary technique. I actually had years of experience. I ripped the weapon from his hand and rolled to my feet.

Sharp had already pulled her own sidearm, and Mara was close behind.

"Stand down," Sharp commanded.

I raised my own weapon to aim at her. "So you can kill me? No, thank you. I'm leaving."

"No, you're not." Her hand was steady on the handgun.

I backed up another step.

"I said stand down," she repeated.

Weiss dragged himself upright. "Just shoot him already."

"Please," Mara said beside him. "Don't make this any harder than it needs to be."

"Oh, I'm sorry," I said. "Is this difficult for you? I hadn't noticed."

"Please," she repeated, but her eyes weren't on me. They were fixed over my shoulder at the security panel on the wall.

I rammed my fist into the circuitry and clapped my hands over my ears as all our failsafes went off in a single brilliant cascade. It was meant to be a safeguard against an enemy raid: flashbangs powerful enough to blind and deafen bloodthirsty rakshasas, and an EMP blast to wipe out their communications and equipment.

Turns out it worked just as well against humans.

My ears bled from the roar of the stun grenades and my balance was blown to shit, but I was better off than the three who lay curled up and blind on the floor. I staggered to the door, now hanging loosely from a crater in the wall. When I emerged onto the puddle-strewn parking lot, I broke into a drunken amble for the nearest cluster of buildings.

I felt like the ground had been swept out from under me. Like I was unanchored. Freefalling.

I'd fucked up. I'd hesitated. I'd felt sympathy for monsters.

But not just monsters. People, too. Decent, honest, innocent people— or as innocent as anyone could be. They were worth a few seconds of hesitation, weren't they? They were worth a momentary compromise, weren't they? And surely— surely the High Synod would see that. They'd tell Weiss he'd been wrong. They'd make him reverse the sentence.

Something twisted in the pit of my stomach.

Damnatio memoriae was only talked about in hushed whispers. I'd heard of more than a dozen men and women who had been stripped of name and identity, who were remembered only for their crimes. I'd cringed at the stories and agreed with their sentences. Of course I did. Those people were despicable. Irredeemable. Unforgivable.

Never once had a sentence been overturned.

My uniform was still damp from the storm, and a cold wind dragged its claws down my spine. I had to keep running, but I didn't know where to run to.

I had nowhere to go.

Everything I'd ever known was suddenly barred to me. I was a fugitive. I'd be murdered on sight by everyone I'd ever known.

Almost everyone.

I had one option left to me. Only one. It was the wrong one. The worst possible one. But it was better than being alone.

Arkay

The hospital's sign language interpreters had their hands full with other patients, so for the sake of translation, the nurses let me stay with Father Gabriel, but they weren't happy about it. Apparently they hadn't forgiven me for trying to strangle that one doctor a few weeks back.

Some people don't know how to let go of a grudge.

As part of the compromise, a pair of burly security guards accompanied us while Father Gabriel was pumped full of painkillers and wheeled across the diagnostics wing. I'd butchered two scarier-looking people earlier that night, and they'd both been armed and ready to kill.

"Don't tell them that," said the memory of Rosario. "They're just here to make the nurses feel safer around you. Don't give them a reason to throw you out."

I conceded her point, though I glared at the flicker in the corner of my eye. I thought I'd gotten rid of that hallucination.

"Sleep deprivation is a bitch," she said. "And you haven't actually been sleeping for more than an hour at a time. So no, I'm not going to be going away for a while."

I'd showered, though. That seemed to have gotten rid of her.

"Showering isn't the same as a full night's sleep, Arkay."

I took my attention back to the nurse.

"It looks like your leg is too swollen to put a cast on it yet," I translated with a flutter of my hands. Father Gabriel's eyes were glazed as they drifted over my signs. "They're going to have you stay in the splint overnight and see how you are in the morning."

"But the parish is an hour away," he slurred. The painkillers hadn't done him any favors. "And I can't drive like this."

I rubbed gently at his shoulder. "You're going to sleep here tonight."

"Oh. Alright, then." There were still bits of plaster in his graying hair. I'd done what I could to clean him up, but he still looked like a house had fallen on him. I didn't look much better.

My usage of words like 'overnight' and 'tomorrow' had been a bit liberal. The X-rays and MRIs took forever and a half to conduct, and by the time I tucked Father Gabriel into a hospital bed, it was close to dawn. After I cleaned myself up in the common shower and changed into fresh clothes from the gift shop, a watery sun started to peek through the oversized windows.

Even the shower hadn't done much to wake me up. And so I dragged myself to the familiar corridors of the ICU and slipped into Rosario's room.

She looked exactly like she had the last time I'd been here, but in the gray light of dawn, I could almost believe she was only sleeping.

I dragged a chair beside her bed and lay my head in her lap. My eyelids were too heavy to stay open any longer.

"I'm sorry, Rosa," I mumbled, taking her hand. "I couldn't stop them from knocking our house down. But I'll get us another one. A better one. Or you can wake up, and we'll go house hunting together."

Not even the hallucination replied. Damn, I was tired.

"Later, though." I gave her hand a squeeze and shut my eyes.

The blare of my cell phone dragged me away from the edge of sleep.

"Hello?" I groaned, dragging the screen to my ear.

"Arkay?" Kindra's voice sounded shrill on the other end of the line. "Oh God, Arkay, are you alright?"

"Huh?"

"The news says another meth lab blew up, but Arkay, that's your neighborhood. That was your house! And I've been inside there, I would know if you two had been cooking meth—"

"It didn't have anything to do with that." I yawned. "Shit happened."

"Were you there when it happened?" she asked. "Are you okay?"

"I'll live."

She lowered her voice. "Arkay, does this have to do with what you told me about? With…"

"Yeah," I said.

"Fuck." I heard the faint click of a stud between her teeth. "Is there anything I can do to help?"

Aside from hanging up the phone and letting me sleep? "Yeah, actually. I had to get out of there in a hurry last night. Mind driving me back to see if any of our stuff is worth saving?"

"Of course," she said. "Yeah. Where are you? When do you want me to swing by?"

"Later," I said. "In a few hours." I didn't bother telling her where I was. That would just start up a fresh round of questions, and I had no energy left to answer them. "I'll call you back when I'm ready for you, okay?"

I was already fumbling to end the call when I heard her assent. I didn't have the energy for this. For any of this. I needed rest, goddammit, and I was about ready to turn off my phone and barricade the door to get it.

"Don't do that," the hallucination said. "The nurses need to come in to turn me over."

"I know," I grumbled. "But sleep really does sound nice right about now."

It wasn't enough that I was having auditory hallucinations, or that eerie flickering in the edges of my vision. I'd even started smelling things that weren't there. Not even good scents, like food or happy memories— no, I got rain and smoke and gunpowder and man sweat.

Very specific man sweat.

I raised my head from Rosario's bed and turned around. Adam stood framed in the doorway, silent and staring. His clothes were still soaked with rain. He looked confused. Conflicted. Almost exactly like he had earlier in the night, when he'd watched me pull Father Gabriel out of the ruins of my house.

Was this just a memory of that moment, then? Just another hallucination?

And more importantly: did I actually give a fuck?

He took a step forward.

The answer was no.

I lunged. He turned and scrambled for the door, but I didn't let him get that far. My claws caught on the collar of his body armor and I hurled him into the opposite wall. While he dragged himself upright, I shut the door and barred it with my chair. His buddies wouldn't save him. Security wouldn't stop me.

I advanced, and he fled to the other corner of the room, toward the shelter of cheap furniture and IV drips.

Toward Rosario.

I leaped after him before he could lay a hand on her, catching his hand in both of mine and swinging him back. He hit the windowsill hard enough to knock the air out of his lungs, but he clung to that surface, staring at the window.

I could see a plan forming in his eyes, in the curve of his stance. A solid blow might crack the glass. There was no fire escape, but we were only on the second story. If he jumped, the fall probably wouldn't kill him.

And even if it did, at least it would be quick about it.

I grabbed him by the shoulders and threw him to the center of the floor, at the foot of Rosario's bed. Fury threatened to leave me mute, but I forced myself to hold onto a modicum of calm. I wanted to stay verbal. I wanted him to hear me talk. I wanted to understand his sobs when he begged.

"You destroyed my home," I snarled, sinking into a crouch over his body. He raised a hand to shield himself, but I caught it and pinned it to the floor. "You butchered my friends." With my other hand I caught his jaw and forced him to look me in the eyes. "*You shot Rosario.*"

I could peel the veins out of his arms and use them to strangle him. I could carve out his lying tongue and thread it through his voice box. I could smash open his skull and show him all the synapses Rosa would never use again.

"Arkay, don't," said a quiet voice. Rosario's voice.

My teeth gnashed less than an inch from Adam's face.

"Arkay, look at him," said the hallucination. "He's not trying to hurt you. He's not even fighting back. You don't have to kill him."

No. Fucking no. The hallucination wasn't real. It didn't get a say in this. Not now. Not when all I had left were echoes and ghosts.

"Rosa is gone!" I snarled. "She never did anything to you! She never hurt anyone, and you lied to her! You used her! You shot her!" With each accusation, I slammed Adam's head into the tile floor. "She's never waking up and she's never coming back, *and it's your fault!*"

The last of the tension left his shoulders. He stared up at me, open and fragile and resigned. "I know."

I could break him. I could kill him. I could mutilate him in a hundred million ways, and it wouldn't be enough.

It would never be enough.

Killing him wouldn't bring her back. Making him suffer wouldn't wake her up.

"Arkay, please," the hallucination said. "She wouldn't have wanted this."

No. Rosario tried to see the best in people, and she forgave them when they didn't live up to that hope. When they hurt her. When they betrayed her. Time and time again, I'd watched her advocate for the most miserable excuses for sentience that this world had to offer.

And for all her good intentions, I'd watched her beaten and battered and bruised. All her forgiveness and mercy and love had gotten her nothing but a body full of scars and a hospital bed.

She deserved better than that. She deserved so much better.

And I couldn't give it to her.

In her last moments she'd been afraid of me. Her last act had been to try to stop me. And it hadn't worked.

And now she was gone and I was alone.

My voice dried into a whisper. "You're a monster."

"I know," Rosa said. Adam closed his eyes. "I'm asking you anyway."

My grip went lax around his throat and my shoulders sagged. Adam hacked and wheezed as air was reintroduced to his lungs, but I ignored him. The hallucination was gone, and it took with it my last hope of hearing Rosario's voice again.

Adam pulled himself unsteadily to his feet, and this time I didn't stop him. Let him crawl back to his fucking cult. I didn't care.

Instead he staggered to the corner behind Rosa's bed and pulled a knife from his belt. I tensed, but he didn't turn it on Rosario. Instead, he slid the blade into the crack between the rubber moldings on the floor and the wall, extracting a thin wire. A flick of his wrist, and the wire was severed.

"The fuck is that?" I asked dully.

"Surveillance camera." He sounded as exhausted as I felt. "It's how we've been monitoring you." He took a moment to steady himself. A rivulet of blood streamed from his split lip. More seeped from underneath his hair. "After what happened last night, they'll be trying to do damage control. They'll send another team after you— a bigger team, and more experienced. And they'll send someone in to get her." He tilted his head at Rosario, and I tensed.

"What do they want with her?" I demanded.

Carefully, he folded the knife and returned it to his belt. "The state she's in now, I don't think she'll be much use to them as bait. More likely they'll want to study her. Find out how she did what she did."

"She didn't *do* anything."

"She made friends with you, didn't she?" he asked. "And ghouls and impundulu and wendigos and… hell… humans aren't supposed to be able to do that. Just walk right up to monsters and… and not die. So they think there's got to be something in her pheromones, or in her eyes, or in the frequency of her voice, that makes people like you not want to kill her on sight."

"How about because she's a person? Because she's gentle and kind and brave and *good*? How about because I love her? Did that ever cross your mind?"

He averted his eyes. No. No, they fucking didn't. "They're regrouping as we speak. They'll be here to take her within a few days at most."

I bared my teeth. "Let them try."

"You don't want that." He set his jaw. "We tried strategy on you, and it didn't work. They'll use brute force next. And they won't stop just because you're holed up inside a hospital."

"Fuckers."

He cringed. "They're just…" He glanced my way and apparently changed his mind. "There's still time to stop them. I can get her out of here before they can get their computers back online."

"You think I'm going to just sit here and let you take her away from me?"

"Then stay put, if you want," he snapped. "Or come along on the transport, or hang onto the side of the helicopter, or do whatever the hell it is dragons do. I'm not here to ask your permission."

I leveled my gaze with his. "Then why are you here?"

He jabbed a finger at Rosario. "Because she didn't deserve what happened to her. And she sure as hell doesn't deserve what they're planning to do to her. So do you think you can stow your vendetta until I get her out of harm's way?"

I stared at him for a long moment, and finally I nodded.

For Rosa.

For Rosa, I could do anything.

~~Adam~~

???

Moving Rosario had always been part of the plan. It required extensive preparation, but that had all been taken care of weeks ago. All the groundwork had been laid, the arrangements prepared, the passwords procured. We only had to give the command, and Rosario would be transferred to an Order-run hospital in Chicago for testing.

Until now, Arkay had been the limiting factor. She'd prowled over Rosario's body like the hospital bed was a mountain of gold, called obsessively to check in on Rosario's progress, and nearly murdered anyone who so much as suggested moving her Potnia Theron. Even if by some miracle we could transport Rosario to another location without

Arkay's knowledge or interference, it would have been a matter of time before the dragon retaliated with a full-blown rampage right through one of the most populated cities in the world.

There would be no covering that up.

"Our orders were to stand by until you could be properly destroyed," I explained to Arkay while I adjusted the forms on a hijacked hospital computer. "Rosario wasn't a priority. It's not like she was going anywhere."

Arkay made a low noise, but I couldn't tell if it was meant as approval or disdain, or if it was just the beginning of a snore. She looked ready to drop.

Weiss hadn't revoked my access to the hospital records. He probably thought he wouldn't need to—either I would redeem myself, or I would die.

The thought made my stomach lurch, and I started talking again. "Of course, with Rosario gone, it'll be obvious what I've done. But even if we schedule the transfer to happen as fast as possible, it'll take some time to prepare her for travel, and that'll give us a chance to change the name on her records. Her hospital bracelet and physical forms might cause some minor problems, but I can handle that." I glanced over my shoulder. Arkay continued to glare at me with glazed eyes. "Being realistic, there's still a chance they might find her, but it'll take them a while. There are more than one hundred and seventy hospitals in the state, and they'll have to search all of them. We can go ahead and alter a few other details, so they can't try to narrow their search to hospitals that currently have comatose Latinas on their patient registries."

I might as well have been speaking Arabic for all that Arkay understood me.

"You know what? How about I take care of the name changes." It didn't look like she could handle using a pen right about now, let alone forge a nurse practitioner's handwriting. "How exactly did you manage to throw me around that room?"

All I got was another grunt. A master conversationalist, that one. I sighed and continued editing the forms.

"Names are all changed. Do you have a preference for which hospital we're sending her to, or is it—"

Arkay pushed me away from the keyboard and started typing in a sudden burst of activity, scrolling down to hide her contribution from me as soon as she'd entered it. Apparently satisfied, she sagged back into her chair.

The keyboard felt fuzzy with static when I touched it again. I ignored her secrecy and glanced at the name of the hospital. It was church-run, in a city maybe an hour north of us. Apart from that, I didn't recognize it.

"Just had that name sitting in your head?" I asked, not expecting a reply.

"Got a friend up there. He makes regular visits to the hospital. For charity 'n shit."

"You mean Father Gabriel?" He'd been transferred to Fort Wayne, hadn't he? Mentally I congratulated myself for keeping his name out of the official records.

"A friend," Arkay grumbled, but it was a weak diversion. We both knew who she meant.

That was the last of our conversation before she dozed off. Her head started off against my shoulder and slid gradually lower until half her body was sprawled across my lap. I worked around her without trouble. Apart from the lap dance that had damned me, I'd never spent much time around her, and now I had no reason to hide my curiosity. She was warmer than I'd expected. Lighter. Softer. Her mild, ungraceful snores seemed almost kittenish.

"Behold the most ruthless and dangerous of monsters," I mused. I could still taste blood on my lip from where she'd split it, and my chest and back would have bruises for days. But it was hard to reconcile that beast with the sleeping woman on top of me.

Maybe Rosario really had done something to me.

Arkay

I woke up to the warmth of a body, the steady rhythm of a heartbeat, and the familiar, cozy scent of home. I cracked open one eyelid: I lay curled up against Rosario's side, my head tucked under her arm, a thin cotton blanket draped up to my shoulders. Rosario's feeding tubes and IV drip had been carefully rearranged so my movements wouldn't disturb them.

Reluctantly, I crawled out of the bed and turned Rosario onto her side. Someone had replaced her hospital bracelet. The new one was bright and unblemished. Maria Sanchez, it said. The clipboard at her feet corroborated the name change, and included instructions for a transfer to a hospital in Fort Wayne.

So that hadn't been a dream.

Father Gabriel had been through surgery while I'd been asleep; he'd needed two screws to put his leg back together properly, but it would heal. That was for the best. He'd need to have his leg looked at regularly for the next few months, and that would give him ample excuse to check in on Rosario.

He'd be happy to do it, he said. It was the closest I would get to consolation. Aside from him, I would be trusting Rosario's life to strangers. I got twitchy just thinking about it.

I stayed with Rosario until the nurses arrived to take her away, flanked by their now-mandatory host of security guards. They smelled of secondhand sickness and disinfectant, and they shared the odd pallor of skin that's spent too long under fluorescent lights. Another shallow comfort: these guys, at least, were real.

It was almost nightfall by the time I returned to the ruins of our home. A few of the walls stood upright, but the roof had collapsed under its own weight, burying everything under debris. I picked through the wreckage for anything I could still use: my clothes, caked in soggy plaster dust; my wallet, buried under the bed; a few waterlogged blankets; the first aid kit and what toiletries I could salvage from the bathroom. Bricks had been tossed aside, evidence of other people looking over the rubble with the same idea. Apparently someone had tried to dig out the TV, only to find it twisted up beyond recognition. Rosario's laptop had been shattered. My own tablet had miraculously survived, probably because of the enormous rubber case that I'd used to protect it from the natural static of my fingers. Among the furniture, only my big pink armchair had survived, though its color had darkened with soot and rain, and it now smelled strongly of smoke.

Kindra offered to let me use her washing machine to clean my belongings, and volunteered her garage to store my armchair until I found a better place to keep it.

She didn't know what she was getting into. I didn't have a job, a social security card, or even a last name. Chances were I wouldn't find a place to stay until summer, when enough of the college kids left town to make homeowners desperate for the income of a new renter. I accepted the offer all the same, and thanked her for it. I really did like that chair. In the meantime, I went back to being homeless.

I'd spent most of my life on the street, revisiting old haunts and exploring my options. It never bothered me before, but now it carried a peculiar discomfort. It was too cold. Too quiet. Too lonely. It hadn't been like this before. I'd never been alone. Not when I'd had Rosa.

I saw Adam weeks later, hunched over a bowl of chili in the corner of a church soup kitchen in Indianapolis. His hair was a noticeable dirty blond now that it had grown out of its buzz cut, and he'd gained a beard to match. His jacket, more than warm enough for the early days of autumn, seemed pathetically light now that the grass started to crunch with cold. He still wore the same combat boots, though they were barely recognizable under all the layers of grime.

"Fancy seeing you here," I said, setting my tray down across from his. He tensed, as if to run. Where he expected to go was beyond me. "Chill, soldier boy. I'm not going to eat you. The food's not that bad."

Father Gabriel had been checking in with me at least once a week, mostly through email and photos. Rosario was safe in her new hospital. Nobody had come by to take her away to some freaky horror lab, which meant I didn't need to dish out a slow, agonizing death for Adam. In the meantime, Rosa would want me to play nice.

Reluctantly Adam settled back into his seat.

"What brings you to this fine establishment?" I asked. "Did the Nazi party cut their grocery budget or something?"

He scowled. "I'm not with the Order anymore."

"Congratulations." I tipped my cup of water to him.

His scowl only deepened. "They threw me out."

"Congratulations anyway."

"Go fuck yourself," he muttered.

"Only as a last resort."

Apparently he took that as an invitation to rant. "It's not like they left references, either. How the hell am I supposed to get a job around here without any history of employment? Or a place to stay? Do you have any idea how much motels cost in this city?"

"Gee, I totally didn't." I crumbled my dry cornbread over my chili. "Try the strip clubs. Most of their dancers are paid under the table, so they don't generally give a fuck about your resume. Might try applying as a bouncer, too, while you're at it, but the pay's shit. Barely over minimum wage without tips. I recommend dancing."

He snorted. I think he meant it as a derisive sound, but I chose to interpret it as agreement.

I waved a hand at an imaginary marquee. "I can see your stage name now: Adam N. Steve. You won't even have to change it all that much."

His amusement soured. "My name isn't Adam."

"I knew it," I said. "So was it like a regular alias, or did you make that one up special?"

"It was my name. It isn't anymore."

I blinked. "Yeah, I'm not following."

He poked bitterly at his chili. "They took it away when they threw me out. I didn't just lose my home, and my family, and the whole of my purpose on this earth. I lost my life. My name. My identity. It's gone."

Well. That explained the stale beer smell.

"They can't just take your name away," I said.

"The Order named me," he said miserably. "And they can unname me. And they did."

I fiddled with my silverware, trying to digest that piece of intelligence. But even after I processed it, the best I could come up with was, "That's stupid."

He glared at me. "You're a dragon. You wouldn't understand. Where did you even get your name?"

"I picked it," I said.

"Out of what, a dictionary?"

I shrugged. "I liked the way it sounded, so it's mine now."

"And you think my system's stupid." He lowered his head and continued sulking.

He really was pathetic, wasn't he? The guy couldn't even eat without someone to give the order.

I watched him poke at his food for a solid fifteen minutes before I spoke up again: "Mephistopheles."

He looked up listlessly. "Hm?"

"That's your name now," I declared.

He blinked. Blinked some more. "You're joking."

"Why not?" I asked. "If those assholes can just pass out names and take them back, then so can I. And I say you're Mephistopheles. Congratulations, you have a name again."

He took a long swig of his water. "You named me after the devil."

"*A* devil," I corrected. "The definite particle implies the king of hell. You're not that special, cupcake."

"You still named me after an unholy abomination."

I gave him a nice long look. "You're a racial supremacist who flunked out of the Nazi party. Meph is about as good as you're gonna get for a while."

He swallowed a spoonful, and another. "So my name is a punishment."

"Hey, at least it sounds badass," I said. "Take something else if it bothers you so much. But as of now, I'm calling you Meph."

He scowled some more, but he'd started eating again.

"Okay," he said at last.

"Okay?"

"Meph is fine. For now." He kept grumbling to himself, but when he stepped away to refill his glass, he took mine, too.

"For the record, you suck at fighting," he said when he returned my cup to me.

"Bullshit." I examined my water for evidence of tampering. "I've beaten the crap out of dozens of people."

"You've overpowered dozens of people," he corrected. "And you caught most of them by surprise, thanks to that helpless little girl routine you've got going on. The Order is going to come back for you one of these days, and when they do, they aren't going to fall for that. They know how to handle a dragon, and you're not even a very big one."

"You're kidding, right? Have you seen me?"

"Yeah. You're tiny. If it weren't for those giant antlers of yours, I'd assume you were still a juvenile. Which means if you actually want to survive what the Order is going to throw at you, you're going to need to work on your technique."

I flicked a stray kidney bean at him. "Has anyone ever told you that you're not a very complimentary person?"

"It's a mess. I'm seeing bits of pieces of what might be capoeira, some savate, a bunch of kung fu that looks like it came out of a bad action movie, and… I'm not even sure what the rest of it is supposed to be, so I'm going to be generous and call it street brawling."

"You're too kind," I drawled. "The Gestapo hasn't come for me yet."

"Only because they're gathering their forces. When they come back, there'll be more than six of them, and they'll be prepared."

I knew what he was doing. He was lonely and miserable, desperate enough to take any hand that reached out to him, even if it belonged to the thing he hated most in the world.

Rosario had always had a soft spot for people like him.

"Sounds like a good reason to skip town," I said. "I'm thinking someplace sunny. Wanna come?"

Book 5:
Forest of the Damned

I was in my senior year of high school when my brother put a shotgun to his head and tried to kill himself.

I say tried, because it didn't work.

I came home from a basketball game and found him on the floor, twitching and rasping. I never saw that much blood in my life— not before, and not since. And more than blood— worse than blood— were the goops of gray stuff. His big, smart, engineer brain was all over the floor.

And he was still alive.

See, he missed all the important bits for keeping you alive— the parts in charge of walking and breathing and shitting and all that. Instead the buckshot scrambled the parts of him that made him my brother.

Things got rough for my family after that. When my parents weren't bawling their eyes out, they were screaming at each other, blaming anyone and everyone for what happened to him. While they were warming up for their divorce, I ditched school and buried myself in video games. I just needed something to distract myself.

And then one day I got this message. This random guy, 3claw, started chatting me up in a chatroom on Battle.net. We hit it off, and exchanged AIM names (yeah, this was way back in ye olden days. Get over it). It was just regular conversation at first, and then it turned personal, and he asked me about my brother. By then I figured I knew him. And it felt good to talk. It was such a relief to be able to vent about it all without feeling like a complete asshole, you know? Like somebody had been aiming a gun at my head all this time, and they finally put it down.

And then 3claw sent me a message: *Do you want your brother to get better?*

Me: *Of course I do*

3claw: *There's a new procedure out. It's still experimental, but it may be able to help him.*

Me: *his brain is gone, man. He's a veg til the day he dies.*

3claw: *Then it can't hurt, can it?*

Me: *whatever*

3claw: *Would you want to try? If there was a chance?*

Me: *I just want my brother back*

3claw: *Is that a yes?*

Me: *I guess???*

3claw: *I guess isn't yes.*

Me: *YES, OKAY? YES I WANT MY BROTHER BACK. but it's not happening. drop it.*

He logged off as soon as I sent it. That was the last time I ever heard from him.

The next morning, the hospital called to tell us that my brother had been taken away to a private research facility—only nobody had ever heard of it. When my parents had them check the records, all that came up was dummy accounts and fakes. This place didn't actually exist. But the doctors swore up and down that the transfer had been authorized by my family.

My parents interrupted their divorce settlement to sue the hospital. Meanwhile, I tried everything to find 3claw. I sent him so many messages my computer froze. I asked around on all the Starcraft forums. A few people heard of him, but nobody knew who he was, or where he was from.

He was just gone.

It started messing with me, you know? Eating me up on the inside. My brother was gone again, and this time it felt like it was all my fault. Like I'd let this 3claw freak get his hands on him, like I'd sold him out without even knowing. I told myself that it wasn't my fault. That I was just a kid, and this 3claw freak was just another weirdo from the internet, and he had had nothing to do with what happened.

Funny how you can tell yourself something for ages and never actually believe it.

So one day I got in my car and got out of there. I didn't have a plan, I just needed to run and keep running.

About forty miles out of Oklahoma, I stopped at a gas station and went inside to grab that foul-ass coffee they always have inside, with enough cream and sugar to cover up the stale bean taste. I went to the front to pay, and I nearly shat myself.

His nametag said Jevon, but that was my brother standing behind the register. This wasn't one of those things where everybody has a twin, or an evil doppelganger, or some guy who looks a lot like him. This guy had my brother's raspberry birthmark over half his face. He had the same bald spots on either side of his chin where he couldn't grow a beard. He had the same big brown puppy dog eyes— both of them, perfectly fine, like he'd never been shot. He didn't have the scars, or the deflated balloon looking patch where the front of his skull used to be, or the drool hanging out of the corner of his mouth. He was real. He was whole.

Except he didn't know me. Not me, or our parents, or our dog. He didn't remember trying to kill himself. And when I tried to talk to him about it, he just looked at me like I was crazy. He even threatened to call the cops on me.

And yeah, I was shouting. "THAT SON OF A BITCH! WHAT THE FUCK DID HE DO TO YOU, TREY? WHAT THE FUCK DID 3CLAW DO TO YOU?"

He'd been completely blank before then, but suddenly you could see the blood drain from his face. His eyes went wide as hubcaps. And then he was on the other side of the counter, grabbing me by the shoulders and dragging me back to my car.

"Leave. Now. And you leave 3claw out of this." I didn't get a word in edgewise before he grabbed a crowbar from inside and ran at me like he wanted to take my head off. "I said get the fuck out of here!"

I came back the next day with a camera. I needed proof it was really him. I needed to show my folks. But when I got there, my brother was gone. I went up to the girl who was restocking iced tea in the coolers.

"Hey, I'm looking for the other guy who works here. Black guy, red birthmark on his face. He goes by Jevon."

She just looked confused. "We've never had anyone like that working here."

"But he was just here," I said. "Came at me with a tire iron. I kicked over the soda by the front— the floors are still sticky."

"Sorry," she said. "It was just Dana and Michelle here yesterday. I can ask them if they saw anyone—"

"No, he was behind the register. He worked here!"

It didn't matter what I said. She had no idea who I was talking about. Neither did the guy who came in to work the next day, or the girl after that, or the weekend guy.

It's like I saw a ghost.

Arkay

I scrolled past the story without much interest. This wasn't the first time I'd read that particular creepypasta, and it wasn't the most well-written version, either. Stories about ThreeClaw cropped up a lot on grief support websites, though the details changed with every retelling. This one was about a brother who'd attempted suicide. The last one had been a sister with ALS. The one before then had been a little kid who got in a car accident. Before that, a husband who'd OD'd on coke. ThreeClaw's name always stayed the same— but then, nobody ever changed Slenderman or the Rake, either.

I continued skimming through the rest of the forum. More fortunate survivors offered their advice on how to talk someone down from the edge. Those left behind shared their grief. A few well-meaning souls suggested probiotics and crystals and looking at trees.

Looking at all the trees in the world wouldn't do Rosario any good.

I minimized the browser and gave my eyes a rest. I'd been trawling these forums for hours, with nothing to show for it except another shitty ghost story. I flopped onto my stomach and buried my face in the scratchy motel blanket. On good days, I might find someone ranting about necromancy or summoning angels or demons or something equally interesting. Not that I had much faith in those sources anymore. I'd been possessed by a demon once. If it could heal people, then it wouldn't have had so much trouble holding onto a host body. The few would-be wizards and summoners I got a hold of wound up being quacks. For all their self-promotion, none of the other users ever declared that they'd been miraculously cured. You'd think if somebody could come back, they would be talking about it.

Laying down on the job didn't sit well with me. With a grunt of frustration, I pulled out my tablet again and started going through my emails. The first pass I deleted without bothering to look: hot singles in my area, exclusive offers to reduce student loan debt that I didn't have, and messages from sketchy dudes who'd responded to my dating profile and got pissed when I didn't reply right away. Equally sketchy women who were very likely preprogrammed bots. Actually interesting suggestions from women who were a few hundred miles out of my range at the moment. I saved those; maybe I'd hit them up again the next time I was near the Rockies.

I had legitimate emails from a folklore professor in Michigan, a museum curator in Ireland, and the dean of a seminary in New Zealand. I skimmed their letters for important details, then marked them unread. I'd respond to them later.

My phone rang, and I scrambled to answer it. "Meph! Tell me you have something. I'm dying in here."

He hesitated. "You said you were fine staying at the motel."

"And now I'm saying I want to get the hell out of here," I said. "What have you got? Did you find our guy?"

"Yes—" He stopped himself before he could add 'ma'am'. That would be awkward. "He's been visiting a property at the edge of the city limits. You were right about the lye pit— he's keeping it well-ventilated, but there's obvious activity going on in a wooden shed behind the cabin."

And Meph hadn't believed me.

This guy looked perfectly respectable, he'd said. He had a good feeling about him, he'd said.

Trial and error taught us that for all his experience hunting and killing people, Meph was really shitty at actually sussing out bad guys. To compensate, we'd established a system. In the mornings, the two of us wandered the most heavily trafficked public spaces in whatever city we found ourselves in that day, and I'd pick out potential evildoers from the crowd. When I gave the signal ("See that guy? No, not that one. The other one. The white guy in the blue shirt. No, the other one. Brown hair. Bad haircut. No, not him—follow my finger, Meph, see where I'm pointing?— yes. Yes, that one. You see him? Good. Yeah, I'm pretty sure he's our guy. Now go do the thing."), we split up. Meph followed our would-be culprit around town, and I retreated to our motel or the nearest place with free Wi-Fi and continued my research. And now that Meph had found actual evidence of wrongdoing, I had an excuse to get out of this damned motel and stretch my legs.

"Text me the address," I said.

"Do you want me to pick you up?" Meph asked.

I scowled at the phone. "Meph, I spent three years living on the streets before I met you. Most of my income came from mugging sexual predators. I think I can handle public transit."

"And if you can find any busses that'll take you into the woods outside of town, you're free to take them," he said. "But I haven't seen any. I wasn't exaggerating— this place is in the middle of nowhere."

"All right, fine," I said. "Come pick me up."

Half an hour later, Meph pulled up behind the wheel of a red Dodge Charger that we'd appropriated from a drug runner in Miami, along with a duffel bag full of cash.

Back when I'd been homeless, I'd let my prey come to me. I got the moral high ground that comes with breaking a man's face in self-defense, but my prizes had been limited to whatever they happened to have in their pockets. Not so anymore.

Meph's surveillance training meant we could follow our targets back to their homes, and once we brought them to justice, we got to take our pick of their belongings. That was where we got most of our stuff these days.

As he drove, the towering office buildings and lines of tightly-packed townhouses gave way to loosely clustered suburbs, which stretched and sprawled into wooded countryside. Mile by mile, the roads narrowed until the steady highway pavement had become a spindly dirt road that ended at our destination.

A click of our lockpick gun— another trophy from a past conquest— and the cabin door opened without a fuss. Our entrance wasn't overheard, judging by the whistled tune rising from the cellar.

It was a simple little one-story deal, the kind of place you might expect to find drunken coeds running from demonic zombies or cannibal hillbillies in a horror movie, though without the broken windows or rotting roof beams. Kind of cozy, really, if you could ignore the reek of bleach and bodily fluids wafting from under the floorboards.

That was how we'd found this guy. For the most part he'd been careful, preying on sex workers and the homeless and other people whose disappearances would go unreported, taking them out here to where they'd never be heard, and thoroughly cleaning up the evidence when he finished with them. He was probably at it now, whistling while he scrubbed somebody's remains off the cellar floor. He'd likely be wearing rubber gloves, plastic booties over his shoes, and one of those weird poncho things to keep the bleach from ruining his clothes, but the fumes of it still clung to his skin and matted his hair, no matter how many times he tried to wash them out. The smell of bleach was like a neon sign, made all the brighter by the sharp tang of lye. And beneath all of that, the unmistakable aroma of blood and fear.

But all of that didn't make for an instant death sentence. A month ago, Meph had spent three days following a woman with the same scent profile, only to discover that she was a hypochondriac dentist who made soap as a hobby. Not this guy, though. I had a good feeling about him. Or a bad one. Whatever.

The cheerful whistling grew louder, accompanied by the percussion of footsteps on stairs. A few moments later the cellar door swung wide, revealing a balding man with thick glasses and a cheerful smile. He looked more like a good neighbor on a sitcom than like a serial killer. But then, that's probably what made him so effective.

He passed me without looking up, apparently too lost in his own thoughts to notice a strange woman sitting in his darkened living room. Several minutes later, he emerged from the bathroom and finally thought to turn on the lights.

"Sonova—" He jumped back, jostling a bookshelf with one shoulder and sending several volumes to the ground.

"Not the son of anyone, actually." I didn't rise from his armchair. "But I'm one hell of a bitch."

He rushed away from the cellar and grabbed a shotgun off the mantle. "Who are you? How the hell did you get in here?"

"That thing isn't loaded, is it?" I didn't bother hiding my disgust. "In the house? That's like firearms safety 101. Don't load a weapon if you don't plan to use it."

"Oh, I plan to use it, alright." Give the man some credit, he bared his teeth in an impressive looking snarl. It didn't last very long, though. Not when the muzzle of Meph's Desert Eagle pressed into the back of his skull.

"Put it down," Meph growled.

The other man's gun slowly sank to point at the braided carpet. His knuckles were white on the forestock. "You the police?"

"Do you see a warrant?" I showed him my hands. "But if you want to call the cops, go right ahead. I'm sure they'd love to see your little workshop down there."

"Then who are you?"

"The turning point," I said. "This is the moment when your life changes. You get to decide what that change looks like." I rose from the chair. "The first option is the obvious one. You go to the police right now and turn yourself in, and you spend the rest of your life locked up where you can't hurt anyone."

"What's the second option?"

"You give up all of this and you start working for me."

There's an old saying known to adventurers, philosophers, and anybody who hasn't been living under a rock all their lives:

He who fights with monsters should look to it that he himself does not become a monster. When you gaze long into an abyss, the abyss also gazes into you.

Nietzsche said it first in 1886, and since then it's been an epigraph on a few thousand pieces of pop culture.

Almost a hundred and thirty years later, I decided the old saying needed a caveat:

Those who are monsters already should see to it that they fight other monsters. If you and the abyss are going to be eye-fucking all day, you might as well exchange phone numbers.

"This whole setup didn't make itself happen," I continued. "And obviously you've been at it long enough that you seem to know what you're doing. You come with us, and you use your talents against people who deserve it."

He laughed. "You think they didn't deserve what they got? You think any goddamn one of them didn't have this coming to 'em?"

I tilted my head. "Already on your way to vigilantism, are you?"

"If it didn't come from me, it would've come from someone else," he said. "Everyone wants what I've got. I'm just the only one smart enough to pull it off."

"Let's just agree to disagree on that," I said.

"Do you think you're better than me? You come barging in here like you're some superhero, like you're not doing exactly what I'm doing?"

I stepped in close, flashing a sharp-toothed smile. "I've laid out your options. Take your—"

I didn't get a chance to finish the sentence before he rammed the butt of his shotgun into Meph's stomach, ducking away from the pistol at his head. I sprang to the side, but not fast enough. A blast of buckshot caught me in the chest with all the force of a cannonball, throwing me into the armchair.

"Arkay!" Meph started toward me.

The serial killer rounded on him, raising his shotgun for a second blast. Meph snapped up to grab the gun out of his hands. Meph should have won a grapple easily, but he was at a bad angle and still short of breath. Slowly the other man inched the barrel of the shotgun closer to the ex-soldier.

I climbed to my feet in time to see a hand closing around the trigger guard.

The movements were instinctive. One moment I was beside the chair; the next, I had the man's head in my hands.

The movies always made it look so tidy. Just grab a person by the head and twist their chin past their shoulders, and they died instantly. The movies had no appreciation for the durability of the human body. The spine was designed to bend, and the entire torso would try to turn before it let the body do an exorcist impression. Actually snapping the neck required strength— a dragon's strength.

His bones crunched. His body spasmed and went limp. But even that didn't kill him.

I wrenched open the cellar door and threw him into his little workshop of horrors. The fall down the stairs probably didn't do him any favors, but I still heard the wet rasping of breath long after his body stopped moving.

Perhaps he'd die of thirst down there. Maybe his lungs would fail, and he'd choke.

In the end, Meph ventured down into the cellar and finished the job himself.

When he came back upstairs, his Desert Eagle was holstered, but his hands were clenched into fists. His face had taken on a green twinge.

"Sick fuck," he muttered, kicking the door shut behind him.

"I'm guessing there's nothing worth taking down there?"

"No."

I couldn't help being morbidly impressed. We'd taken down a lot of creeps since we'd started working together. Most of them didn't get this kind of reaction out of Meph.

There was a script for people getting upset like this. Rosario had explained it to me a long time ago: I was supposed to say 'do you want to talk about it?' and then nod politely and mirror his facial expressions while he talked— or if he said no, then I was supposed to not bring it up for at least a day.

Before I could decide whether or not I wanted to comfort Meph, he'd already started searching the cabin for valuables. The fact that he'd ignored the massive gun locker in the front room told me he wanted a distraction.

Before I could think of something suitably attention-grabbing, he stopped. "I could have shot him."

"Hm?" I squatted in front of the gun safe. Looks like the Hannibal wannabe kept it unlocked. That was just plain irresponsible. Somebody could lose a finger or something.

"As soon as he went for the gun. I should have shot him."

"No, you shouldn't have. We hadn't given him the choice yet."

"The fucker didn't deserve one."

"You know the rules," I said. "If you get a second chance, everybody gets a second chance."

He slammed a drawer back into a dresser harder than absolutely necessary. "They never take it."

"You did."

"That man was a serial killer," he snapped.

"And you're a mass murderer." I pulled a series of ammo cans out of the safe, along with a fancy hunting knife. "There's not a whole lot of higher ground to stand on, Meph."

"It's not the same," he said. "I thought I was doing the right thing."

I snorted. "Of course you did. Because nothing says 'God is on my side' quite like starting a gang war, right?"

He turned his back on me, and another drawer slammed.

Oh. Right. Not helping.

I went outside to stow two of the ammo cans in the trunk. While I was there, I stripped off my hoodie, the ruined bulletproof vest I'd worn beneath it, and the sweat-soaked undershirt beneath that. Entirely naked from the waist up, I stepped back into the cabin. I didn't glance at Meph as I grabbed the next set, but his abrupt silence let me know the exact moment he noticed me.

Rosario would have known a hundred ways to handle this situation. She had a talent for knowing exactly what people needed, and exactly how to give it to them.

I had a much more limited understanding of the human psyche, but my usual tactic proved decently effective. Which surprised me— you'd think by now he would be desensitized.

"You cold?" He probably had meant that to sound cool, rather than like a caveman grunt.

"The asshole ruined my vest," I said. "And I liked that vest, too. Do you have any idea how hard it is to find these things in my size? And ones that fit under my clothes?"

"Some idea, yes." He took a step toward me, then turned away, swallowing. He was still gawking when I came back and took the rest of our scavenged supplies out of his hands.

Seriously, it was like taking the battery out of a frozen cell phone. Instant reset.

I didn't repress the flare of satisfaction I felt when I walked out the door. He hated himself for looking at me, so I gave him every possible opportunity to look.

Just because we were on the same side didn't mean I'd forgiven him for what he'd done to Rosario. Sure, she would have wanted him to have a chance to redeem himself, and for her sake, I'd given it to him. So far he was even doing a pretty good job of it. But redemption was supposed to be a process, and I intended to make it as painful for him as losing Rosario had been for me.

Also the look on his face was priceless.

"Did you get all our stuff from the motel before you went out, or do we need to head back?" I asked.

He blinked, trying to regain his focus. Poor babe. "I— no, it's in the back already."

"Good boy," I said, standing on tiptoe to pat his head. "Shall we go?"

He nodded dumbly, and I waltzed back to the car to put on a sweater.

Meph

We'd just passed the last exit into Syracuse when my vision started swimming. We'd only been on the road four hours, but I was exhausted.

"Are you feeling up to driving?" I asked, glancing at the passenger side. Beside me, Arkay slumped in her seat, her arms pulled into her sweater and her head resting against the window. I sighed and pulled into the next exit, keeping my eyes open for the first motel that didn't look like it belonged to a national chain. The one I found looked dangerously unwholesome, but the manager accepted cash without asking any questions.

"Come on, Arkay," I said, easing open the car door and unbuckling her from the seat. "Let's get you into a bed."

Her eyes cracked open. "Hm?"

"Get up. We're stopping for the night."

She gave a vague hum of assent, and I half-led, half-carried her into the room and deposit her on top of the bed. When I came back from the car with our duffel bags, she'd managed to crawl under the blankets— and out of her clothes, judging by the pile of cotton at my feet.

I swallowed and stepped into the bathroom to change into a loose shirt and pajama pants, because one of us had to think about basic modesty.

Our sleeping arrangements were always a source of anxiety for me. Bad enough that I had to sleep with a man-eating monster in the same room, but we had to share the same bed. Even if Arkay had decided to let me live, it would only take one nightmare for her to eviscerate me. And what if my hands wandered while I slept? Would she lash out at me?

Or would she return the gesture?

Not that I should have been thinking about any kind of intimacy in the first place. The Order had sentenced me to death for the mere suggestion that I could harbor attraction to a dragon. It was wrong to even consider the idea. Disgusting. Ridiculous. And besides, the whole line of questions had turned out to be moot.

I crawled under the covers beside her, and she shifted to fit against the contours of my body. Her legs looped around my knees, and her head nestled comfortably against my shoulder.

Arkay saw me as a dog who slept at the foot of her bed— welcome company, but nothing more. She curled closer to me when she got cold. She changed in front of me without concern. When I stammered, she laughed.

If she realized how deeply she affected me, she didn't seem to care.

I woke up to a vantage point of Arkay's lap. She was sitting up in bed, her back against the headboard, her phone in one hand while the other rested idly on my shoulder. I caught a few glimpses of her screen, but I had other thoughts to occupy me. Namely the fact that she hadn't bothered putting on a shirt yet.

She had a nice body. Soft ocher skin; small, perky breasts; the slender musculature of an acrobat; and a constellation of scars. Flat silver lines around her wrists, from when she'd broken through handcuffs. Raised starbursts that puckered around the memory of a bullet. Angry red lines that showed off where she'd been grazed, slashed, and clawed at.

There was no hope of stripping in her future anymore, but that didn't seem to bother her. All her battle scars hadn't made any obvious dents in her confidence or her vanity, and they didn't keep her from wandering off to spend the night with strangers.

But not today. Today she was here, with my head on her lap, and I allowed myself to bask in that. I had a dozen reasons to worry and feel guilty, but none of them seemed relevant at that moment. None of them seemed worth dredging up to think about.

At least, not until Arkay stiffened.

I blinked the sleep out of my eyes. "Something wrong?"

She didn't answer. Her eyes flicked rapidly across the tiny screen.

"Arkay?"

She changed her grip on the phone and tried to navigate it— and when that failed, she jerked out from under me and dug her tablet out of her bag.

"Arkay?" I sat up. "What's going on?"

"There are two hundred artifacts that could possibly be the holy grail," she snapped without looking up. While the tablet loaded one page, she tapped again on her phone. "Most of them are in Europe. There are upwards of a thousand artifacts that supposedly contain unicorn horn in museums and private collections, but obviously there's no way to tell if they're real without testing them. And what would you even test them against? It's not like I've got a unicorn sitting around that I can grab a DNA sample from. Same goes for any journals belonging to Nicholas Flamel, Thomas Aquinas, or any other actually successful alchemist— which of course would be useless anyway, unless we could get the journals decoded and translated in any reasonable time frame."

"Okay?" I tried to connect Catholic artifacts, extinct homicidal equines, and medieval philosophers, but came up with a jumble of useless data. It was too early for this. "I'm sorry?"

"Fucking slow internet!" She hurled her phone across the room, and it bounced off the door with a clatter. Even with the thick rubber case, I was surprised it didn't shatter on impact. "You told me the Order has been chasing all things supernatural for centuries. They have to have found something since then. The fountain of youth. The Club of Dagda. The Ausadhirdipyamanas. Panacea. Phoenix down. *Anything.*"

I stared, dumbfounded. She wasn't making any sense. She'd been fine a few moments ago, and now she was pacing across the motel room, stopping only to dart back to her tablet and type in another command. I couldn't imagine what could get her so worked up so quickly, aside from—

Oh.

Oh shit.

"Did something happen to Rosario?"

She looked up, frustrated and confused, like she'd been speaking to me in French and only just realized it. Finally she translated for me— slowly, like she didn't expect me to understand. "She has pneumonia."

"Oh."

"Father Gabriel's been checking up on her. He sends emails."

I climbed carefully out of the bed. Arkay was at her most dangerous when Rosario was involved. It was one of the many reasons I had pointedly never asked about her condition all these months, and Arkay had never before volunteered anything.

"She's in a hospital," I said gently. "It's the best place for her right now."

"No, it's not." She turned back to the tablet. "This isn't the first set of complications. She had major trauma to her vital organs, catastrophic blood loss, infections, and that's not even starting on the dehydration and vitamin deficiencies that are common for coma patients." She started pacing again. "They're fighting just to keep her alive, and it's a fight they're losing. They can't fix her. They don't think it's even possible, because everything they know about science and medicine says that she's never waking up, but they're wrong." She threw her tablet at the bed. Her breath came in shallow gasps, like she'd run a mile. Electricity charged the air around us, snapping at my fingertips when I reached out to grip her shoulders. "They're wrong, because they don't even know that *I* exist, which means that there are a hundred million other things they don't know about. But I do— and I'm going to find it. I'm not giving up on her, Meph." She pulled back to start pacing again, but my hold kept her anchored in place.

She'd been researching this for a while— maybe since she first brought Rosario to the hospital. All that time, this had been eating away at her, and she'd never said anything about it to me.

Of course not. I was the one who shot Rosario in the first place.

"The Order's got to know something," Arkay said quietly.

I swallowed. "The mortality rate is high in the Order," I said. "If we— they— did, they wouldn't have lost so many people over the years."

"Bullshit."

"I'm sorry, Arkay." But sorry didn't change anything. Sorry didn't undo the damage in Rosario's brain, or slow the gradual deterioration of her body. "Not all fairy tales are based on reality. Sometimes they're just stories."

Her eyes narrowed. Her mouth twisted into a thoughtful frown. Abruptly she ripped herself out of my grip and dove back at her tablet.

"Arkay?"

"There's a story people tell online," she said without raising her eyes from the screen. "It's like Slenderman mixed with Rumplestiltskin. He kidnaps people who are sick and dying, and he says he can bring them back. Or she. It changes." She shoved the tablet at my face, too close for me to make out the words. "ThreeClaw. Ever heard of them?"

I gawked. She couldn't be serious. "I— I've never heard that story."

"It only really gets passed around on medical forums. Grief support groups, that kind of thing. And it's not like anybody listens to it— you don't go believing everything you read online— but there could be something behind it, right?"

"There... is. Something." *God save me.*

Arkay jerked upright. "So you do know the story?"

"I have heard of ThreeClaw," I said cautiously. "But none of the rest."

"So there's a chance!" Her eyes were wide and painfully bright. I couldn't stand to disappoint her when she looked at me like that.

"ThreeClaw was a... I think the best word for it would be a mob boss. Back in the seventies, it gathered a massive following of nonhumans— mostly smugglers and thugs." I didn't know how else to put it into words Arkay could understand. ThreeClaw was a nightmare even among monsters. It insinuated itself into warring factions as a peacekeeper, and then swallowed both sides into its army. It forced human and monster alike into subservience, and publicly butchered anyone who didn't comply. "Arkay, if ThreeClaw was taking people, then it probably wasn't trying to help them."

I'd meant it as a subtle hint to let go of that hope, but Arkay wouldn't be dissuaded.

"Maybe not," she said. "But mobsters have mob doctors. And if this person really did have a decently sized following, then they'd have some top notch medical supplies on hand in case something happens. It sounds like a lead to me."

Oh hell.

"Arkay, wait," I said quickly. "You don't know what you're getting into."

"Then you can fill me in on the way there." She pulled on a shirt from her duffel bag and stuffed the rest of her belongings inside. "Where do they live? Are they in the country, or somewhere else?"

"ThreeClaw is dead." I let the words hang between us. "The Order took it down half a decade ago. It's gone." It took the Order forty years and hundreds of casualties to do it, too.

Arkay paused for a moment of thoughtful silence. "Did they take down the whole organization, or just the boss?"

"What?"

"Which one?" she asked.

I massaged the bridge of my nose. How did I get involved in this? "ThreeClaw's Hoarde is still around," I admitted.

Arkay frowned. "Wait. Hold that thought. Do you mean horde as in raid, pillage and burn? Or hoard as in eight million cats and newspapers to the ceiling?"

"Both," I said wearily. "ThreeClaw considered its followers part of its holdings." I wrote out the word on a complimentary note pad that we'd swiped out from a classier motel a few weeks back.

Arkay tilted her head at the word. "Because nothing demands respect quite like cracking a pun. So if these guys are still around, do you know where?"

I sat heavily on the bed. "You're really planning to do this."

"I spent six months emailing every relevant history buff on the planet who would give me the time of day, and this is the closest I've come to an actual lead. Which part of that gave you the impression that I didn't plan to follow through?"

I pinched the bridge of my nose. This wasn't a conversation I wanted to have. "The Hoarde's headquarters are in an underground cavern. They call it Felldeep, and it isn't exactly secret. The Order has been sending strike teams in for decades— not insubstantial ones, either— and the number of people who've come back alive is in the single digits, and none of them got past what we'd assumed was the front entrance. Walking in there is a death sentence."

"Maybe for them," she said. "You've never sent a dragon."

"We don't even know if this will give you anything worth having. You're risking a ninety-nine percent mortality rate for a low probability of success. I'm sure if we just keep looking, something else will come up."

"I've been looking." Her tone was calm, but razor sharp. "And this is it. If you don't want to come, then you can stay right here. But first you're going to give me the address."

I turned my gaze to the window. I couldn't look at her anymore.

If I went with Arkay, we would both almost certainly be killed.

If I didn't, then no matter whether she succeeded or failed, I would be left alone.

She was already heading for the door.

"Wait," I said. "I don't actually know where Felldeep is. I don't have the place's address memorized."

She didn't even pause.

"Give me a day," I said. "Twenty-four hours to research so we can actually be prepared."

Finally she stopped. "You're coming, then?"

"Yes. I'm coming."

May God have mercy on my soul.

Arkay

Meph didn't have a computer of his own beyond his phone, and the Order's fancy websites were apparently too data-intensive to run on my tablet (a load of horse shit, I was sure), so we wound up spending the next two days wandering the halls of a public library. It would have taken us only one, but the library had shitty wiring and hadn't bothered to properly ground its workstations. When I got too excited too close to one, the whole row of computers fried. I kept my distance after that, clinging to my sensible tablet and its nice protective rubber case.

"So let me get this straight," I said, taking a break from researching ThreeClaw the old-fashioned way— via Google. "They kick you out. They take away your name. They freakin' try to kill you. But they don't bother changing your login information?"

"Of course they did," he grumbled. It was still a sore spot, apparently. "I'm not using my login, I'm using Mara's." His old handler had been one of his closest friends, though that hadn't been enough for her to stand up for Meph when he got the boot.

I tutted. "That's the first rule of computer security, man. Never give out your password. I'm disappointed."

"She didn't like filing reports," he said defensively.

"And you did?" What was I saying? "Of course you did, you big dork."

He glared.

"You're also supposed to change your passwords every six months or so," I pointed out.

"If you can find me a person who actually does that, I'd be happy to meet them."

The rest of my findings weren't particularly helpful. Most were creepypastas in the same vein that I'd found before. A few were usernames in forums and on gaming sites, which seemed more likely to belong to random teenagers than to a supernatural Al Capone, unless ThreeClaw had absolutely no grasp of basic grammar.

"You got anything?" I asked after an hour of dead ends.

"Bits and pieces. It looks like ThreeClaw's enforcer is in charge these days. Nadezhda Ruslanova Alkaev."

"That's a mouthful."

"Which is probably why she's usually identified by her rank."

"What, they just call her Enforcer?" I asked. Admittedly, it would be easier to say in one breath.

"Apparently within the Hoarde, her rank is Fext."

"Fext," I repeated. *"Fext?* Is that like a more intense version of a sext?"

"It's an old term— derived from the German word for bulletproof. They're supposed to be invincible warriors."

"Does it say the etymology of the word right there, or did you just have that nugget of information floating around in your head?"

"It's not too far off the mark, either," he said, ignoring me. "She's been recorded in at least four dozen combat situations since 1989, and there aren't any obvious scars or disabilities on file. It looks like she got hit by a Claymore in the early 2000s. Next time they saw her, she didn't have so much as a papercut." He clicked open a few files. "There's some speculation that she's undead. Some kind of ghost, maybe."

"Or they could just have a whole warehouse full of Fext clones," I mused. "Replace her with a new one every time she gets killed." I snickered. *"Fext."*

He gave me a side-eyed glare. "You do realize that you named yourself after a part of the alphabet. And you named me after a demon. You're not exactly the shining paragon of nomenclature."

"But aren't you glad I didn't call you Fext?" I asked.

He rolled his eyes and returned his attention to his computer.

Personally, I'd had my fill of staring at screens for the day, and I wandered off to prowl the stacks. For some reason, people kept assuming that I didn't like reading, but I generally enjoyed books.

I didn't know how to talk when I first met Rosario. Not for any reason in particular— before then, I'd never had a reason to get to know any humans, and so learning the language seemed like a waste of energy. I picked up the language fairly quickly once I set my mind to it, though. I didn't need to follow her around for long before I learned phrases like "are you okay?" and "spare some change?" and "fuck off, dickwad, I'm trying to sleep".

I was proud of that last one. It was a long sentence for a beginner, and an effective one for getting a point across. Rosario was less enthusiastic about my accomplishment, and she started taking me to the library to supplement my vocabulary. Before then she'd been reluctant to put me in an enclosed space for any length of time, but the days were getting cold and neither of us could stand being out in the snow for long. And so every morning we would march up the granite steps and into the abstract wonderland that was the children's section. I'd set up our stuff on a squiggly bench that we used so often that the librarians started calling it ours, and Rosario would retrieve a stack of books, and she would sit down on the squiggly chair and read to me, eight hours a day, from the moment the library opened until it closed for the night. She read me picture books and showed me picture dictionaries, pointing to each image until I linked the object and the word. When my comprehension improved, she moved on to chapter books and abridged classics. Within the space of a school year, I'd gone from not knowing a word of English to reading *The Strange Case of Dr. Jekyll and Mr. Hyde* while Rosario updated her blog.

These days, I could only peruse the shelves for titles to download later. We never stuck around any one place long enough to finish a book, and Rosario would have disapproved of borrowing a book without returning it.

"Any other hilarious details we need to know about?" I asked once the silence got too boring.

"None that are consistent," he said. "These reports are a mess. Some of them say the Felldeep is a few hundred square yards, some of them say it covers several dozen miles. It could be a base of operations, or an entire underground compound. And they don't even agree on whether or not it's underground."

"What, no windows?"

"Apparently not." Something popped up on his screen. He leaned in, frowning, and then sat back again. "I'll make a list of the supplies we'll need and pick them up tonight."

Meph

I dropped off Arkay at the bar with a wad of twenties and a promise that I would be back soon.

I could only hope I would be back soon.

While I'd been logged into the Order's servers, a message had popped up:

I know you're reading this.
I tracked your IP.
What the hell are you doing in NY?
—M

I should have realized Mara would be online. It always took her forever to file her reports— one of the reasons she'd always persuaded me to do them for her. Apparently that hadn't changed much.

But she shouldn't be talking to me at all, not even over email.

I was the worst kind of apostate. If I ever made contact with another member of the Order, they would kill me on sight.

But Mara was a friend. Or the closest I had to a friend, aside from Arkay.

M

Are you okay?

They know what happened with me wasn't your fault, right?

How is everyone?

I didn't know how to sign it. Adam wasn't my name anymore, and she didn't know me as Meph. She'd probably be as repulsed to know I'd been renamed by a dragon as by the reference to a demon.

Instead I sent it unsigned.

I can't talk here, she wrote back.

Where can I reach you?

I hesitated. This could be a trap. An email address or a phone number could be tracked, as easily as she'd tracked the computer I was using. This could be the preamble to an ambush.

But we'd be marching into certain death tomorrow anyway.

I gave her my phone number.

Call me after 8 my time.

The green clock on my dashboard read 8:06. Arkay was prowling some faraway bar for a dose of nightly comfort, and I had an excuse to be gone for however long Mara wanted to talk. I paced in the vast parking lot of a Lowe's and counted the moments.

Finally the phone rang— some shrill pop tune Arkay had programmed into it as a prank, which I'd never gotten around to changing back.

I let the call go through and put the phone to my ear without a word.

"Hello?" Mara asked cautiously. "Are you there?"

It almost hurt to hear her voice again. "Yeah. I'm here."

"God help you," she said. "What did you do? What were you thinking?"

I should have expected an interrogation. "You're going to have to be more specific, Mara."

"You want specific?" she snapped. "Let's start with how you abducted the Hernandez girl."

Arkay would have bristled at hearing Rosario referred to like she was a child.

"I had to, Mara." I sagged against the hood of the car. "They wanted to bring her back to headquarters."

"Exactly! That was what we wanted, remember?"

"Not if it meant vivisection," I said. "You know what kind of information they wanted. Bone marrow, brain tissue— that's not the kind of thing you can get out of a person in one piece. Not in the quantities they were asking for. I couldn't let them do that to her."

"No, but you could sneak her out of a hospital and hide her God-only-knows-where. And for what? The Hernandez girl isn't going to complain about it. She can't even feel it. She's a vegetable. At least if you'd left her to us, she could have done some good before she went out."

This morning flashed before my eyes: Arkay, frantic and pacing, grasping desperately for straws. Her eyes so painfully wide and bright when I gave her a scrap of hope to cling to.

"I'm sure you believe that," I said quietly. I tried to change the subject. "Are you doing alright, Mara? I hope they weren't too hard on you after what happened."

"They demoted me, if that's what you're asking." She snorted. "It didn't stick, though. They threw me at a Mishibizhiw in Quebec. The damn thing took out three quarters of the team before it went down, but the rest of us got commendations. Now I'm back to where I was. Back where I belong."

"Good," I said faintly. "You deserve it."

She paused. "You can come back, too."

The words shot through me like lightning. "Did the ruling get overturned?"

"No, not yet. The Synod upheld the decision. But it doesn't have to be permanent. There's still a way out of this."

"I don't see how." I fell back against the car again. "A damnatio memoriae has never been revoked, Mara."

"You'd be amazed what the higher ups can forgive when you bag a dragon."

A lead weight dropped into my stomach.

"You're the expert on Arkay," she continued. "And you're resourceful as fuck when you want to be. You can find it again, and you can bring it down. You can tell the Synod that this whole fiasco was a misunderstanding. That you were just biding your time until you made your move. They'll understand."

Hope hit me like a slap in the face, soured by revulsion. Kill Arkay?

Yes, she was a dragon— but she'd named me. She'd protected me. She'd forgiven me, or as close to it as she was capable. She'd given me something to work for when I didn't know what to do with myself. And for all her eccentricities, I had never once seen her do anything that I could honestly call evil. She never went after anyone without evidence. Never took them out without first offering them a choice.

Murdering her now, without provocation, after everything we'd done together— that would be cold-blooded betrayal.

It would be wrong.

I shoved the remnants of hope away so I could think clearly. "I don't think they will, Mara."

"They've been willing to listen so far," she said.

Another slap. "God. Mara, what did you do?"

"I made a case for you. A good one. The evidence Weiss used against you was circumstantial at best, and he never gave you a chance to say your piece. If you bring them the dragon, then you can prove that everything you've done was just a means to an end. And yeah, you'll be in hot water for unorthodoxy, but they can live with that. You'll be able to come back where you belong. Back home."

The word was the final gut punch that floored me.

Home.

I could go *home.*

Back to the Order. Back to stability and family. Back to everything I'd ever believed in.

My knuckles were white around my phone. My hands shook. If I hadn't been leaning against the car, my knees wouldn't have been able to hold me.

I could have my name back. My job. My purpose.

I could go back to standing between the common man and the monsters that lurked in the dark.

Only…

Only I hadn't really stopped, had I? The monsters I was fighting now were more often kidnappers, serial killers, human traffickers, not supernaturally gifted but still insidious.

That had to count for something, didn't it?

Not all monsters were inhuman, after all.

And not all inhumans were monsters.

"Are you still there?" Mara's voice was distant. I'd let the phone fall away from my ear.

"Yeah," I rasped.

"You can do this," she said. "You can find the dragon. I know you can."

"Finding her won't be the problem." The words were lifeless and empty.

"I can find you some decent firearms," she said. "We don't use our full arsenal all the time. I'm sure nobody would notice if a Barrett went missing."

"It's not that," I said. "Mara, I don't know if I can do that." The other end of the line fell silent. "I know where she is, Mara. And she's not— I don't think she's the kind of dragon we should be going after. It wouldn't be helping anyone. You saw her, Mara. She's—she's *different*. She's not like—"

"Oh my God," Mara said quietly. "You really have been sleeping with it."

"I—" I couldn't lie to her about how I'd woken up this morning— and most mornings, since Arkay and I had figured out our sleeping arrangements. "I haven't been having sex with her."

"But you want to."

"It's not—" I stumbled over the words.

She let out a low, disbelieving laugh. "Really? What is it, then? Explain it to me. Tell me why you don't want to kill the man-eating reptile."

"She doesn't eat people," I said. "She tries to help them. To save them. Maybe she wasn't always like this. Maybe Rosario did something to her, but she's—" I didn't know the words. "It's almost like she's human."

"But it *isn't* human," she said. "You understand that, don't you? It can't feel like humans do."

"You haven't seen her like I have."

"You sure about that? Because I was watching it right there with you, before you fucked things up. And you know what I saw? An overactive sex drive and the possessive reflexes of a hoarding instinct. And that's it. Perfectly typical behavior for a dragon. For any dragon. I know these last few months have been hard on you. I know you don't handle isolation well. But don't let this thing trick you into thinking it cares about you. It's a dragon. They're not capable of love."

But Mara hadn't seen Arkay half mad with grief at Rosario's bedside, wailing and gnashing her teeth like her very soul had been ripped to shreds. She hadn't seen Arkay get shot and stabbed in the name of honoring Rosario's philosophy. She hadn't seen Arkay pacing like a madwoman, terrified beyond reason by the prospect that Rosario would never wake up.

Arkay didn't love me. She probably never would. But not because she couldn't.

"I don't expect you to understand," I said.

"I understand just fine," Mara said. "This thing is manipulating you. It knows you're talented, and it knows you've got access to the Order's files, and it's feeding you manufactured affection to make you help it. It's using you. You have to see that."

"Mara—"

"Get out of there," she said. "Please. Get out while you still can."

Arkay

"Turn here," Meph said.

I frowned. "Seriously?"

"Seriously."

Reluctantly I turned into the exit that veered slightly off the highway. Seven hours of driving had brought us to the complete middle of nowhere: a lonely rest stop tucked in between the mountains of West Virginia. A trio of semi-trucks lounged in the far edge of one parking lot. In the other, a minivan and a U-Haul truck occupied opposite corners. It looked exactly the same as every other rest stop we'd passed in the last six months. The same urinal-cake smell wafting out of the men's room, the same awkward coffee/cocoa/soup dispenser tucked in with the vending machines, the same racks full of brochures for local tourist traps. Not exactly the kind of place you'd expect to find mustache-twirling villains.

"You're sure this is the place?" I asked again. "It's so… benign."

"I think that's the point," Meph said. "It's supposed to be the last place you'd expect it to be. But these are the coordinates I got off the database." He ran his hand absently over a map of the state, his fingers tracing the gaudy 'You are here!' sticker. "There's another town not too far from here. Do you want to hit a motel before we go in?"

"No." It occurred to me a moment too late that maybe he hadn't been asking entirely for my benefit. He'd done most of the driving on the way here. "Do you need to sleep?"

He glanced back at the car through the oversized windows. "We're already here. We might as well get this over with."

I adjusted my duffel bag, and the water sloshed in the several canteens that dangled from the straps. We'd never brought food and water with us before. We'd never been on a raid that lasted more than an hour, and that was including the one time with the drug dealer's pet tiger.

Cameras watched us from every corner of the rest stop, and they probably didn't belong to the Department of Transportation. According to Meph, the Order had tried putting up their own surveillance on the area. It took them three weeks to realize that the same handful of cars kept coming and going every day. The Hoarde's operatives had spliced themselves into the network and replaced all the video all with a looped feed, and then mailed a box of disassembled cameras to the Order's New York office. They probably already knew we'd arrived.

No point in being sneaky, then.

Between the men's and women's restrooms stood the door to a cramped maintenance closet. Inside, rolls of toilet paper as big around as my waist lay stacked almost to the ceiling. Glass cleaner and floor polish shared shelf space with piles of toilet brushes and plungers. A bag of road salt slouched against one corner. On the far wall stood a fuse box, an emergency phone, and a pair of valves.

Just two. One was marked Water Main. The other wasn't marked at all.

I reached out and gave it a hard twist counterclockwise. It barely resisted, turning with a series of clicks rather than a squeak. Something else clicked at our feet, and a trap door slid open, widening a few inches for every turn of the valve.

"That's it?" I asked. "No pass codes? No key? No 'you must answer questions three'?"

"No." Meph peered down into the tunnel. "You know, there might still be some alternatives we haven't considered, in case you want to turn back now. Have you tried True Love's Kiss?"

It was meant as a joke, but I glared at him. "That was like the third thing I tried." I even had Rosa's girlfriend try it, in case 'True Love' excluded aromantics for some bullshit reason. It didn't work for her, either. Apparently, comas don't work the same in real life as they do in fairy tales. "If you don't want to come, then don't. But I'm going."

"It was worth a shot." Meph lowered his bag into the darkness and followed after it on a wooden ladder.

I felt a bit disappointed. "Is it booby trapped, at least?"

"Seeing as I've landed safely, I'm going to say the answer is no. Come on, the ladder's steady."

I declined the ladder, jumping instead into the opening. I landed on solid stone maybe fifteen feet down.

"Shit!" Meph pulled tighter against the ladder. "Warn me before you do that!"

"It's not like I hit you." I hoisted my duffel over my shoulder.

"No, but you could have."

The maintenance closet's single bare light bulb filled the space with a murky yellow glow. It looked like a tunnel, easily as tall as it was wide, heading back and gradually down. It felt mildly chilly, almost pleasant after the June heat.

Meph laid his hand on the seam where the smooth stone had been patched with rougher concrete. "The first time the Order came down here, the team tried to clear the tunnel with a grenade. Then they got down here and realized there wasn't anything to fight off. Not yet, anyway."

"No guards?" I asked. He shook his head. "No locks, either. Seems like shitty security to me." Overhead, the trapdoor began creeping shut with a mechanical click. "Well, let's see what makes this fortress so damn impregnable."

I'd expected something to replace the glow of the murky light bulb— halogen tubes, or glowing fungus, or *something*. Even Christmas lights would have been welcome. Instead, all we got were the military-grade glow sticks Meph pulled out of his duffel. Which was fantastic. Now we looked like a pair of teenage hopefuls at the world's loneliest rave.

It was surreal. The tunnel was large enough that the far corners were steeped in shadow. The darkness loomed like a physical presence, huge and oppressive. For a while, the only sounds in the tunnel were the soft rustle of clothes and the steady clap of boots on stone. After a while, I started to wonder how long we'd been walking, and I realized I had no idea. We could have been marching for twenty minutes or forty. Maybe longer than that. We had to have covered at least a mile— maybe two? Three?

I pulled out my phone. The screen, still set to its daylight brightness, left my eyes watering before I hastily turned it down.

"What are you doing?" Meph asked. "You're not going to get any service down here." His voice sounded tinny and hollow as it bounced off the walls.

"I'm not trying to make a phone call," I said. "Do you know what time we started?"

"Five, maybe? Six?"

I frowned. "So we've either been down here for half an hour, or an hour and a half.

"That can't be right," he said.

I showed him the phone. "Apparently this tunnel goes on forever. Wait." Something occurred to me. "It can't *actually* go on forever, can it? Because never-ending hallways are actually a thing in horror movies."

He hesitated. "No? Of course not."

It didn't exactly inspire confidence.

We kept walking, though we might as well have been on a treadmill. The tunnel didn't change or shift. I'd started to build up a sweat from our endless walking, and the cold air left me shivering.

"So here's a theory," I said, checking my phone again. Twenty minutes since my last peek, and another seven percent less battery. Stupid piece of crap. "Maybe that thing the surveillance team saw wasn't a looped video feed. Maybe this whole area is part of a time loop, and we got caught in it. We're just going to keep walking down the same stretch of tunnel forever."

"Have I ever mentioned that you're a pleasure to be around?" Meph asked dryly. "Stop putting ideas in my head."

"Freaking out yet?"

"I'm going to be a lot less useful to you if I'm jumping at every sound."

Aw. My little Meph was getting scared. It would be adorable, if I hadn't been giving myself the creeps, too.

"How about a conversation, then?" I asked. "Tell me about this ThreeClaw person."

He looked uncomfortable. "What about it?"

"What's with the name?"

"It only had one arm," he said. "The other had been removed at the shoulder— which left three limbs. Supposedly, three claws."

"So not human-ish?" I asked.

"A dragon." Meph's voice started to settle into a more relaxed register, the way it usually did when he started nerding out. "At least, it claimed to be a dragon. We never found any evidence of it presenting in anything but a humanoid form."

"Seems like a weird thing to lie about," I said.

"Not really. It's politics. Most of the different subclasses of monsters have their own hierarchies. Fae have their courts, trolls have their own set of laws, ghouls have theirs, and so forth— and that's not even getting into regional differences.

It seems like the only thing they can all agree on is that it's not smart to piss off dragons. So the highest authority in a mixed crowd would generally be a dragon."

I snorted. "Not that I saw."

"Are you sure about that?" he asked. "Those potlucks you used to hold had some of the most diverse attendance we've seen outside of the Hoarde. I saw monsters there that had generation-long vendettas against each other, with no sign of fighting."

"Well, yeah," I said. "But that's because of Rosario. She doesn't put up with that shit."

"Maybe," he said. "But did any of them ever show you disrespect after they knew what you were?"

"Not really? But it's not like they were bowing and scraping, either." I switched the strap of my duffel bag to my opposite shoulder. I should have worn a backpack.

"Generally people don't expect to do much bowing at a potluck," he pointed out. "There's a firebreather operating out of Germany who calls itself the Contessa. It seems to think it's royalty, and nobody who disagrees lives long enough to talk about it. I've heard its territory described as a palace."

I liked the idea of a palace. A big one, with koi ponds and water slides. I lingered on the image for a moment, before I realized the conversation had died down.

"Do a lot of dragons have palaces?" I asked.

"Only a few that I've heard of," he said. "The Contessa, a handful in Asia. ThreeClaw had the Felldeep. I'd heard of one in Brazil that had the locals build it a temple. But they're the exception. From what I've heard, most dragons live wild."

"Palaces are definitely the better option there."

Meph raised an eyebrow.

"I used to do that," I said. "I don't recommend it. You have to hunt every time you want to eat, and half the time the stuff you eat is either sick or poisoned. And when you get too sick to hunt, you go hungry. It's not like there's takeout in the middle of the woods or anything."

"I didn't know that." Meph's voice was quiet.

"Really? I thought it would be pretty obvious. You need money to order pizza, for one thing."

"That you used to live wild," he said. "I assumed you'd always been with Rosario. You never talk about your life before that."

I shrugged. "I hunted, I ate, I slept, and eventually I got sick. Things got more interesting when I met Rosario. What more is there to say?"

Meph

"Are you alright?" I asked.

"Fine." Arkay's heavy breathing made that hard to believe.

"We can switch bags if you want." Maybe it had been a mistake to pack the spare ammunition and extra water in her pack. She'd never complained about carrying heavy loads before. But then, we'd never done this much walking at one time, and the tunnel had turned abruptly into a staircase.

"I'm fine," she repeated.

"A rest wouldn't hurt," I tried, but she only glared at me. "Look, you're not going to be much use if we get ambushed and you're exhausted."

She stormed past me with a burst of speed. "Which part of 'I'm fine' don't you understand?"

"You're tired," I said. "And you get hostile and snappish when you're tired, and I'm the one you take it out on. So forgive me if I've got a vested interest in seeing you rested."

"For the love of fuck, I'm not that—" She stopped short, and took a step up onto a wide landing. "Okay, so maybe I am."

"Arkay?"

She lowered her bag and dug her phone out of her pocket. The glow of the screen cast a fluorescent halo around her head. "Meph? What time does the sun set around here?"

"Around nine," I said automatically. "Why?"

"It's a little after seven." I could hear the frown in her voice. "So we're not outside."

If we were, we would have felt it. Outside, the air was thick and hot from a rainless summer. Down here the air was cold and clammy, an eternal fifty-two degrees Fahrenheit.

"We're still underground," I said cautiously. "Are you sure you're feeling alright?"

"That's what I'm trying to figure out." A tall, thin shadow resolved before her. As she drew closer, the light from her glow stick gave it shape and texture. "Meph, are you seeing this?"

I stared. "That's a tree."

"So that would be a yes."

"That's a tree," I repeated. "We're underground."

"Your powers of deduction leave me speechless."

What I'd mistaken for a landing was an enormous cavern. The ceiling stretched past the reach of my light, nothing but the shadows of leafless branches against inky blackness. Our glow sticks caught the edges of more trees: the diamond-pocked bark of aspens; the gray furrows of hemlock and ash; the smooth blue-gray of beech. A carpet of pine needles softened our footsteps, but there were no other leaves— neither on the ground nor the trees, even though we were in the thick of June.

I dug at the detritus with the toe of my boot. Underneath the layer of needles and dirt, the tree trunk sank directly into a layer of concrete, just like in the tunnel. "I think the Order's been here."

"That's reassuring," Arkay said. "Any of those reports of yours mention a big-ass forest?"

"No, they didn't." Which meant nobody who came this far had ever come back.

A sharp cracking sound filtered through the trees. Maybe something had stepped on a branch— but it sounded an awful lot like a shattering bone.

Arkay crouched beside her bag. "So it looks to me like we've got two major options. Either we can try sneaking around in the dark and get stalked by some nocturnal nightmare, or we can shoot up a couple flares and actually see what we've got to work with."

"And instantly reveal our positions to everything and anything in these damned trees," I pointed out.

"There were cameras watching us come down here, and there's only one exit from the tunnel. Unless whoever runs this place has shitty security guards, they already know we're here. And anything that lives in these trees knows anyway. We're not exactly being quiet, Meph."

I tried to come up with a better argument, but Arkay was already moving away from the bag, holding a magnesium flare. She ripped away the cord at the end, and the flare blazed like a miniature sun in her hands, gushing sparks that smoldered in the pine needles at our feet. The forest lit up with a brilliant red glow, and I peered away from the light to try and find the edges of the cave. Billows of smoke blocked my view of the ceiling overhead. Around us, the light ended before the trees did. Sinewy trunks and branches blocked the light on every side, so the red glow ended in sharp edges that shifted as Arkay moved the flare. The effect wasn't unlike an enormous mouth full of gnashing teeth.

I caught a shape in the distance, watching us from between the trees. I moved toward it, but a sudden movement caught my attention.

One of the shadows peeled free of the splintered dark and moved deliberately to one side. I waited for the light to frame the shape, but when it crossed into the shadow of another tree, the light ended abruptly, like it had been blocked by a screen. As I stared, the shadow jumped to another tree, closer this time. Still the light didn't come back.

"Arkay?" I backed up a step.

The shadow I'd been watching wasn't the only one like it. They danced around us, carving away our circle of light a few feet at a time, creeping ever nearer.

Arkay crouched into a fighting stance, her face contorted into a snarl, but the shadows didn't seem to notice. Within minutes, a fifty-foot diameter became twenty, then fifteen, then ten. Shapes darted across the bark of the tree. Skittering and reptilian, they flashed their jaws against the light and left nothing but darkness in their wake. Arkay lunged. Her claws raked through dead wood and sent splinters flying, but the darkness kept coming.

"Arkay, they're after the light," I said in a rush.

"No shit!" The words hissed through sharp teeth.

"No— I mean—" I gave up. There was no getting through to her when she was like this. So I did the only sensible thing and grabbed the flare out of her hand, hurling it into the trees.

Once again we were plunged into darkness. Arkay gave a final hiss, but finally straightened beside me. After the brilliant glow of the flare, I could barely make out the movement by the light of our glow sticks.

"The fuck was that?" Arkay demanded.

"Living shadows," I said. "They eat light. And things that create it."

"Like flares?"

"Like us," I said.

"What about these?" Her glow stick went dark as her hand closed around it.

"Apparently not bright enough to be tempting," I said. At least, that's what the training manuals said. "They're minor monsters. Vermin."

"Sure they are," Arkay grumbled, leaning close to me.

Too late I made the connection.

Almost a year ago, Arkay had been possessed by a shadow demon. We'd been able to exorcise her, but not before it took control of her body and nearly murdered Rosario. Most of the time she pretended to be unaffected by the trauma, but we slept in the same bed. I was fluent in the sounds of her nightmares.

The scent of woodsmoke distracted me from my sympathy. In the distance, new flames bloomed around the discarded flare, crawling across the forest floor and climbing up the trunk of a tree.

I blanched. The dead, dry trees would go up like kindling. The pine needles would burn even faster. Within minutes, this whole damned forest would be an inferno.

I grabbed Arkay's arm. Maybe if we could get down the stairs, we could escape the worst of the heat and smoke. Maybe we could get back to the tunnel's entrance before we asphyxiated.

Oh God, I'd killed us both.

But before I could open my mouth, a massive shape closed over the flame. Sparks flew through the air and glowed briefly on the pine needles before they, too, were smothered. There was that sound again— the *snap, crack, crack* of breaking bones.

"That wasn't another shadow just now, was it?" Arkay asked quietly.

I swallowed.

I didn't need to answer.

A rational person would have taken this opportunity to turn back and regroup, maybe get our hands on some infrared goggles. But we were down here for Rosario, which meant Arkay was anything but rational.

She slung her bag over her shoulder and marched into the darkness, led by the light of a single tactical glow stick and her own dogged determination. According to my compass, we'd been heading mostly northwest.

"Any idea where you're going?" I asked.

"Nope."

Of course not.

"Do you— Arkay, get down!" A figure appeared in the trees, humanoid and barely visible in the light of our glow sticks. Arkay crouched to spring, and in an instant I had my firearm unholstered and aimed. The figure didn't move.

"On your knees," Arkay commanded.

No reply.

"Who the hell are you?"

Still nothing.

"The fuck is wrong with you?" she asked, this time more to herself than to the stranger. She advanced a few steps, and the faint light washed over its face.

Or rather, its lack of a face.

It was a mannequin, made of yellowed cotton and wrapped in solid olive army fatigues that looked like they belonged in a history museum. Stuffing and a metal frame peeked out through a rash of gunshots on its chest.

"Well, that's creepy as fuck," Arkay observed.

"What the hell is that thing?" I asked. "And... why?"

"Maybe it's like those terra cotta warriors. You know, in China?" She sniffed at it. "I just know it's been down here for ages."

"Do you smell anything?"

She paused to give me a disapproving look over her shoulder. "It's a forest. I smell lots of things."

"Well?" I asked. "Anything important?"

"Trees. You. Me. Smoke. And a whole bunch of other things that I've never actually seen before, so how the fuck should I know what they smell like?"

With that gentle reassurance to soothe my nerves, I tightened my grip on my Desert Eagle.

The mannequin wasn't the only one like it. Now that we knew to look for them, we spotted others perched in tree branches as though to watch us. One wore medieval French plate mail. Another wore the mangled uniform that used to be standard issue in the Order.

It was still stained with its owner's blood.

We'd been walking for close to a half hour when Arkay stopped short. "Meph!"

I leaped to her side, my firearm raised for a quick shot. "What is it? What's out there?"

"Over there!" She pointed into the trees. "It's a deer!"

I blinked, lowering the weapon. I'd known her for more than a year. I'd spent half that time watching her every move through endless camera displays, and the other half sleeping in her fucking bed. And yet I still had a hard time discerning a gasp of alarm from a giddy schoolgirl squeal.

How the hell had Rosario done this? Sure, she was a Potnia Theron, but there had to be some kind of trick to this, wasn't there?

It just wasn't fair.

"Look at it," Arkay cooed, pulling me close. "It's been ages since I've seen a deer up close. It's so pretty!"

I had every reason not to put up with this shit. Instead I squinted into the dark. "Where?"

"Right in front of us."

"I don't see it."

"Right there. There's a leg, and there's the other leg, and there are its hooves— see?" As she pointed them out, she traced the outlines of the shapes with her fingers. Only that couldn't be right. Yes, those two lines looked roughly like the forelegs of a deer, but they were obviously trees. The things she called hooves were each the size of car tires.

But then one of those trees bent and pulled itself out of the ground.

"Hell," I whispered, raising my glow stick. The long legs widened and came to a halt at a massive white belly, bristled with fur. Another shape moved at the corner of my vision. I'd mistaken it for a fallen tree, but no— it was a neck. A goddamn reindeer nosed at the forest floor. And yes, it *would* have been pretty— if it wasn't the size of a two-story building. Large, tawny ears flicked in our direction. Its antlers were taller than I was, and branched in patterns so complex that they seemed almost fractal, but they looked disproportionately small on its enormous head. A juvenile, perhaps. A fawn.

Dear God, what did the full-grown version look like?

Arkay didn't seem to share my horror. While I made my observations, she'd been digging in her bag, and now she came out with a cupped fistful of granola.

"Here, Bambi," she cooed, clucking with her tongue.

Oh no. If she threatened the thing, if she provoked it, it would come after us. I didn't want to find out just how sharp those fractal antlers could be. "Arkay, wait!"

But she was already at the edge of the shadows, presenting a fistful of dried fruit and granola to the enormous deer. It stilled, watching her with large inky eyes that didn't reflect the light of the glow sticks quite right. Then it stretched its neck and daintily nibbled the treats out of her hand.

Arkay giggled. "Look at that, Meph. It likes me." The deer shifted to snuffle at her pockets, and she ran her palms along its face. "You have to try this, Meph. Its nose feels like velvet."

Behold Arkay, the great and terrible dragon, most evil and dangerous of all monsters, giggling over a deer like she was a child in a petting zoo.

This was what my life had become.

I crept closer, one hand still on my firearm. I'd been wrong about its eyes: they didn't reflect light so much as swallow it. The points of illumination came from within. Pinpricks of starlight clustered into swirling nebulae in its huge, inky eyes.

I reached out my hand to touch it, the deer tensed and bounded away. It moved gracefully, somehow keeping those enormous antlers from catching on the branches. Its bucket sized hooves barely made a noise as it disappeared into the dark.

Arkay

I wasn't sure how long we'd been walking. My phone's battery was dying, and without it, we had no way to mark the passage of time except with the trees and the random scents that crossed our path. Noises rustled in the distance, like footsteps on the soft ground, but that could be anything.

I could feel every ounce of the duffel bag as it dragged at my shoulders. Our brief water breaks only reminded me how much I didn't like carrying the damned thing, and we weren't depleting our canteens nearly fast enough to get rid of the extra weight.

"Okay," I said. "I'm calling it. We're making camp for the night."

"Are you sure?" Meph asked.

Like I'd say so otherwise.

"We've been walking for ages," I said. "Let's get some sleep and try again in the morning. Or when we wake up. Whatever. Time is weird down here."

I lowered my bag, finding the long cylinders of the flares by touch more than by sight. The light would only last us a few moments before the shadows scarfed it up, but at least that would give us an idea of our surroundings. A rip of the cord, and it burst into flame and began belching bitter metallic-smelling smoke.

"Shit!" Meph yelled, punctuating the shout with a trio of gunshots. At the edge of the narrowing circle of light, a shape fell out of the trees and plummeted to the ground with a chitinous crunch. "What the hell is that?"

I pocketed another flare and crept closer, wrapping myself in scales for protection. It was the size of the lions at the zoo, and it looked like the kind of nightmare you'd have after watching *The Thing*. Red-black cruor seeped from a cluster of gunshot wounds in a bulbous, muscular thorax. From that central point stretched five sinewy, many-jointed limbs, now curled up like the legs of a dead spider. Protrusions covered its body. I took them for barnacles or warts, but then one slitted open and peered at me. And then others did the same.

They were eyes. Dozens upon dozens of human eyes.

The punctured flesh contorted and bulged, pushing the bullets out of its body with a wet sucking sound.

"Jesus Christ," Meph whispered.

This was the part where we were supposed to run, but I couldn't make myself move. I could only stare, horrified, as its body continued to gurgle and twist. Sharp, white chunks of bone jutted through its hide. Teeth. Canines and molars and incisors arranged themselves in a twisted imitation of a human mouth. Then the top of its body folded in on itself with a massive crack, and the thing flashed us a grotesque grin. Its legs bent around it at unnatural angles, and when they reached the limit of their joints, the bones snapped with a sickening crack.

The circle of light closed in around us as the living shadows gnawed it into nothing. They'd be coming after us next.

They hadn't reached us yet, but I could already feel them, oily and cold. They would feel the same way Kele had when the demon had crawled under my skin and stripped away my free will. When it had left me trapped and flailing inside my own body.

The memory rose like bile. Hot, sharp, and corrosive.

That fucking demon hadn't managed to smother me. I'd butchered the damn thing. I'd ripped it to shreds. How dare these slithering little shades try to touch me?

I hurled the flare away, and let them chase after its light like dogs after a tennis ball.

Meph tugged at my shoulder. "Arkay, we need to get out of here."

The collar of my shirt pulled uncomfortably at my throat. He'd been trying to pull at me for a while now, hadn't he?

I unlocked my joints and let him pull me away. The acquiescence had been too sudden. He overbalanced, stumbling sharply to the side.

All of the thing's eyes turned to leer at him. Its newly formed mouth drew a hissing, rattling breath.

For an instant Meph stood frozen, matching the eldritch abomination's stare. And then he turned and ran, dragging me behind him.

The thing took off after us, its five legs twisting underneath it in a scurrying gallop.

I couldn't get any traction on the soft pine needles, slipping and skidding with every step. Meph didn't seem to share my problem, but he had my wrist in a death grip, and he sprinted between the trees, all but smacking me into their trunks. It was all I could do to stay on my feet. Keeping up with him wasn't an option. And the thing was closing in on us with every second.

This wasn't working.

I dug my heels in and wrenched my hand out of his grip.

"Arkay!" Meph grabbed at me again, but I ducked under his grip and turned to face the thing in the dark.

Fuck no, I wouldn't be chased around like a rabbit. I was the predator here. I pulled back my arm and threw a punch that could shatter bone.

In fact, it did shatter bone. It also smashed through the leathery hide and ruptured a few organs. The thing skidded to a halt, impaled on my arm up to the elbow, and it blinked at me.

It looked surprised. Not the blank confusion of shock—just everyday, ordinary, "please tell me you did it for the vine" surprise.

I yanked my arm out of its torso. Now that I was covered in the stuff, I recognized the scent of the monster as human. Not one human, though, but dozens, maybe more, mixed and separated and remolded into a completely different shape. The goo on my arm reeked of blood and spinal fluid, urea and gastric juices, all blended together in a soupy mix.

This was wrong. It shouldn't be alive, it shouldn't function, it shouldn't even be able to move.

So how the hell was I supposed to kill it?

New plan: get the fuck out of there.

I took off, hauling myself into the trees. It could probably climb, but it was bigger than me. Heavier. As long as I kept to the smaller branches, it couldn't follow me.

It was a good plan. A solid one.

So how was I supposed to know it wouldn't bother following me?

Meph

I tried to shout again, but I choked on the words. I had to keep running.

That unholy aberration was still chasing me. Every second it grew louder— the crack of its bones, the uneven skittering of its footsteps, the clacking of its teeth. Dear god, it smelled like an operating table.

Terror ran like ice water through my veins. It wasn't just going to kill me. It would unmake me. Unravel my most component parts and splice them into that abomination.

Snap. Skitter. Crack.

Branches reached out of the dark to claw at me, dragging me back. I tore myself out of their grip, but they kept bits of my clothes, my hair, my equipment. A branch caught me across the neck, and I flailed wildly to disentangle myself. When I took off again, the darkness closed in around me.

The glow stick. I'd left it behind.

Snap. Skitter. Crack.

No time to go back. I kept running, gripping blindly at the foliage.

I struck a wall. Trapped. No way forward, and only that thing behind. I turned sharply to the left and kept moving, one hand on the wall to guide my way.

Snap. Skitter. Crack.

Oh God, it was gaining.

My hand caught on something, sinking into a crack in the stone. A seam. Beyond, a metal bar.

A ladder?

No, a door. I scrabbled madly at it, my sweating palms slick on the cold metal.

It turned, and the stone door swung in toward me.

I heaved it open and dove through, slamming it shut behind me. Abruptly my ears popped and my stomach lurched. My foot caught on a stone, and I went sprawling.

I lay motionless, madly trying to suppress my gasps for air.

If I stayed still, maybe the thing wouldn't see me.

Arkay

"Meph?" I shouted. The sound faded too quickly in the enormous space, swallowed as abruptly as the shadows had devoured our lights.

He didn't answer.

I lowered myself onto the pine-needle-strewn floor and inhaled, but no luck. My nose wasn't meant for tracking on the best of days, and at the moment it was overpowered by the gunk that covered my arm.

I caught a glimmer of light, barely visible in the distance, and rushed toward it. It was his glow stick, caught in the branches of an old oak.

"Meph?" I called again. "Come on, Meph! Answer me!"

Still nothing.

Maybe he couldn't reply. Yelling into the dark would get my attention, but I wouldn't be the only one to notice.

New plan. I hoisted myself back into the trees and climbed again, heading straight up. The dry tree creaked underneath me as I reached the smallest branches. I moved even higher, and my footholds threatened to break underneath my weight.

I broke through the canopy. Nowhere to go but up.

I grabbed one of the flares I'd pocketed and yanked at the cord. Without the trees to block my view, I could finally see the whole of the forest.

The canopy stretched out around me, pressing against the smooth walls of an enormous cavern. A few trees continued above the others, their enormous trunks disappearing into perfectly-sized holes in the stone over my head. Light bounced off a smooth, uneven ceiling. I was near the edge of the forest, maybe a hundred yards or so from the stone wall. The forest stretched for more than a mile in the other direction and kept going, though the light was being steadily devoured by the living shadows.

I scanned the trees, but there was no rustle of movement, no spot of light to give away Meph's location.

But I did spot something else.

A metallic pole speared the air to my left, climbing from the forest floor into the ceiling. A spiral staircase wrapped around its support, ending in a platform above the trees. A bridge stretched from the platform to the nearby wall, suspended by rows of chain that dangled like vines from the ceiling.

"That looks promising," I muttered to myself.

This place was built like the inside of an Egyptian pyramid: a hidden entrance, a long tunnel, a grand gallery with its assortment of booby traps. Following that pattern, I could expect the very top to have the pharaoh's chamber.

No self-respecting dragon would settle for any less.

I took careful aim and hurled the flare. It hit the platform, but rolled off and down the stairs. It fell like a shooting star into the forest, and the living shadows gave chase. Not a perfect throw, but at least it was still vaguely in the right direction.

I descended back into the canopy, climbing the interlocking branches toward the dying light. A few moments later it vanished, punctuated with the crack of breaking bones, but I was finally close enough that the faint light of my glow stick caught the metal railing, and soon after I was on the stairs and on my way to the platform.

The bridge rattled underfoot, swinging wide in time with every step we took. But for once the path was clear of trees and debris, and I matched my strides to the rhythm of the bridge.

Down below, an enormous deer raised its head above the trees and stretched out its neck to sniff at me. Its attention felt more like a passerby gawking at a car accident than a vote of confidence. I had no supplies, no backup, and this bridge felt unnervingly similar to the moment of respite before a boss battle in a video game.

The bridge led to a hole in the sheer rock face— the mouth of yet another tunnel. Unlike the other tunnel, though, it veered sharply right after a few feet, and then moved just as abruptly to the left, a sharp zigzag that left me disoriented. But with every step, the darkness thinned, becoming first a murky gloom, then easing slowly into a soft twilight glow. Around every corner, it grew brighter. It was refracted light, blocked off from the absolute dark of the cavern by half a dozen twists and turns. I sped up, anxious to be able to see again.

But when I finally rounded the corner, I had no idea what I was looking at. The tunnel yawned into another massive chamber, this one a tangle of spiral staircases and elevated walkways, woven in and around and through each other so closely that I couldn't tell where one ended and another began. Adding to the confusion, the paths blended seamlessly with stone statues and brass sculptures, all of them of dragons, all with only three legs. It seemed like the kind of place M.C. Escher would draw, if he didn't get a migraine just from looking at it.

I padded quietly through the chamber, but my footsteps were echoed by the soft rhythm of bare feet on smooth stone. Holding my breath, I crept toward the source of the sound.

A woman in white moved gracefully across the floor, her long blond tresses whipping behind her with every turn. She was tall and as powerfully muscled as a ballerina, and for a moment I thought she had to be dancing. But no. I recognized the sweep of her leg, the slice of her arm. Those were martial arts forms, like the ones Meph had taught me, but infinitely more complex and precise. Her eyes were shut, but she whirled around the complex layout of the room with ethereal grace, never so much as brushing the interlocking sculptures.

Footsteps clattered through the twisting hallway, faintly at first, but growing steadily louder and closer. I ducked closer into the shelter of the statue.

A crowd of people rushed into the chamber in a brisk military jog, all of them decked out in modified Dragon Skin body armor. The bulk of the company scattered around the perimeter of the room, while one— an Indian woman with fierce eyes and close-cropped hair— approached the blonde.

"Fext," she said. "Terry's raising the alert. There's been a breach."

The blond woman, Fext, paused in her ritual and opened her ice-blue eyes. "Has Ivan been informed?" she asked through a light Russian accent.

"Yes, Ma'am. He's got the residential wing and the market under lockdown."

Fext pulled a ponytail holder from her pocket and tied back her hair. "Do we know who's behind it?"

"We're still working on it," the other woman said. "But all we've got is the process of elimination at the moment. By all means, they look like freelancers."

"Might be the Contessa's mercenaries." Fext scowled. "That scavenging bitch."

The other woman hesitated. "Fext, if they *are* hers—"

"Then we will give them back to her in body bags," Fext said icily. "She knows the protocols for sending an envoy. If she can't be bothered to respect our rules, then we have no obligation to return her toys."

The other woman swallowed. In the far corners, some of the other soldiers exchanged glances. Smart little boys and girls. They knew better than to piss off a dragon.

Fext ignored her subordinate's uncertainty. "Do we know what they are after? Which way they're heading?"

The soldier pulled back slightly, guarded. "Terry spotted one of them heading to the doors. They believe a second may have been coming here." She glanced past Fext, at the flashes of the rest of her company that were visible through the architecture. "Did they not come past you?"

"I didn't see anyone." Fext narrowed her eyes, not woman enough to admit she'd been off in her own world when I'd arrived. But if the slip embarrassed her, she didn't show it. "Widen the search. If they came in here, they may be after something in ThreeClaw's apartments." A handful of the soldiers hurried to the far corner, away from the entrance we'd used. Meanwhile Fext hoisted herself over the handrail of one of the spiral stairs and started climbing, sweeping her gaze from side to side. I held my breath and pressed closer against the statue. This place was a kaleidoscope. Even if Fext had a better vantage point, she couldn't possibly pick us out of the chaos.

The thought had barely formed when she froze and her eyes locked on mine.

Well, shit.

"There!" Fext shouted.

The soldiers rushed me, but I grabbed the nearest railing and swung myself into the air. Two steps, and I leaped onto the next walkway up, and the next. Climbing had been my specialty even before I made a living shimmying up an oiled pole. The soldiers scrambled after me, but they were slow and plodding by comparison.

All but one.

Fext climbed up after me, leaping from rail to ledge like a gymnast. I moved faster, but she knew this place. While I scrambled across the shortest distance between points, she loped easily across the smoothest terrain with half the energy and twice the speed.

It was only a matter of time before she caught me, so I stopped running.

I lunged for the thin support pillar that held up one of the curling statues. Inertia kept me going, but I twisted that momentum into a tight spin that would have made any stripper proud. When Fext followed after me, I swung both my feet into her stomach, driving the air out of her lungs. She should have crumpled. Instead, she grabbed my legs and hung on tight. If she was going to fall, she'd take me with her.

I snarled at her. If the bitch wanted to fall together, then I'd let her have her way. I thrashed my whole body, ramming her against the pillar, and then I let go.

I was familiar with pain. I'd been shot, stabbed, possessed, and hit by cars. I'd even got in a fight with a tiger once. A fall was nothing.

At least, not normally.

Fext let go of me, but only for an instant, long enough to grab me and force me underneath her. I dug my claws into her and thrashed, but not fast enough. We hit the floor, and all of her weight smashed into me.

Shock and surprise came first. The fall knocked the wind out of me, and I was left gasping for air that didn't reach my lungs, stunned by my own confusion.

Then came the pain. It pulsed across my body in waves, deep and sharp and burning. A new wave of agony stabbed my chest every time I tried to suck in a breath.

I tried to sit up and let air into my lungs, but my right arm refused to obey me, answering instead with even more pain.

Fext looked no worse for the wear, probably because I had cushioned her fall.

Her stare moved from my face to my injured arm and back like she didn't know what she was looking at. While she reacquainted herself with my injuries, she didn't notice my other arm was perfectly fine. I lashed out, raking my claws across her face. She pulled back, crushing the air out of my lungs a second time. But instead of scrambling away, she pinned me down. Her weight on my wounded arm sent white sparks across my eyes and ripped a howl from my throat. When my vision cleared, her face filled my field of view. I could only see her eyes— one blood-filled and ruined, the other wide and impossibly blue.

I tried to struggle, but I couldn't look away. I blinked, but the image of them seemed burned into my retinas. I couldn't see anything else.

And then, I couldn't see anything at all.

Meph

I lay flat on the forest floor, listening for the skitter of deformed legs and the crack of breaking bones, but nothing came. Maybe that thing had forgotten about me.

Gradually my pulse calmed and my breathing slowed. Panic subsided, and in its place was a different kind of anxiety. Arkay was out there somewhere. Had it caught her? Was that why it hadn't come after me?

She's a dragon, I told myself. *Most fierce and dangerous of all monsters.*

I wondered if whoever had made that designation knew about that thing that lurked in the shadows.

It didn't matter. Arkay would be fine. I had to keep believing that, or I'd lose my mind. Arkay was fine. Right now I needed to focus on staying alive.

I pulled myself onto my hands and knees and tried to get my bearings. The air had gained a cool humidity that it hadn't had before, as well as a smell: flowers, fallen leaves, and wet earth. Light filtered through the canopy above me, casting the trees into blue-tinted shadows.

Moonlight, I realized. The door must have opened out onto the side of the mountain. I was outside. I turned back to look where I'd come, but with no success. The forest was brighter than the inky blackness of the cavern, but my eyes still couldn't pierce the shadows.

Maybe come daylight I could find the door and try again.

The thought made my heart pound, and I jerked back into the dappled moonlight. I couldn't go back. That thing was still in there.

No. Better to stay out here and wait for Arkay to come out. We'd been grossly unprepared for the Felldeep. We needed to get out of here and regroup. If we did come back, we would do it with the proper supplies. Infra-red goggles, perhaps. And a rocket launcher.

I'd make a list and run it by Arkay when she came out.

Unless she came out through a different door, somewhere else on the mountain.

I checked my phone. No signal.

Better to get to a town and leave her a message there. She'd probably do the same. It was the smart thing to do.

I backed away from the memory of the door and followed the pull of gravity down the slope.

Arkay

I woke up in a hospital bed, feeling like I'd been on the underside of a mosh pit. My chest ached with every shallow breath I took. My right arm was numb, but not enough to ward off a distant stabbing pain.

I tried to sit up, but found myself strapped to the bed. I counted four leather cuffs around each arm, some of them positioned awkwardly around a splint. Six more cuffs wrapped around each leg.

A chair creaked, and I looked up. Fext glared at me from a chair at the far end of the room. The claw marks I'd left on her face, the ones that should have left her half blind and permanently disfigured, were barely scratches over a black eye.

Woah. Deja vu.

"Very impressive," I told her. "You've got a nice Doctor Evil vibe going on, but I'm gonna have to dock you some points for originality. I'm pretty sure I saw this exact scene in, like, *eight* horror movies."

"So you keep telling me," she said flatly.

Not deja vu?

Fext got out of her chair and started toward me.

This had all happened before. I woke up, I made a horror movie reference, she stood and leaned over me, and then... blue. Big blue eyes.

She leaned over the bed, and I turned my head aside. "This sleeping beauty is already awake, thanks."

She tried to grab at my chin, but I snapped at her finger with sharpened teeth. Let's see her healing factor grow one of *those* back.

A soft knock came from the door. "Nadia?"

"I'm busy," Fext growled, grabbing again at my face and almost losing her thumb in the process.

The door creaked open. "Nadia, do you need help?"

"I almost have her." She grabbed me by the hair and yanked my head back. She tried to look me in the eyes again, but I ripped my head out of her grip and repaid her hair pulling with a bar-brawl headbutt. It cost me a bit of hair, but it was worth it to hear her swearing in Russian as she pulled away.

"Perhaps that won't be necessary," said the other man, stepping into view. He was a shorter man in spectacles and a lab coat. He looked Filipino, if I had to guess, middle-aged, but aged prematurely by chronic stress. Deep lines framed mouth and bloodshot eyes. Gray streaked his neatly-cut black hair. Mild pudge sat oddly on his slender frame, like he'd lost a lot of weight and then gained it all back again.

"Hello," he said softly. "I do apologize for the present situation. I assure you, we mean you no harm."

"And I'm sure strapping me to a bed is just your idea of foreplay."

His face colored, and he pulled away, blinking rapidly. "No! No, of course not. Please understand, the straps are for your own protection. You seem to be very... active upon waking. You've got a collapsed lung, and your arm is broken in three places. You must stay still if they're too heal properly."

"Sounds great," I said. "Let me go, and I'll go sit still on my own time."

"We will," he said hastily. "Just wait a few more hours. As soon as we finish our tests, you'll be free to go."

Hell no.

It had taken months and copious quantities of alcohol for Meph to tell me what kind of tests got done on so-called monsters. No way were they doing that to me.

"I've got a better idea." The last syllables garbled as my jaw grew into a muzzle and my teeth grew into fangs. Antlers shot out of my skull and speared my pillow. My limbs thickened with muscle and scales, pulling my restraints taut.

Fext swore.

The doctor blanched. "Nadia, get her down!"

Fext leaped on top of me, trying to pin me to the bed.

For an instant, her eyes met mine, and I was caught in the impossible blue. But the spell lasted only a moment. More pressing was the stabbing pain in my arms and legs. The leather bands carved into my limbs, cutting skin and circulation, but then the straps ripped through entirely, and I hurled her away.

I forced myself to focus. Meph had told me about this kind of thing before: poludnica, who could knock you unconscious with a glance.

That would make things complicated.

I leaped off the bed, squeezing my eyes shut as soon as I hit the floor, and kept growing. In a heartbeat, I was fifteen feet long. Twenty. Twenty-five.

"Wait, please!" the doctor cried. "This is a hospital!" His voice collapsed into a gasp as he was shoved into a wall by my bulk.

"Quinn, this isn't the—" Fext abruptly stopped talking when I pinned her underneath one of my claws. I threw the tuft of my tail over her face for good measure to hide those stupid eyes. In my spite, I lost track of the doctor. He reappeared barely a foot from my muzzle, so close I could taste him when I inhaled. Fear soured his scent.

I opened my eyes, but I had to cross them to see him properly.

"Please," he repeated. Slowly, deliberately, he sank to his knees. "I surrender. We were wrong to attempt to subdue you. Please accept my most humble apologies."

My tongue flicked out, catching all the nuances of his scent. He looked down, all but prostrate. "My name is Quinque Magbantay, and I'm the head doctor in Felldeep. The staff and patients in this facility are my responsibility. Please do not bring your wrath down on them for my wrongdoing."

I was starting to like this guy.

I let out a puff of air and jerked my head at Fext.

"Nadia?" He looked uncertain. "She's here because I asked her to be. I take all fault for her actions against you, as well. And I beg you, please don't kill her."

It wasn't the begging that won me over, though. It wasn't the bowing and scraping, or the full-blown kowtow, either.

It was just such a Rosa thing to do.

I caught Fext's side between my teeth and gave her a solid jolt of electricity. It wasn't enough to stop her heart, but it would keep her down for a while. In the next moment, I was tiny and humanoid again, standing over Doctor Magbantay with as much authority as I could manage while cradling a broken arm and wheezing like an old vacuum cleaner.

"I have questions," I growled. Electricity crackled across my skin. "You're going to answer them. Is that clear?"

"Extremely," he said.

I tried to order my thoughts. "The people who came here with me. Where are they?" I'd only come with Meph, but he didn't need to know that.

"You're the only one we found."

"We were being chased by a freaky spider monster," I said.

"Yes, Terry." He nodded. "They already reported in, but they never caught anyone."

"Terry? That thing looks like it walked out of the Necronomicon, and you named it *Terry?*"

"They named themselves, really," he said. "They're really quite friendly to those who have clearance to be here. They said there'd been signs that someone had recently used one of our doors to the outside. But that carries its own problems. Not all of those doors lead to places in the immediate vicinity."

I officially stopped caring. Meph hadn't been caught and he hadn't been eaten. I'd find him later. "You were experimenting on me. Why?"

"No! Never. You were bleeding. We collected a blood sample and ran a DNA profile. It's still processing now."

"What the fuck would possess you to do that?"

He hesitated. "You... you possess a certain resemblance to our old leader. To ThreeClaw." He said the name with an odd weight, like he half expected thunder and trumpets or something. He almost managed to hide his disappointment when nothing happened. "We believed you might be a relation. A daughter. A sister. A niece, perhaps."

I narrowed my eyes. "Why does it matter?"

"Because she's gone," he said slowly. "And if you are... related to her, then that has... certain implications."

"I don't do Socratic dialogue, dumbass," I growled. "Stop hedging and get to the fucking point."

He swallowed. "You stand to inherit her holdings. Her lands, her money, her followers. The entirety of ThreeClaw's Hoarde."

"Say what now?" That didn't make sense. Dragons didn't make wills, and we didn't inherit. We conquered. We claimed. "What was with the warm welcome over there?" I waved an arm at the still unconscious woman.

He cringed. "Nadia is... not so enthusiastic about the Hoarde changing hands. She's confident that ThreeClaw will still come back someday. But I think it's time to accept that that isn't going to happen." He looked pained. "Nadia can dislike the circumstances, but she can't argue against them. The Hoarde is yours."

"Hold on," I said. Where was all this coming from? Even King Arthur had to yank cutlery out of a rock. "What makes you think I want it?"

He blinked. "Why wouldn't you?"

"Why would I?" I asked. It didn't matter if this place was big and fancy. These people were just handing it off to the first person willing to take it. It had nothing to do with my prowess or my conquest or even my intention. I was just a warm body to fill whatever vacancy they had open. It wouldn't be mine, not the way Rosa and Meph were mine. Not the way Our Lady had been mine. Worse, I'd belong to them. Nobody owned a dragon. "You can keep your evil empire. I've got shit to do."

"But think what you could accomplish with our resources—"

"You mean like traveling the country and catching serial killers? Because I'm already doing that."

"Your influence was limited," he said. "With the Hoarde—"

"What is this, an infomercial?" I glowered. "You're really going for the hard sell here."

"We're desperate." He flashed a grin that probably should have looked self-deprecating, but wound up looking utterly miserable. "Our organization was built on the assurance that we would always have ThreeClaw to watch over us. Half our pacts and treaties are invalid without a dragon to give them legitimacy. We've spent seven years trying to persuade our allies that ThreeClaw is still around, that she'll be back any day now, but confidence in our word is crumbling. We're one major disaster away from falling apart."

"That's very sad for you," I said. "Behold all the fucks I give."

"We're at war," he said. "There are people out there who want to kill us— who want to kill everyone who isn't human. If we fall, then the people under our protection will be systematically hunted down and murdered."

Rosa would want to reach out to these people. Maybe, once she'd recovered, we could do that. Until then, she was my only priority. I couldn't take care of her if I was playing substitute for some other dragon's estate.

"That's not my problem." I crossed my arms. A mild ache shot through my elbow, and I glanced down. The splint had come off during my struggle, but I hadn't noticed. Aside from some discomfort, it looked fine. "You said my arm was broken."

Doctor Magbantay looked at me like he'd had an epiphany. "It was."

Oh shit. How long did bones take to mend properly? It was upward of a month usually, wasn't it? I scrambled for my phone, now buried amid the splinters of a bedside table. "How long did you guys put me out?" Rosa's condition was fragile. If it took a turn while I was unconscious—

"Only a few hours," Doctor Magbantay said. "No more than half a day."

I turned on the phone anyway. The date and time confirmed it, but my unlock screen showed about a dozen missed calls and texts. Before I could read the names attached to them, the phone died. Stupid shitty battery.

"ThreeClaw brought me into her Hoarde because I had been making strides in medical research," he continued. "Under her patronage, I made a breakthrough. We called it Styx."

I jabbed my finger into the charger port and sent a current into the phone. It wasn't good for it by any means—three guesses why I had such crappy battery life in the first place— but at least it worked for a quick jump.

"Just making sure," I said absently. "But do you mean sticks as in twiggy things, Styx as in the band, or as in the river of the dead? Because given ThreeClaw's naming conventions so far, it could be all of the above."

He blinked. "The… er… the river."

"So it was a poison or something?"

One percent. Not enough battery to read all those texts, let alone listen to a voicemail.

"Just the opposite," he said. "A restorative. A substance with the power to break down damaged cells and regenerate living tissues according to their genetic blueprint."

I looked up from the phone.

"You can actually do that?" I asked. "Regenerate people?"

"It only works on living tissue, of course," he said. "Once a person has died, there's nothing that can be done for them, short of necromancy."

"But you can fix things."

"It isn't a perfect cure," he said. "It can't unmake genetic conditions or preserve corrective surgeries, and targeting a specific focus for the regenerative properties is limited at best—"

"But it works." I pulled my hands behind my back to keep them from shaking. "Even on brain tissue? Could it repair brain damage?"

I knew the answer before he nodded. I'd read about it. A boy who'd shot himself in the head had been up and walking, good as new.

Rosario could be just like that. She could wake up and come back and be alive.

I could save her. It had taken me six months, but I could finally save her.

"You have to understand, there are major problems…"

He was starting to sound like the lawyer voice at the end of a commercial for some new prescription. *Do not use if you are pregnant or may become pregnant, yadda yadda yadda.* He kept talking, but my attention had reverted back to my phone. I'd gotten up to five percent battery. Still not great, but good enough. I swiped the screen to open my messages.

They were all from Father Gabriel.

Antibiotics aren't working.

The infection has spread into Rosario's bloodstream.

Her liver is failing.

Please hurry. She doesn't have long.

Every muscle in my body tensed. Static crawled on my skin.

"Are you alright?" Magbantay sounded wary.

Nothing was alright. Rosario needed me.

"I think we're done here." My voice was flat and unyielding. "There's only one thing you have that I want. So I'm going to take that part of my *inheritance* and get out of here, and save your cranky coworker a few headaches."

"But— wait—"

My teeth sharpened. "You people have a way to fix brain damage. I want it. And I'm only asking nicely once."

"And you'll get it," he said hastily. "As soon as the tests come back. What you're asking for is rare and powerful. I can't turn it over to you until we're certain of who you really are. Just a few more hours."

"Or I could go all big and scaly all the way up and down this hospital." I flashed a ruthless grin. "Would that be proof enough for you, or do you need something a bit bigger?"

He blanched.

"I'm not leaving this building without a dose of Styx," I said. "The only real question is, are you going to hand it over, or will I have to take it by force?"

Meph

Sunlight rose over the mountaintops when I reached a town. It was a small thing, with odd names on road signs and narrow cobblestone walkways that branched off the cobblestone roads. The houses I passed had an unusual uniformity, with pastel paint on flat plaster facades, and wooden roofs that seemed unnecessarily steep. It didn't look like any of the towns Arkay and I had passed through together. But then, we'd stuck to the main roads. Maybe this was normal for rural Appalachia.

I checked my phone again. No signal.

People were starting to come out of their homes. A woman in jean shorts jogged past me, and I signaled to her.

"Hey," I said. She slowed and stopped, pulling earbuds out of her ears. "I'm not getting any signal. Do you know anywhere near here that has a payphone?

Her brow furrowed. "Sorry," she said in a heavy accent. "My English is... not so good. Can you say again slowly?"

I looked over my shoulder. Behind me, a shop owner was opening a store front. A few English words popped out at me from the displays, but around them was pure gibberish.

I spoke again, slowly. "I got lost. Where am I?"

"Das ist Pommelsbrunn," she said.

Shit. Oh shit.

"Did I..." *Oh shit oh shit oh shit.* "Did I cross any borders?"

"No," she said. "We are still in Deutschland."

Fuck.

Arkay

Terry— yes, that *was* in fact the eldritch abomination's name— led me back to the tunnel where I'd come in, but they kept a safe distance away from me all the while. The whole silent march would have been seriously awkward if I had enough mental capacity left to care.

The car was still parked outside the rest stop, still loaded with our gear. No sign that Meph had gotten here first. I sent him a barrage of texts, explaining where I was going and where he should meet me. I didn't have time to wait for him. Rosa needed me.

And then I drove. The landscape rushed past me, forests and mountains melting into endless flat farmland, dotted in places by cities and towns. My vision blurred, but I only stopped long enough to splash water on my face and chug an energy drink before I kept going. Even ignoring the speed limit, it took me six hours to reach the state border, and another half hour after that before I was in Fort Wayne, pulling into the parking lot at St. Joe's Hospital.

"I'm here for Maria Sanchez," I announced, marching past the information desk without a pause to sign in. I knew these hallways, and some of the staff recognized me, too. I'd stopped by a few times over the past few months, usually while Meph spent the day tailing a potential bad guy on foot.

Hopefully this would be my last visit.

I pushed open the door of Rosario's hospital room. Father Gabriel startled awake in his chair, almost knocking over a vase full of lilacs on the table beside him. He must have been with her all night.

"Arkay," he said aloud, his hands tracing my name sign. "You came. I was afraid…"

How is she? I signed, watching him from the corner of my eye as I approached the bed.

"She's… It's good that you're here."

Rosario lay on her back, her hands at her sides. Her skin had turned a sickly yellow, and her breath crackled and wheezed past the tube in her mouth. According to the EKG clipped to her finger, her pulse was unsteady and slow. The sharp tang of infection tainted her scent.

I brushed oil-heavy hair behind her ear. "It's alright, Rosa. You're gonna be okay."

"I've given her last rites," Father Gabriel said, signing the words out of habit. "I know that doesn't mean anything to you—"

It matters to her. Thank you. And thank you for staying with her.

But she wouldn't be needing a priest anymore.

I opened the leather case Doctor Magbantay had given me, pulling out a hypodermic needle and a vial of Styx. It was small, but I wouldn't need much.

I filled a syringe and emptied it into the IV's injection port. For a moment the saline solution inside took on a faint blue tint, but then the serum dispersed and the color faded into innocuous clarity.

"Arkay?" Father Gabriel picked up the unlabeled vial. "What was that?"

I smiled. "This is what's going to save her."

An hour later, Rosario was still out cold. The Styx hadn't done any glowy magic or anything, but already I could see it working. Her heartbeat had grown steady and strong, and her skin had lost the jaundiced yellow and returned to a healthy russet glow. Even the bite scar on her arm was starting to fade. I added another syringe to the IV. Hopefully that would help her along.

I tried to fill Father Gabriel in on what had happened, but I was fading fast. I'd made the entirety of the six-hour drive in one shot, stopping only for gas and bathroom breaks, and I'd been exhausted before I even started. It didn't help that in the last six months, my ASL had gotten rusty. I was halfway through fingerspelling 'eldritch abomination' when the last of my willpower gave out, and I nodded off against the priest's chest.

When I came to, Father Gabriel was gone. I'd been eased over to lean against the bedside table, my jacket rolled up under my head as a pillow, and a thin hospital blanket draped over my shoulders. I blinked hazily at nothing for a few minutes. Damn, I'd needed that nap.

I sat up and stretched, wiping a line of drool off my lips, when something flickered in the corner of my eye. I tensed. This wouldn't be the first time that sleep deprivation had me seeing things, but usually the hallucinations happened before I passed out in somebody else's lap. I caught the flicker again: the minute shift of a face turning to watch me.

Rosario was sitting up in bed. Her eyes were open and leaking tears. A recently ejected feeding tube lay tangled on the blanket, still wet with spit.

I jolted upright, and in an instant I was at her side. She gasped at the sudden motion, but I caught her and pulled her into a hug.

"It's okay, Rosa," I whispered into her hair. "Everything's okay. You're safe now. I'm never letting anyone hurt you again."

Hands pressed against my shoulders, pushing me away.

Immediately I tensed. "Are you alright? Are you having trouble breathing?" She'd had pneumonia a little bit ago. My punctured lung had recovered before I'd crossed the border to Ohio, but mine had only been collapsed for a few hours; she'd had problems for months. Maybe she'd need longer to be back to her old self. "It's gonna be okay. This stuff is still working through your system. Just give it a little time. You're gonna be good as new."

But even though she was breathing hard, it wasn't a gasp for breath. Her face was pale. Her eyes were wide.

She looked afraid.

"It's okay," I said softly. "Things are gonna be confusing for a bit, but that's okay. You've been asleep for a long time. But nobody's gonna hurt you. Not ever again." I reached out to touch her, but she cringed away, almost falling off the side of the bed in her hurry to get away from me.

I pulled back like I'd been burned.

"Are—" Something cold and dark welled in my chest. "Are you scared of me?"

She didn't answer. But with that look in her eyes, she didn't need to.

"I'm not gonna hurt you, Rosa. I would never." I shrank down, making myself as small as I could manage. "And I know that's not enough for you. I know what you said the last time you saw me. But I'm not like that anymore. I've been working on it. I'm better now. I'm controlling my temper. I'm helping people. I'm trying to do the things you would want me to do. And it's hard, Rosa. It's so damn hard, and I don't always know what the right thing is, but I'm trying, Rosa. I want to be the kind of person you don't have to be afraid of. Please believe me."

She didn't reply.

"Please, Rosa," I whispered. "Please. If there's a problem, I'll fix it. If it's something I've done, I'll stop. I'll make it right. Please, Rosa, just say something."

But she didn't make a sound. She just stared at me, scared and confused, looking at me like—

No.

Please no.

She looked at me like I was a stranger.

The cold sensation in my chest took form. "Rosa?"

I reached out to touch her, and she flinched away.

"Rosa, it's me. It's Arkay. Your dragon." I caught her hand and held it against my cheek. Maybe if she could feel me, or smell me, she'd remember who I was.

She had to remember me.

The door burst open, and Rosario flinched back again, wrapping her arms around her chest. A crowd of nurses filled the room, Father Gabriel behind them.

"Oh my God," one of them started.

"Jesus Christ," another said. "It's a miracle."

Rosario cowered, her knees pulled in front of her like a shield. She looked frantically from one face to the next, her eyes wide and terrified.

I wanted to get between her and the strangers. I wanted to flash my claws and drive them away with a snarl. I wanted to protect her from all the things that scared her.

But now I was one of those things.

"It's okay, Rosa," I whispered, getting off the bed and backing away. "They're only here to help. You're going to be okay."

My heart hammered in my chest. My ribs felt too tight around my lungs. I couldn't breathe. Shapes blurred and scents congealed into incoherence.

I took off, rushing out of the room and down the hospital halls. If I was going to go nonverbal, it needed to not be in Rosario's hospital room. I needed room to breathe.

Rosario was going to be okay. She was just groggy. I'd give her some time, and she'd remember me. That was all she needed. Just time. Just a little time.

I dragged myself through a plate glass door and emerged into an enclosed courtyard. I braced myself against my knees and gulped down mouthfuls of air. The scent of cut grass and summer washed against the taste of bile on my tongue.

The door opened again behind me. Probably some nurse wanting to know if I was okay. I wanted to tell them to fuck off, but I couldn't form words.

Fabric brushed against concrete walls with a faint scratching sound. The other form stood there, unmoving, for the long minutes it took me to collect myself.

"It hurts, doesn't it?" said a voice with a thin Russian accent.

I swallowed my gasping breaths and whirled to face Fext. She leaned against the wall, her arms crossed, her blue eyes cold.

"How the hell did you get here?" I demanded.

"GPS tracker in the case." When I bared my teeth, she shrugged. "Don't take it personally, they're all bugged. It's the most important medical breakthrough since penicillin. Did you really think we'd risk losing a sample?" She pushed off the wall and walked around me in a slow, distant arc, careful to keep well out of striking range. "There are faster ways to get around than driving, by the way. If you'd bothered listening to Quinn, you would know that. You would know a lot of things right now. What is happening to your friend, for example."

I snarled. "You stay the hell away from her."

"I am not here for your friend," she said, unaffected by my fury. "Your tests came back. Quinn believes you should be made aware of the results."

"Let me save you the trouble: I'm not really your fucking ThreeClaw's niece or whatever, and you want your fucking wonder-drug back." I dug it out of my pocket and shoved it into her chest. "Congratulations. Now get lost."

"You really should have let Quinn get a word in edgewise." Fext studied the bottle nonchalantly. "He would have warned you not to use it on your friend."

My hackles rose. "Why not?"

"Because it works very well on broken bones and bullet holes, but you need to be careful about the dose. And whatever you do, don't use it on head injuries."

My teeth were bared and razor sharp.

"We call it *tabula rasa*," she continued. "A blank slate. It turns out that brain tissue is like paper in a book. Rip it out, and we can always put in new pages. But the words that are written there—those can never be replaced."

I tasted blood and bile, but I swallowed it back. "You're wrong."

Rosa was just groggy. She was freaked out from waking up in a hospital. She was going to be okay. We were going to go back to the way things were. I was going to make things alright again.

"Are you sure about that?" An odd look crossed Fext's face, and she stepped closer. "Look at me. Really, truly look at me. Do you remember me at all?"

"Of course I do," I said. "You broke my fucking arm."

She moved closer still. "But that's all you remember? Is there anything else in there about me? Anything at all?"

"What the hell do you want from me?" I demanded.

For one brief second she was in my face, looking into my eyes like she thought something might have been written on my retinas. The next second, she pulled away.

"You were mostly right," she said, her arms folding in front of her chest. "You aren't ThreeClaw's niece, or her sister, or her daughter, or any kind of relation at all."

Good fucking riddance. I was about to say as much when she cut me off.

"You're ThreeClaw."

I snorted. "And you're delusional."

"Are you sure about that?" She pulled away further. "Your DNA is a perfect match for hers."

"Then you fucked up your stupid test," I said. "I'm not her. I would know."

"Would you?" she asked. "Think back. How far do you remember? How long have you known your friend up there? More than seven years?" I turned away from her. I couldn't deal with this right now. "Can you remember ever being a child?"

No. No, I couldn't.

"ThreeClaw made a habit of leaving on business without warning, and she would be gone without word for months at a time. Seven years ago, she didn't come back. Seven years ago, the Order started boasting about putting a bullet between her eyes. Where were you when that happened?"

It would have been before I'd met Rosa. Back when time had no meaning and seasons weren't worth committing to memory.

I needed a drink. "This conversation is over."

"Ignoring it won't change the fact," she said to my retreating back. "You are ThreeClaw."

"And I don't give a flying fuck," I said. "I already told your doctor friend. I don't care if I'm ThreeClaw, or her stepdaughter, or Elvis fucking Presley. I've got my own shit to do."

"Like tending to your friend?" she observed. "She will need physical therapy to relearn command of basic motor functions. Speech therapy to get her talking again. All of it will take time. But then, I suppose you already know that. How long did it take you to learn to talk?"

I ground my teeth. I wanted to punch her, but forced my fist to remain clenched at my side. Starting a fight now would only get me thrown out of the hospital. I couldn't afford that. Rosario needed me.

"You've had your chance to gloat," I growled. "Now take your fucking Styx and leave."

"I intend to." She stepped closer, towering over me. Fucking tall people. "But I recommend you come with me when you do. And I recommend that you bring your friend."

"Are you threatening me?"

"A woman just miraculously recovered from a coma," she said. "That is going to make the news. You have perhaps a day before the Order of Saint Michael comes looking for her. There is a fifty percent chance that she's going to need to learn how to walk. Exactly how long do you think you can outrun them when you have to carry her?"

As long as I had to. Those bastards were never going to touch her again.

"And the alternative is what, exactly?" I demanded. "I shove her in that cave of yours? Hide her in the dark for the rest of her life?"

"If you insist," she said. "Or you could put her in a house. Someplace with a garden, and bodyguards. With the Hoarde's resources, you would be able to arrange it."

I narrowed my eyes. "And you'd be tickled pink to do that for me, wouldn't you?"

"I think Quinn made our situation clear," she said. "You need a safe place for your friend to recover. We need a dragon. Any questions?"

I had plenty of questions, and a few decent one-liners. They jumbled and swirled around each other until I had no idea where to start.

Instinct told me to send her packing in as many pieces as it took to get her off my tail. Instinct told me to grab Rosa and run for it. I could find a safe place and nurse her back to health and she'd be okay again.

But how was I even supposed to do that?

On the streets, panhandling for food and hiding in abandoned buildings for warmth?

Robbing drug dealers and serial killers and hoping I didn't get into another gang war like I had with Paternoster?

Looking over my shoulder for the rest of my life in case the Order found us again?

I could do it just fine. Meph wouldn't have a problem.

But I couldn't just do that to Rosario. I couldn't put her back on the street, back into the cold, back on the run. Not when an alternative was just sitting there within arm's reach.

I looked back up at Fext.

Even if I was this ThreeClaw person, her Hoarde still wasn't mine. But Rosa was. And it was my responsibility to take care of her.

So I shut my eyes, sighed, and started with the questions Rosario would have asked. "How many licensed therapists do you have on staff?"

I could hear the frown in Fext's voice. "Did... you want to talk to someone?"

After everything that had happened, that would probably be a good idea. But the fact that she had to ask in the first place didn't inspire confidence. I opened my eyes. "If there's an actual war on, then the amount of people with PTSD is going to be through the roof. I want them identified, and I want them treated by competent therapists who aren't going to write them off as delusional the first time they say 'my boss is a dragon'."

Fext narrowed her eyes again, but not in disapproval. Possibly she was reconsidering what she'd just gotten into. "Anything else?"

"Hire enough that people can actually see them in a reasonable timeframe. None of that booking three months in advance bullshit."

"That's going to cost a lot of money," she said.

I gave her a look. "Apparently you have enough to buy a house and hire multiple full-time bodyguards. Rearrange the fucking budget if you have to."

Fext regarded me with a long, pensive stare. "Is this your acceptance, then?"

"It's a compromise."

Slowly, deliberately, Fext nodded. "I'll see what I can do."

It wasn't much. It definitely wasn't perfect.
But it was for Rosario. And that was what mattered.

Book 6:
Aglaeca

Arkay

A pair of were-hyenas emerged from the pitch black tunnel and stepped onto the carpet of a newly-installed walkway. The path wouldn't lead them anywhere useful. It ran all over the receiving chamber, through a maze of intertwining walkways, up the backs of marble dragons and down spiral staircases. The room was as gaudy as it was huge, so saturated with shapes and shadows that neither of my guests noticed me perched in the antlers of a nearby statue.

The woman's name was Basima Taban, and she was the head of a clan of were-hyenas living in Sudan. She was small and bent with age, her frail figure wrapped in the folds of her bright green toub. Her face and hands were toughened into dark leather, but she walked with her head held high. Her adult son Zahir walked beside her, his suit tie the same shade as her wrap.

"Welcome, my honored guests." I raised my voice enough to echo off the far corners of the chamber. Zahir jerked his head trying to follow the sound, but his mother continued her walk toward the heart of the room. I saved her the trouble of finding me. A long leap carried me over the nose of the statue, and I landed in a crouch on the floor before them with a flashy smile. "I hope your journey was comfortable."

Zahir jumped, but his mother was unfazed by my display. She shook my hand, giving my shoulders two steady pats, and I returned the gesture.

"Far more comfortable than those little airplanes," she said warmly. "I thank you for giving us passage."

"My doors are always welcome to you and your clan," I said.

Her son hesitated, but a glance at Basima convinced him to take my hand. "It's an honor to meet the legendary ThreeClaw."

My grin shifted into a practiced enigmatic smile. "Please, call me Arkay." It was neither confirmation nor denial. Let them decide for themselves what that meant. "If you'll come with me, refreshments are this way."

According to my cultural consultant, this dinner meeting was supposed to have two parts. The latter, where we talked about logistics and trading favors, was the easy part. It was the actual dinner part that gave me trouble.

My handlers had compiled a list of all the things I wasn't allowed to talk about in front of potential allies. At the very top of the list: my time living on the streets, my career as a stripper, and the fact that I'd spent six months working closely with an ex-Order militant— altogether, five of the seven years I could actually remember of my life.

"My son and I only recently left a celebration," Basima told me. "His nephew is commemorating the birth of his second daughter. My ninth great-grandchild."

"My congratulations to you and your family," I said. "You must be very proud."

She beamed at me, and laid her hand on mine. "Tell me, Arkay. Do you have any children of your own?"

I had no clue. Apparently ThreeClaw had disappeared often enough and long enough that it was possible, but nobody had ever heard of any. Thanks to the regenerative properties of Styx, even Doctor Magbantay couldn't say for sure whether I'd had kids, and the dude was a freakin' gynecologist.

But I couldn't talk about that, either.

"No." I hoped my smile looked more warm than strained. "I haven't been so... blessed."

"Perhaps that's a blessing of its own," she said, patting my hand gently. "Motherhood is a great responsibility, and leadership is another. Bearing both can be a heavy burden."

"But one that I'm sure you bore admirably," I said, glancing at the cultural consultant in the corner of the room to make sure I was staying on the right track. She flashed a brief thumbs up and signaled for me to keep going. "You must have so many stories."

As the dinner wore on and tea was served, I got a clearer impression of the purpose behind our meeting. Three of Basima's grandchildren had been accepted into American universities for engineering, and as eager as they were to venture out in the great wide world, the rest of the clan wasn't comfortable about them straying that far from the family.

"We're especially concerned about the youngest," she said. "Our Farah is going to MIT this fall."

"Impressive," I observed.

"Indeed it is. But not a year ago, a man was found dead in…" She stopped to consult with her son in Arabic.

"The news called it a 'murder dungeon'," Zahir clarified. "His *own* dungeon, they said."

"A serial killer," Basima said. "Not an hour's walk from what will be our Farah's dormitory. And he wasn't even discovered until after he'd died."

I knew about the event. I was half of the reason he was dead. Unfortunately, the other half was a *persona non grata* in this crowd. I glanced at my consultant again, but she didn't seem to notice my unspoken question.

I offered Basima a comforting smile. "We won't let anything happen to her. Or to any of your grandchildren. Perhaps you'd feel better if they were accompanied?"

"Yes, yes," she said. "I think I would."

Nadia

With the end of the day came a mountain of paperwork, and that meant another evening spent filling it out in the Felldeep's primary conference room. The work might have been better suited for an office, with a computer or a filing cabinet or even a requisite drawer full of writing utensils, but after all these years, I couldn't convince myself to fill out forms anywhere else. The place had become too intertwined with the rituals of my work.

The room had been built to accommodate almost any race among our allies. The doors were wide enough for the mass of a wheelchair and the broad shoulders of a troll. The light fixtures were embedded directly into the high ceilings, so as not to swing into the faces of oni and frost giants. The soft, short carpet had been specially selected to offer traction to hooved feet and not snag claws. Behind the paneled walls were closets stuffed with chairs made for more than a dozen heights and body types, each ready to replace the ones already arranged around the long conference table. A large screen took up most of the wall at the far end of the room, outfitted with cameras and microphones for video conferences. At the moment, the darkened screen reflected nothing but my own form, stooped over a stack of requisition forms. I'd only needed enough lights to illuminate my workspace, which left the rest of the room was drenched in shadow.

Footsteps approached the conference room door. They were familiar enough not to warrant alarm. I could almost place their owner, but not quite. Frowning, I glanced up.

My heart stopped. She was right there, cloaked in darkness and turned away from me to close the door, but I knew her instantly. Every inch of her signaled me like a beacon— the curve of her jaw, the planes of her shoulders, the arch of her spine. I pulled away from the desk, but I couldn't decide whether to run to her side or sink to my knees.

She was back. My master. My dragon. My Aglaeca—

She stepped into the light and the moment ended, and she went back to being Arkay.

I forced my eyes back onto the papers in front of me.

"Add another commission to the pile." Her voice was less deceptive. She spoke faster than ThreeClaw always had, more carelessly, and with a higher pitch. Most days, she sounded more like a child than the warrior she had once been. She grabbed a pen and a blank set of forms out of a hidden panel in the wall. She flopped gracelessly into the bright pink armchair at the head of the table. "We need a security detail on three students coming into the country this fall."

While she got situated, I rearranged an expense report to cover the memo I'd been reading. My contacts in Germany had been tracking a young American man across the country. He was obviously out of his depth, with less than a rudimentary grasp on the local language and no money that wasn't procured by either theft or begging. Despite his ineptitude, his demeanor said Orderling.

At least, it had until he'd wandered into the Black Forest. No member of the Order, disenfranchised or otherwise, ever walked out of the Contessa's territory alive.

No point wasting any more resources looking for Arkay's lost pet. I jotted down a note to scrub those side projects. Better to focus on things that actually mattered.

Arkay glanced at me with passing interest, but I didn't give her the chance to inquire.

"You look tired," I said, trying to keep my tone light. "Did she try to haggle with you?"

"Haggling I can handle," Arkay said. "In fact, I probably could have managed that whole three-hour meeting with a twenty-minute phone call. Remind me why we needed to drag them all the way out here?"

'All the way out here' wasn't very far. When ThreeClaw had commissioned the construction of the Felldeep, she'd had it equipped with a network of enchanted doors. One of them opened into a marketplace in Chad; another led to a computer store in Cairo. Neither of those was exactly within walking distance for the Sudanese were-hyenas, but the journey was nothing compared to a flight across the Atlantic.

"In person is better," I said. "They needed to see your face."

Arkay jotted a sulky note on the forms and bobbed her head at the screen on the far wall. "A video conference, then."

"We've been over this, Arkay."

In the first months after ThreeClaw left, we didn't realize anything was wrong. After all, it wasn't the first time she'd disappeared without a word. But then the months stretched into years, and our allies stopped accepting our assurances that the great and terrible ThreeClaw would be back any day now. We tried using forged signatures and doppelgangers, but even that illusion could only be stretched so far before it stopped working.

If we wanted to rebuild our credibility, we had to flaunt our dragon to our allies. They had to be able to see and smell and touch her— things that couldn't be done over a video feed.

While Arkay summarized her encounter in the fewest possible words, I gathered a pile of documents and pushed it across the table toward her.

"What's this?" she asked blankly.

"Background reading for Friday. You will be meeting with a family of kushtaka."

"You have got to be kidding me," she muttered, glancing at the first few pages on proper etiquette for greeting shapeshifting Alaskan otter-people. "You couldn't possibly do this yourself, could you?"

I didn't even look up. "According to their family's taxonomy, poludnica are a subcategory of fae, which they refuse to deal with as a consequence of an incident with

French faerie in in the 1760s. The details should be in the reading."

"Yeah, but according to Quinn's Index, poludnica *aren't* fae." She sounded entirely too proud of herself for that piece of trivia, like she wanted a reward for doing the bare minimum expected of her.

"Just because his research is considered the standard here doesn't mean it's universally accepted," I said.

"Then have Quinn talk to them," she said. "He's the head doctor. That's like double authority figure status. And he can convince them to use his Index so they don't keep calling you things you're not. Everybody wins."

I refused to dignify her with a roll of my eyes. "I'm sure everyone would, if they weren't so adamant about their position against abortion. They won't meet with an aswang, and especially not one with Quinque's resume."

Arkay flopped back in her chair. "Oh, for the love of fuck."

"To put it succinctly, yes." I moved on to the next set of forms. "If anyone else could have done this work, it would already be done."

"Fine. Fine. I'll meet with the..." She glanced at the papers again. "...the kushtaka. Whatever." She stared at the papers like they had personally insulted her. "Will this be another set of obvious yes-or-no questions, or will there be actual negotiations this time?"

"Be patient," I said. "You will get as much as I think you can handle."

She lowered the packet. "You don't think I can handle more than a dinner party?"

Hardly. A dinner party suggested multiple guests from a variety of factions, and she didn't have nearly the political prowess to navigate such a complicated event. What she'd just participated in was more like a business lunch.

"I'm giving you tasks that are more suited to your skill level," I rephrased.

That was meant to sound diplomatic. Arkay merely snorted. "What? Did you make ThreeClaw sit through this bullshit, too?"

My nostrils flared with a sharp exhale. Nobody had to make ThreeClaw do anything, and nobody could have managed it if they'd tried.

"ThreeClaw had sixty years' worth of maturity and experience to draw upon," I said. "You are virtually a child. We have to adjust accordingly."

Arkay sat upright. "I'm a grown-ass adult."

"You think dick jokes are the height of comedy," I said. "You're mentally and emotionally unfit to fulfill these duties. Until that changes, you'll continue performing tasks that Quinn and I believe you can handle."

"I don't care what you think I can handle," she said icily. "I am a motherfucking dragon."

"Then I recommend you start acting like it."

"By all means." She threw out her arms in invitation. "I'm strong. I'm scary. This is not up for debate. So why am I having tea parties with foreign dignitaries in this mausoleum when I should be kicking ass out there?"

Mausoleum? I almost laughed. No. Mausoleums were for burying the dead, for sanctifying their legacy and honoring their memory. All we had left of ThreeClaw was Arkay. And as nerve-grating as she was, we couldn't let something happen to her.

"You're welcome to come on combat missions with me," I said. "As soon as you agree to start using Styx, so we can be sure you'll actually survive them."

"That shit is poison."

"Then you're staying down here where it's safe."

She crossed her arms. "Unless I walk out of here."

"By all means," I said coolly. "And while you're at it, you can look for another way to take care of that Rosario girl. I wish you the best of luck staying ahead of the Or—" The word cut off abruptly as a clawed hand closed around my throat.

Hot breath rasped inches from my ear. "Rosario is not some fucking carrot you get to dangle in front of me." Her voice was low, the words distorted by razor fangs. She could crush my throat, and I'd be helpless to stop her.

Would you do it, Aglaeca? Would you really kill me?

"Go ahead and keep showboating." I tried to sit up, but her weight bore me down, forcing my face against the table. "You're only proving my point."

"You keep telling yourself that," she growled.

"The moment you run out of words to say, you make a fist. How would you manage if that stopped being an option? What would you do if I let you go out there, and you came back in a wheelchair?"

"You got something against people with disabilities?" she demanded.

"Not at all." I drove my elbow into her gut and twisted out of her grip. ThreeClaw could have stopped me, but Arkay didn't have the skill. She stumbled backward, and I rose from my chair. "There are plenty of people who could pull off being a warlord blind, or in a wheelchair, or with any of a thousand impairments. Having one arm never slowed ThreeClaw down. But then, she was brilliant. But what do you have? Your wit? Your *delightful* personality? What skills do you have that don't involve either fucking or fighting? And considering you could barely do the latter when you came here, I'm forced to assume you spent most of your time—"

I expected the kick that threw me into the opposite wall. I probably could have evaded it, but I didn't.

My limbs ached as I scraped myself off the floor. My lungs burned with each slow, measured breath. It was good pain: sharp, concrete, focused. Manageable.

"As I was saying," I began, but Arkay whirled away from me and stormed from the conference room, leaving a rain of flying papers in her wake.

Calmly, quietly, I began gathering the scattered documents, but my hand hesitated over one. A map of southern Germany, tracking the progress of a man named Mephistopheles.

With careful, measured motions, I ripped it to shreds.

I would rather run the Hoarde on my own than be beholden to Arkay. And if I could have done it, I would have.

There was a time when were-hyenas and kushtaka would never have dreamed of denying me an audience. They wouldn't have dared.

On the far end of the conference room lay a patch of carpet that was a few shades lighter than the rest, bleached when bloodstains had been scrubbed out of the fibers. The enforcer of a ghoul family had tried to bully me out of a political meeting. I don't remember what slurs he'd thrown my way—not because they were unimportant, but because they were barely out of his mouth before they twisted into screams.

I could still see him, at least six inches taller than ThreeClaw but brought to his knees before her. Her hand was on his chest, her claws embedded so deep in his flesh that I could hear them scrape against his collar bone. Her expression was so cold it was nearly blank, utterly unaffected by his gasps of pain.

"My Fext is my right hand," she said, her voice as level as the edge of a knife. "Disobedience to her is disobedience to me. Any disrespect will be punished accordingly." Her wrist turned and her fingers curled. The ghoul's arm rose as his collarbone was twisted against its tendons. She could rip it out of his body with a single pull. She would, if he gave her half a reason. He begged for mercy, but she didn't pay attention to him. Her eyes were on the don who stood behind him.

I remember counting the seconds. The ghoul and the dragon stared each other down while the enforcer filled the air with his screams. The don looked away first.

"My family's most sincere apologies to you, ThreeClaw, and to your Fext. I assure you, it won't happen again."

I remember waiting until long after the meeting ended and the ghouls had both gone before I dared to speak. "Your right hand, Aglaeca?"

Her smile was so thin it was nearly invisible, like the first light of a crescent moon. "I was starting to worry nobody had caught that. There wasn't even a groan."

"I think there was plenty of groaning," I said. "And some screaming. And crying. And I think he may have pissed himself."

She gave a quick exhalation that might have been a laugh, but then her expression sobered. "Let me know if anyone speaks to you that way again."

"I don't think they will."

"Not for a while," she agreed. "But be on the lookout anyway. Disrespect is like a weed. It must be dealt with immediately, or it will spread."

And it had spread. For seven years, other organizations had been defying us with impunity, and it was growing by the day. ThreeClaw would be furious with me for letting her empire fall so low.

Even worse: she would be disappointed.

Arkay

I escaped into the receiving room, where a series of hulking, three-limbed statues loomed over me with Nadia's same brand of judgmental arrogance. Bastards, every single one of them. I had half a mind to knock the rest of their claws off. Tear them all down and turn them into rubble.

I dragged myself up the length of one of the brass dragons, using its mane and antlers as a ladder to carry me to a hidden panel in the ceiling. When I pawed at it, the latch refused to budge. I wanted to punch a hole right through the panel, but I knew better than to try smashing my way through an enchanted gateway. I took a deep breath and tried again, giving the latch a series of very careful wiggles until it finally let me through.

Stupid piece of junk.

The trapdoor was one of three that honeycombed my floor. Another couple dozen doors lined the walls, though most of them only opened to reveal solid limestone. The spells that operated them had been systematically disabled, some of them pre-emptively, the rest as a consequence of me wandering into places I wasn't supposed to go.

Nadia said it was for my protection. The doors in the Felldeep were so convoluted and confusing that it was easy to take a wrong turn and wind up halfway across the world. That was how we'd lost Meph, after all. We'd tracked him to a patch of about a dozen doors in one corner of the Forest; depending on which door he went through, he could be on any one of four separate continents.

But as much as I appreciated not getting locked out in the Arctic Circle, the room unnerved me. That's the funny thing about rows of doors that don't go anywhere: pretty soon, they start looking an awful lot like the bars of a cage. The rest of the interior didn't exactly make it feel homey. The furniture was left over from when ThreeClaw lived here, and her tastes had apparently veered toward utilitarian neutrality. It wasn't like I had any possessions of my own to add to the mix. Most of my stuff got destroyed in a fire a year ago, and after that I'd been living out of a car with Meph. I'd tried keeping my pink armchair in here for a while, but it felt out of place, like the last item left to shove into a moving van before it drove out of town. At least in the conference room it looked kinda quirky, instead of sad.

I threw myself onto the indifferent white sheets of the bed, pulled my tablet off the side table, and opened my inbox, trying distract myself from my already shitty mood. There were a few emails from my network of folklorists and historians, though their messages had lost their sense of urgency.

I skipped them and opened the next email down.

Hello Arkay,

I started my new job today, and it looks like everything is going well. The people here are friendly, and I'm not the only ghoul working here. Actually, this Friday a bunch of us are going out to a vegan place that just opened up down the street. Everyone here seems to be pretty open about who and what we are. It feels nice, not having to hide.

I know there's an Order building right downtown, but for the first time since Matheson, I actually feel safe. A pair of Hoarde rakshasa came by the morgue the other day and gave me their phone numbers in case I had any problems (and one of them is really cute— I'll let you know more as that develops).

I don't know how you did it, but thank you so much for getting me this job. The morgue's a fifteen-minute drive from the rehab institute, so I'll be able to come look in on Rosario as often as they'll let me in.

It's a bit more of a drive from Fort Wayne, but Father Gabriel is hoping to make the trip at least once a month, maybe more. I'll let the two of you figure out the details.

Rosa's doing well. Her therapists are nice people, and they're all really impressed with how quickly she's improving. Now that she's fluent in English, her speech therapist is starting her on Spanish and ASL. He hopes that might jog some memories.

She doesn't remember me, but I guess we didn't know each other very long. Maybe if you come see her, it might spark something.

I'd received a similar email from Kindra, Rosario's… girlfriend? Ex-girlfriend? I didn't know what to call her anymore, but she had taken up an apprenticeship in a tattoo parlor in the same area. Whatever their relationship at this point, she still wanted to be a part of Rosa's life. Her last email had been a short one:

That was weeks ago. I'd tried sneaking away from Nadia's endless assignments, only to wind up lost in the Forest for half the day. By the time I managed to get myself within arm's reach of a working vehicle, their movie marathon was long over.

Danielle told me that was fine. She said Rosa didn't even notice I wasn't there. She meant it in a good way.

Besides, it didn't matter. The most important thing was that Rosario was comfortable with Danielle and Kindra. If anything went haywire with the Hoarde, they were my first line of defense. One text, and the two of them would be at Rosa's side within an hour, ready to whisk her off to the farthest corners of the country. Sure, the Hoarde's bodyguards were technically capable of protecting Rosario if it came down to it. I just couldn't trust them to care about her.

I needed to get off this track before I made myself mad again. I opened the next email.

RK—

We've got a new arrival at the Valley. Looks like he's starving but he refuses to eat. I don't know if he's got a head thing going on or if he's one of those ghouls you told me about, but either way, it sounds like you're his best shot right now.

—Mike Jones, Mayor

PS. I've been spreading the word as far out as St. Louis about Meph, but still no luck. Susan's planning to hop a train to California later this month, and I gave her your email. Maybe she'll find something.

I buried my head in the sheet and sighed before opening up a reply.

Mike,

Thanks for looking. Keep your eyes open.

I'll have someone drop by the Valley within a week, but I'm shooting for tomorrow.

Arkay

I wrote up a second email to our outreach specialist, and added a note to send a care package, too: food, cold weather gear, a few new tents, and a shipping crate full of the socks and menstrual products that were always in short supply.

My finger lingered over the 'send' button.

Did Meph have socks?

The thought struck a nerve. He'd only been homeless for a few weeks before we'd teamed up, and he'd royally sucked at it. He didn't know the thousand little tricks that helped keep you alive on the streets, and he was too stubborn to ask for help.

I was still holding out hope that he'd connect with veterans somewhere, maybe find some common ground, but in four months nobody had heard of him. I'd tried asking around the Hoarde, but without much luck. Some people acted like I'd told a joke. Most of them got stiff and cold, and told me in clipped tones that they'd look into it. As if they cared what happened to Order reject.

Who needed them? I'd find him my own way.

Hopefully he could hold out that long.

Meph

A heavy, metallic creak announced the opening of the reinforced steel door at the top of the stairs. Below, the dim hallway brightened momentarily with the spillover of light from somewhere above. Two pairs of footsteps descended, coming to a halt at the door to my cell. Two men, one black and one Arab, but otherwise identical. Both stood well over six feet tall, both wore the same tailored suits in the same shade of crimson, both were groomed like they were ready to attend a gala, and both carried AK-47s. Every inch of them was visible through the pane of bullet-proof glass that formed the front of my cell.

"The Contessa invites you to dine with her," said the black man, his voice softened by a mild British accent.

His expression was perfectly composed, cold without the indiscretion of a scowl. I knew how to get a rise out of him. I'd done it before, when I'd told him that his Contessa could go fuck herself. But whatever else he'd wanted to do to me, he'd simply turned around and walked away, and taken my daily rations of food and water with him.

I'd missed too many meals lately.

"Sure," I grunted. His eyes narrowed, and I nearly rolled mine. "Inform the Contessa that I'd be delighted." I couldn't quite keep the sneer out of my tone.

"On your feet," said the other, gesturing with his rifle. I dragged my feet, nearly falling as the blood rushed from my head. How long had I been crouched in that corner?

"Out here." The two men stood on opposite sides of the door, far enough apart that I couldn't catch them both in a bull rush. I could try anyway, but I'd likely wind up full of lead. Around the corner was a simple bathroom, pointedly devoid of doors or curtains. Basic toiletries adorned the sink: soap, a toothbrush and toothpaste, shaving cream, and a disposable razor.

I stared blankly at them.

"Get yourself cleaned up." He nodded at the shower.

"Some privacy first?" I asked. With some time and tinkering, I might be able to dismantle the razor into a weapon, or at least do something with that can of shaving cream.

"We're staying here," the black man said, raising his rifle. "Clean up and get dressed."

"You have to be joking," I muttered.

His expression hardened, as did his grip on the weapon.

I could make a stand for the sake of principle, but dignity didn't compare to the pangs in my stomach or the rasp of thirst in my voice. The last several days had made my circumstances painfully clear. If I didn't eat with the Contessa, I wouldn't eat at all.

I stripped out of clothes that were likely beyond saving. They'd been heavy with sweat and grime long before I'd been dragged here, and my incarceration had done nothing to improve the smell. Now the odor of my waste bucket clung to the fabric like a miasma.

I tried to ignore the hostile eyes and focus instead on the hot water and the feel of soap on my skin, the simple relief of being clean for the first time in far too long. I didn't want to be obvious, in case they decided to drag me away before I finished, but I gulped down as much water as I could while I cleaned up.

By the time I stepped out of the shower, my clothes had disappeared, replaced by a length of wine-colored fabric that hung from a velvet hanger. A tuxedo, I discovered when I gave it a closer examination, dark red and trimmed with black and gold.

"Put it on," said the British guard. I didn't have much choice, judging by the way he shifted his grip on his rifle.

The suit fit better than it had any right to, as did the shoes I'd been given.

They marched me up the stairs at gunpoint, through plainly decorated servant's quarters and into the more lavish front rooms of a manor house. Plush carpet muffled our footsteps. Paintings and tapestries crowded the walls. Enormous windows displayed artistic views of a forest, each glimpse framed by stained-glass dragons observing their domain.

They led me into a grand dining hall, as opulent and overwrought as the rest of the estate, and its centerpiece was a table that could have seated a small army. At its head, framed by the mantel of a gaping fireplace, sat a chair that could only be described as a throne. Seated therein was an imposing woman, tall and muscular, with ringlets of dark hair cascading down her back. She had the curves of a goddess, wrapped in a floor-length gown the color of glowing coals.

Every detail about her— the arch of her brows, the smoke of her eyes, the set of her shoulders— demanded attention and respect.

"Thank you, Safi, Garrett." A twist of her finger dismissed them to the corners of the room, and she turned her attention to me. "Come, *mein Häftling*. Sit. Have a drink. You must be thirsty."

You made sure of it, I wanted to snarl, but instead I grunted an affirmative, creeping into the only available chair. A glass of wine sat before me. Gingerly I picked it up and took a gulp. It was strong and so dry that it only made me more thirsty.

"Have some more," she insisted, fixing me with calculating eyes as I took a second, smaller sip. Her stare didn't leave me until I'd finished the glass.

As soon as I put it down, she made another subtle gesture, and a flurry of servants swarmed the table. A place setting appeared before me, and more importantly, a bowl of thick, salty soup and a basket of bread. I grabbed a pair of rolls immediately, keeping one safe in my hand while I tore into the other.

"Don't eat so quickly," she chided. "I would hate for you to choke." Her tone was soft, but absolute authority hardened her smile into a threat.

Slowly I pried my hands off the dinner rolls and forced myself to chew thoroughly and wash it down with a drink before I took my next bite. I kept my eyes on the servants who refilled my glass, ready to stab them with a fork if they tried to take my food away.

It occurred to me a moment later that the sharp-bladed knife would make a decent weapon.

I watched her carefully for signs of another command, but she merely smiled at me like I'd performed a trick. Carefully I picked up a spoon and began on the soup. Hunger told me to gulp it down, but I didn't dare. The Contessa's iron gaze never left me, even as she daintily consumed her own portion.

"My colors suit you," she said.

My soup bowl was nearly empty. I sopped up the last drops with bread. This could hold me over until the next meal, couldn't it? "I look like a waiter."

If I'd insulted the Contessa, she only smiled. "A charming profession. And so smartly dressed." She trailed her fingers across the sleeves of a passing servant, and his face flushed the same shade as his jacket. "But I believe your talents are otherwise inclined."

"Why am I here?" I asked.

"Americans," she said with a dismissive wave of her hand. "So eager to get to business. Dinner is a time for conversation." Her eyes were cold and unforgiving, and I took another swallow of wine. "Tell me, *Häftling*. What brings you to Germany?"

"A door," I said flatly. She flashed a smile that was too refined to be a glare. "I got lost."

"And you wandered into my lands," she said. "How fortunate for you. The world is a dangerous place for one of your background. Not all hosts would be as gracious as I have been."

I've seen better.

"Really?" She asked. "Do tell."

Shit. I hadn't meant to say that out loud.

"You were saying?" She prompted again.

Carelessness was going to get me killed. If I wanted to get out of this alive, I needed to be smart. I forced back the fuzziness inside my head and tried to focus.

I'd read up on dragons, back when I'd been in training, and I'd brushed up when I'd started working with Rosario. Traditionally they were solitary predators, though that was such an understatement that it bordered on ludicrous. Their animosity toward other dragons was the stuff of legends. They couldn't be within a mile of each other without resorting to homicide, not even to breed.

I could use that against her.

"You've been gracious, sure," I said. "But the last dragon I spent time with was much more accommodating."

She arched a perfectly manicured eyebrow. "You forget yourself. You are my *Häftling*, not only my guest."

"Wasn't hers, either," I said. "More like one part refugee, one part prisoner of war. But she was still awfully friendly about it."

My glass refilled. "And who was this most magnanimous of hosts?"

The room was starting to swim, and I took another swallow to steady it. It didn't work. "A Japanese river dragon in the American Midwest. Might have heard of her. Goes by Arkay."

The Contessa flashed a thin-lipped smile. "Her reputation hasn't yet reached this far, it seems."

"You sure about that?" I asked. "Seems like everyone in the Order knows about her. All the way to the top. Even Archduchess Stavros was involved with trying to take her down."

The Contessa sat back, crossing her legs with such a look of disdain that I half-expected to see her tail lashing under the table. "Was she now?"

"Last I heard? Yes. Yes, she was." Actually, she'd been more concerned with my court-martial, but I wasn't about to tell the dragon that. There were only so many names I could drop before I got into outright lies, and I had no idea how equipped she was to check my facts.

"Then it seems I have been gravely misinformed." She tilted her head to one side, resting her cheek on one knuckle, and gestured for my glass to be refilled. "Come, *Häftling*. Tell me more about this Arkay."

Nadia

I knocked on the door of Arkay's apartment.

No answer.

I knocked again, and then a third time, and still received no reply. I tried the doorknob, and it turned easily. An unlocked door had always been an invitation to come inside, at least when ThreeClaw had lived here. She'd valued discretion almost as much as she valued her privacy. It was part of the reason she'd insisted that I keep my own apartment, even though there was a time when I'd spent more time in hers than my own.

It's not her, I reminded myself. *This is Arkay. The rules are different for her.*

Exactly, I argued back. *She's a child. She needs authority and guidance. You need to be the one to provide it for her.*

I took a deep breath and pushed open the door. The lights were on and almost painfully bright, but I could have navigated the room in the dark. ThreeClaw's personal belongings had been packed into storage and some of the furniture had been moved slightly, but otherwise it remained exactly as ThreeClaw had left it.

There were no additional pictures, no odds and ends, no trophies of victories past. As haphazard as Arkay was in every other aspect of her life, her room was almost eerily devoid of clutter. A few dirty dishes lay in the sink, but they seemed surreal, almost out of place. The apartment looked more like something out of a catalogue than a place where a dragon had lived for four months.

"Arkay?" I called softly.

Still no answer.

I approached the bedroom. Another knock was met by still more silence, and I opened the bedroom door.

She lay sprawled across the bed, still fully dressed, her face pressed against the black screen of a rubber-encased tablet. Her short, shaggy hair had settled in in a wild disarray, further disheveled every time she twitched and shuddered in her sleep.

ThreeClaw had never slept well on her own. War had left her ever-vigilant, and only the presence of another body seemed to soothe her nerves. As far as I knew, she'd never told a soul about it. Maybe she didn't fully realize it herself.

I wanted to reach out to her, to smooth her flyaway hair, to ease her back into a more soothing sleep.

Except that this wasn't ThreeClaw, and she had a job to do.

I cleared my throat. "Arkay, wake up."

ThreeClaw would have rolled from the bed, ready to spring into action. Arkay merely flopped onto her back and leaned up onto her elbows, blinking blearily around the room before her eyes focused on me.

"Fuck," she yawned. "Can you get any creepier?"

I ignored the barb and showed her the phone, the screen still ticking off the seconds while the woman on the other end remained on hold. "There's a call for you."

"What?" Arkay peered at the clock on the wall, though it took her several seconds to register that it was three in the morning. "Who the fuck would be calling…" I could pinpoint the exact moment her system spiked with adrenaline. Her posture straightened, her eyes dilated, and her expression became sharp and alert. "Did something happen? Is Rosario okay?" She acted like a strategic weapon was at stake, rather than a single human woman.

"No news on Rosario," I said, keeping the emotion out of my voice. "The call is from one of our allies." I used the term loosely. "An important one. This isn't someone we can ignore until morning."

Arkay wilted. "You have got to be fucking kidding me."

"Try not to start a war," I said, and I took the phone off hold. "You're on speaker, Your Grace."

Your Grace? Arkay mouthed silently back at me.

"Thank you, Nadezda." The Contessa rolled my name on her tongue the way a child might savor a favorite candy.

"I am speaking to Arkay, then? I've heard so very much about you."

"It's three AM," Arkay said flatly. "Why are you calling me?" The closest she could come to diplomacy was a full sentence without the word 'fuck' in it.

I glared at her. Which part of 'don't start a war' was difficult to grasp?

"Is it so late?" I could hear the simper on the Contessa's lips. "It's so easy to forget the difference in time between our countries. A mistake I'm sure you've made often— that is, if you've had dealings outside of your own borders?"

Arkay deepened her glower.

Don't you dare, I mouthed at her.

"Who the hell is this fucker?" Arkay hissed in tones that were likely meant to be inaudible.

They weren't.

"Merely an interested party bidding you welcome to your new home," said the voice on the phone. She sounded amused more than offended; I couldn't tell if that was better or worse.

"Arkay," I said tightly. "This is the Contessa. The dragon of the Black Forest."

If she'd ever had a name beyond that title, she didn't need one.

Before the Order came to power, the world had been teeming with dragons, but very few ever made it past their teenage years. Instinct drove them to venture out and claim a territory of their own, and usually that meant challenging an older, larger dragon for their own land. Roughly ninety percent died in that first fight. The remaining ten percent would typically be killed off within a decade, either by a younger dragon or by human dragonslayers.

The Contessa had held the Black Forest for more than a century. She was one of only seven to accomplish that in all of recorded history.

"It's so good to hear that the Hoarde is finally under new management," the Contessa continued. "My deepest regards. Oh, and Nadezda, dear, while I have you on the phone, I wanted to assure you that my previous offer still stands. If you find yourself wanting to escape your present situation, know that I'm only a phone call away."

My stomach dropped. My shoulders tightened. It was a backhanded offer at the best of times, but this— this was cruel. She'd advertised subversion and betrayal in front of another dragon. She'd proclaimed me untrustworthy and seditious. ThreeClaw would have seen the slander for what it was, but Arkay?

I couldn't be sure.

"I don't think that will be necessary," I said, hardening my voice into ice to hide my anxiety.

The Contessa tutted. "Your loyalty is admirable, but unfortunately misguided. I'm afraid your new master can't take care of you the way you deserve."

"You want to say that again?" Arkay demanded, her hackles rising.

"No need for posturing, *Schlängelchen*. I already know you're new to all this. And this Hoarde of yours is entirely too much responsibility for you. There's no shame in acknowledging that. The real shame comes in failing so spectacularly to care for your charges."

"What are you talking about?"

"Why, the poor, starved puppy I found on my doorstep." The Contessa's voice held a smile. "He did mention an Arkay, but I dearly hope that wasn't you. I'm sure the name is fairly common in your country."

The hairs on my neck stood on end, and I tasted ozone. Electricity crackled in the air. The call fuzzed into static and dropped entirely.

Arkay had leaped from her bed, her lips peeled back in a snarl, her claws out and ready to shred. "She has Meph."

That was what she took out of this conversation?

She'd listened to a barrage of insults and barbs with indifference. She'd been accused of neglect without more than a sneer. She'd been told that I— her first lieutenant, her closest advisor, her greatest supporter— was poised to betray her, and she didn't bat an eye.

Because she didn't care. Not about responsibility or pride. Not about me.

Just some miserable Order castaway.

"Put her back on the line," Arkay growled.

"No." My phone's screen was frozen, the shapes fuzzy and the colors distorted. It would probably have to be reset, assuming it survived at all.

"Then give me her fucking number and I'll do it myself. That crawling bitch has Meph."

"Let her have him." The word tasted like acid on my tongue.

Abruptly Arkay was too close, her eyes narrow and sharp. "You wanna try that again?"

"He's an Orderling," I said. "The faster she kills him off, the better off we all are."

"He's reformed."

"You think that actually matters?" I spat. "Do you have any idea how many innocent people die every day because of the likes of him? ThreeClaw dedicated her life to ending their reign of terror. If one more of their kind dies, then I call that a victory."

She pulled back, her expression unreadable and cold.

"Funny," she said. "He used to say the same thing about people like you."

Meph

I regained consciousness and regretted it instantly. The inside of my mouth felt lined with carpet; my throat felt like sandpaper. Sunlight streamed through a nearby window, and every shaft of light sent a stabbing pain through my skull. I wanted to vomit, but the taste of acid in my mouth suggested that had happened already.

Jesus Christ, what did she do to me?

I burrowed into the warm dark of a blanket. It was soft and plush, though damp from sweat, and it reeked of stale wine. I stayed under until the threat of smothering forced me to creep into the painful brightness of the room.

I'd been laid in an elegant four-poster bed and covered in a thick feather comforter. The sheets underneath me were a higher thread count than I was used to; Arkay could probably have given me an exact number, but I could only ascertain that they were luxurious and soft. I'd also been dressed in silk pajamas, though I didn't dare think too hard about how or when that had happened.

A pitcher of water sat on the bedside table, accompanied by an already-filled glass and a note written on gold-embossed stationary: *In vino veritas, in aqua sanitas.* In wine there is truth, in water there is health.

"Fuck you." I downed the glass, only to find the inside of my mouth assaulted by the sting of unexpected carbonation. I spat it out, choking and spluttering.

I sniffed at the glass. It didn't smell unusual. It didn't taste like anything unnatural, either. Just ordinary carbonated water. It had been fairly common when I'd been making my way through Germany, but I hadn't had anything like that since I'd been captured by the Contessa's guards. For the last few weeks, I'd been lucky to get water at all.

There was no way in hell she'd let me go this easily. What was she playing at?

I drank as much of the offered water as I could stomach, then valiantly braved the rest of the suite. The walls were papered in an intricate burgundy and black design that looked vaguely Victorian, though it lacked any obvious signs of age. The bedroom furniture was all wood, all of it expertly carved and stained nearly black, and tastefully accented with gold leaf. Beyond a lacquered door was an expansive bathroom, complete with a bathtub large enough that it must have been intended for at least two occupants. Beyond another door lay a sitting room in the same style. But that was as far as I could go. The next door was locked.

I might be able to break the door down, assuming it wasn't reinforced, though that would probably summon the guards. I could snap the legs off one of those chairs and make a decent club, but it wouldn't do much against AK-47s. I could try smashing my way through the stained-glass windows, but there'd be no squeezing through the artistically wrought iron bars just beyond.

I hadn't been released, only moved to a nicer cage.

At least this one had access to a shower.

I felt significantly more human once I'd gotten cleaned up, though I noticed with unease that someone had followed me into the bathroom. There had been no sound, no glimpse of movement, no sign of an intruder, but my discarded pajamas had been removed from the bathroom floor and replaced, once again, by a red tuxedo.

I didn't like where this was going.

Awkwardly I put on the provided clothing and stepped back outside.

The sitting room had been empty a few minutes before. Now a tea service had been laid out across a coffee table, and a pair of armed guards stood at attention on either side of the locked door.

The Contessa sat on the black leather sofa. Her gown was a deep ruby, the same shade as her satisfied grin. "Good morning, *mein Häftling*. I trust you slept well."

"I wouldn't know," I said.

She tittered. "Such a fascinating conversation we had last night. You were quite talkative."

"You got me drunk." The accusation was aimed as much at myself as at her. I shouldn't have been so fast to talk. I should have trained up on advanced counter-interrogation techniques when I'd had the chance. Instead, I'd accepted the Order's standard training. I'd always assumed I'd be willing to go through with it if the occasion ever arose. As it turned out, I was more amenable to wearing gaudy tuxedos and meekly drinking tea than I was to suicide.

The Contessa smiled, completely ignoring my retort. "I'm particularly intrigued by what you had to say about your dear Arkay…"

"You stay away from her," I snapped.

The guards shifted, adjusting the rifles in their hands, but the Contessa only laughed. "So protective! And I was worried you would be entirely untrained. This is a lovely surprise."

I narrowed my eyes.

"It's fitting, really. An ambitious little thing like herself, it's only natural she'd find herself a few good hounds. Your breeding makes you an unusual choice, of course, but…" She tilted her head to the side. "Given her background, I can understand her preference for pit bulls. It must be quite a strong preference, considering the effort she's put into procuring you."

What effort? Arkay had taken me on out of pity and some misguided attempt to honor Rosario's memory. I was an afterthought to her.

The dog metaphor was an uncomfortably accurate one, though. I needed to change the subject before it got unbearable.

"Is this another interrogation?" I asked, nodding at the tea. "Because I'm not drinking that." They'd probably spiked it with sodium thiopental or something.

The Contessa tittered. "Of course not, dear. I'm here to make you an offer."

"You're joking." I'd been wondering if she'd just have her guards pour it down my throat, or whether that would compromise her elegant facade.

"Never," she said. "I am a woman in the business of filling needs. And you, my dear, are so very unfulfilled."

The last time a woman had talked to me like that, she'd been a dancer in Arkay's old strip club. Not the kind of association I wanted to make with the dragon who'd starved and imprisoned me for the past several weeks. "I don't want anything you could possibly give me."

Her lips parted, revealing perfect white teeth. "Not even the Order?"

I made every effort to keep emotion off my face. "Like I said. Nothing you could possibly give me."

"Nothing is impossible for the suitably resourceful." Her smile widened. "Especially not when I've done it before."

She was lying. She was one of the Order's greatest enemies, not a member of the High Synod. And besides, even if I might have entertained fantasies while drugged, I was sober enough to know better. "Even if they wanted me back, I don't belong there. The Order is broken."

"Indeed it is," she said. "And it's in desperate need of repair. A task, I think, that would befit a man such as yourself."

I glared. "I'm sure."

"Your drunken ramblings impressed me, *Häftling*. You have dreams. Your ideals are so often smothered in individuals of your breeding, but they instill in you a potential that should be appropriately harnessed." Her glance dipped momentarily. "There are other ways to take advantage of your talents, I'm sure. But that would hardly be an efficient use for them."

I felt the sudden urge to cross my legs. "You want to use me?"

"You have always been used, without reservation or pity." She leaned forward, and I would have edged away if I hadn't been blocked by the back of the couch. "But unlike your previous master, I intend for you to be well rewarded for your efforts. I think you've gone long enough living off scraps."

"Is that why you opted not to feed me?" I asked.

"A woman does not reach my position by wasting resources on impotent assets. Fortunately, you find yourself in possession of a unique potential. I suggest you make use of it."

Or else I would go back to starving in a cell.

She smiled sweetly. "But that shouldn't be difficult for you. You have dreams. You could bring the Order back to what it always should have been: a shield between the innocent lambs and the beasts that would consume them."

I swallowed, but said nothing. Apparently she took that as an answer, because she gave my leg a congenial pat.

"Consider my offer, *Häftling*. We will discuss it again at dinner."

Arkay

I hurled my bed into the air, and it collapsed into mattress, frame, and bed spring as it hit the wall. Something splintered, and there was a puff of drywall dust in the dim light, but I was too furious to care.

She had Meph. She had Meph! She had him and she was keeping him from me and she was doing who knew what to him. He was mine, god-fucking-dammit, and she couldn't have him! How dare she take what was mine and dangle him in front of me like that?

I'd rip that coal-sucker's eyes out!

And Nadia!

She knew I'd been looking for him. She'd been helping me look. And now she got off telling me to just leave him?

Fuck, she didn't even bother looking surprised when the Contessa dropped that bomb on me. Did she know already, or did she honestly give so few fucks that she couldn't even bother to fake a reaction?

Fuck her, then. Fuck them all. I'd been an idiot to ask her for help in the first place. Now that I knew the Contessa had him, I could do the rest on my own. Then I could get him somewhere safe, and grab Rosario, and get the hell out of this prison.

First, though, I needed a plan. Success required plans, and good planning required recon.

I pulled up my phone and dialed the Hoarde's archive. It was one of the few places I was actually allowed to go, mostly so I could do background reading for all the political bullshit Nadia had me doing. And thanks to world-wide political ties with people who couldn't respect fucking time zones, they had to have someone on staff around the clock.

After four rings, the archivist on duty picked up. "M'ello?" yawned a voice on the other end.

I seethed. "This is Arkay. As in dragon."

I caught a muffled "shit!" from the other end, along with some hasty scrambling. When the young man spoke again, he sounded far more professional. "Yes, ma'am. How can I be of assistance to you today? Tonight. I mean tonight."

"I just got a phone call from a piece of work who calls herself the Contessa. Know of her?"

I heard him swallow. "I've heard of her, yes."

"Good," I said. "Bring me everything you have on her."

It was time the Contessa and I were properly introduced.

Nadia

For the next week, I kept myself busy. A family of kobolds in Chicago wanted help recovering a precious family heirloom, a new dragon had come to power in the Amazon, and a syndicate of oni wanted to renegotiate our trade agreement. All of that required meetings, paperwork, and administration. I barely had a chance to eat before I collapsed into bed at night, so keeping my mind off Arkay should have been easy.

Should have been.

Instead I found myself lying awake for hours, silently fuming at the ceiling. I was coming in late to appointments because I would be reminded of Arkay on the walk over and lost track of time while I silently seethed. I relieved my frustrations in the gym, only to wind up pulling muscles and straining joints.

My mental processes were grinding down, my reaction times were flagging, and my productivity was reaching an all-time low. I suspected I was developing an ulcer, though regular doses of Styx kept healing it before it had the chance to fester.

I was effectively immortal thanks to the drug, and Arkay was *still* taking years off my life.

Maybe I should take the Contessa's offer, I thought bitterly. *See how well Arkay handles the Hoarde without me around to keep the wheels turning.*

Let the Contessa— I only managed to entertain the idea for a moment before the satisfaction of spite drained away. The Contessa wouldn't just claim me for her own. She would break me down into my component parts and remake me in her own image. She would peel away every vein of loyalty and affection I had for ThreeClaw, and replace them with a fanatic devotion to my new master.

Arkay was utterly useless, but she had neither the patience nor intelligence for that kind of domination.

I shook my head. There weren't enough hours in my day to waste on dramatics. I was only even entertaining this nonsense because I was tired. I needed coffee, and then I'd be thinking clearly again.

I left the conference room that acted as my office and headed to the bazaar.

The Felldeep's marketplace had started out as a staff cafeteria in the early days of the Hoarde, both imposing and practical to suit ThreeClaw's sensibilities. But as the Hoarde grew, the Felldeep became home to an ever larger population of refugees, most of whom had brought their own culinary habits. Kiosks spread like weeds around the kitchens, and the air was dense with a clutter of smells. Habañero long pork battled for space with halal kebap. Pickled ginger stood side by side with gingerbread. Further away from the kitchens, novelties and daily wares joined the mess, until the overcrowded cafeteria resembled a market square more than an organized structure.

I wasn't the only one who needed a drink, apparently. The little coffee stand already boasted a long line that wrapped around a display of Matcha whisks and lingered thoughtfully beside a waist-high stack of prayer rugs.

I pulled out my phone— might as well look through my emails while I waited— when a voice caught my attention.

"So anyway..." Up ahead, a young kappa huddled with the most conspiratorial air he could without losing his place in line. "A few days ago, someone who said she was Arkay called me up during the night shift, right? Like four in the morning. And she asked for like everything we had on the Contessa, and fast. So of course I had to deliver it— I almost needed a wheelbarrow to get it all— and she answered the door and everything."

"Holy crap. You saw her?" asked a waifish succubus who worked in IT. "What did she look like?"

"Are you sure it was her?" asked a handsome impundulu, his beaded braids clicking around his face

"Of course I'm sure." The kappa said, nodding carefully to keep the water from spilling out of the indentation in his head. "She introduced herself as Arkay. Who would lie about that?"

"It could have been a doppelganger," the impundulu pointed out. "It wouldn't be the first one. Do you remember that one who called herself ThreeClaw a couple years back? It was when the Olympics were on."

"That wasn't a doppelganger," said the succubus. "That was really ThreeClaw."

"It was not," said the kappa. "The Order had already killed her by then."

"No, they only said they did. They lied about it. Everyone knows that."

"Then why do we suddenly have another dragon?" the impundulu asked. "If ThreeClaw was still here, she wouldn't have it." He was getting agitated enough that tiny feathers were starting to add flashes of stark white to his midnight skin, and electricity began crackling in his long hair.

"I thought Arkay was ThreeClaw," the succubus said.

"Then why would she change her name?" the kappa asked. "Besides, she had both arms. Everyone knows ThreeClaw only had one."

"Maybe she grew it back and decided to change her name," the succubus said. "Dragons can do that, you know."

"That's not dragons, it's newts."

"My cousin said it was dragons."

"Has your cousin ever even seen a dragon up close?"

Their argument was drawing attention, and not just from the other people in line. Passersby abandoned discretion to lean in, their interest piqued by gossip.

"As fascinating as I find this discussion," I broke in coolly. "It does leave certain questions unanswered."

For the briefest of moments, the three nodded cheerfully along with my contribution, blindly accepting another voice into their conversation. The impundulu looked up first, his face going ashen and his pinprick feathers puffing up in alarm when he realized who I was. The succubus caught his expression and glanced abruptly at me, and her full lips snapped shut. The kappa had his back to me, but I could see his body stiffen as realization washed over him.

"Foremost," I continued. "Do the Felldeep's archives not ensure the same rights of privacy observed by other libraries, or has that recently changed without my having been informed?"

The kappa swallowed, and the water held in his skull rippled.

"Secondly, do you find it important to publicize the confidential research conducted by *all* your patrons, or merely those you deem to be *celebrities*?" The last word came out a hiss.

The kappa turned and nearly crashed into his compatriots. "I didn't— I wasn't—"

I ignored his stammers. "And perhaps most importantly, is this flagrant disregard for your vocation a personal matter, or has this become common behavior among the other members of your staff?"

"I— I—" He stared at me with wide eyes, his short dark hair plastered to his face with both sweat and spilt water.

"Get yourself cleaned up and report to security," I said. "Ivan will want to know exactly how much information has been leaking from the archives."

The last of the color drained from the kappa's face, and he swayed. Automatically the succubus and the impundulu stepped closer, wary in case he fainted outright. It was an appropriate reaction to meeting our head of security. I liked to think I cultivated an air of intimidation, but it was hard to compete with an eight-foot-tall minotaur.

I dismissed the kappa with a wave of my hand, and the succubus and impundulu helped him out of line. Our audience dissipated. Those in line averted their eyes and huddled into whispers, while others ducked their heads and hurried on their way. With any luck, the topic of conversation would be more invested in security breaches and spycraft, rather than Arkay.

Meanwhile, I got out of line. Arkay had bypassed her supervisors to call the archives directly. That required investigation.

I passed through one of the enormous doors in the walls of the bazaar, and found myself in a long hallway lined with security cameras and even more doors. More hallways exactly like it connected every single chamber in the Felldeep. If an enemy ever managed to breach one of the public areas, we'd be able to remotely break the enchantments on the doors, entombing the intruders in a small, unventilated space under fifty feet of solid rock. Only ThreeClaw's apartments connected directly to the public spaces, though most of those had been sealed when Arkay moved in. We'd worked hard to maintain the Hoarde's credibility during ThreeClaw's absence. The last thing I needed was for Arkay to mingle with our employees and prove that we'd taken on an incompetent dragon.

I turned left into the administrative wing, then passed down another long hallway to the familiar door. It didn't open.

Irate, I knocked. "Arkay, open the door."

A voice filtered through the door, speaking too low for me to make out the words.

"I said let me in."

The door opened just wide enough for Arkay to slip through and snap it shut behind her. She probably meant to block the view, but she was too short to conceal much from me. Piles of books and papers were spread across the coffee table in the familiar patterns of research.

"Don't tell me I've got another phone call already," she said, her tone acidic in its sweetness. "It's barely ten in the morning. Did somebody mix up their time zones or something?"

I narrowed my eyes. "It sounds like you've been making plenty of calls of your own."

"I've been known to do that on occasion," she said evenly.

"I'm sure you have. And tell me, are you enjoying the collected works of the Contessa?"

She raised her eyebrows in a parody of mild interest. "Keeping tabs of the books I read? Real classy."

"You called the archives behind my back."

"Oh, wiretapping. My mistake." She snorted. "I've called the archives plenty of times. How the hell is it a problem now?"

"Because before you were talking to seasoned archivists who took pride in their discretion. This time you called an idiot newbie who got stuck on the night shift and felt the need to share what he'd learned over breakfast."

"Who fucking cares?" she demanded. "I got a middle-of-the-night threatening phone call from another dragon, and

I'm doing actual research to figure out who the hell I'm dealing with. If that kid wants to tell all his friends, then whoop-dee-fucking-doo. Guess what? Your new dragon's actually doing her fucking job!"

"If that's all he saw, that would be fantastic," I snapped. "But you couldn't be bothered to order the materials and leave well enough alone. You had to invite him into your bedroom. Were you even dressed at the time?"

Her eyes narrowed. "Why wouldn't I be?"

Who was she trying to fool? "You think we didn't do a background check when we brought you on? Did you really think you could hide that from us?"

"I haven't been hiding anything."

"You were a pole dancer!" My voice nearly cracked into a shriek. "You used to take pride in yourself, you used to have dignity, and now you're a few dollars short of a—a streetwalker!"

I was ready for a gasp, a blush, a look of horror, anything to show she still had an ounce of shame. But apparently she'd lost all sense of shame when she'd lost her self-respect.

"You have no problem hiring a sex worker, but you don't want all your friends to know. Can't say I've never heard that one before." She watched me like I was an enemy, but her head tilted coyly to one side. "By the way, I've just got to know. All this spying on me and sneaking around, did you learn that working for the KGB, or are you just trying to impress Putin? Because if you're thinking of switching jobs, I would be delighted to write you a letter of recommendation." She put her thumb and forefinger together. "Because you are doing a bang-up job."

How dare she. *How dare she.*

I'd dedicated my life to ThreeClaw. I'd given up my country to be with her. I had risked sanity and identity to uphold her legacy. And this pathetic, egotistic, self-righteous *child* had the nerve— the audacity—

"You're a disgrace," I breathed, too furious even to vocalize.

"You keep telling yourself that, comrade. You're still the one desperate enough to ask me for help."

Meph

For days, almost nothing changed.

The door stayed locked and guarded. The windows remained barred. When I damaged something that had been given to me, it was taken away. Every evening, I was marched to the grand dining hall to eat with the Contessa. When I behaved politely and didn't argue, I was rewarded with regular meals, though always simple and small compared to the lavish feasts I shared with her.

When I protested at all, even subtly, I was forbidden food until our next meeting.

It was an obvious ploy, a variety of manipulation in use since the first wolves were domesticated into dogs, and I was prepared for it.

I was less prepared for the silence.

Now that the Contessa had her sights on me, my guards vanished entirely to the other side of the door. They appeared only during meal times, and always without a word. They never laid a hand on me, but with the firepower they carried, they didn't need to. In their absence, I was starting to crave human contact. Any kind of human contact.

Even contact that wasn't so human.

The Contessa knew. When I did what she wanted, she had my place setting arranged at her right hand, and she favored me with fond glances and animated conversation. Her fingers brushed my hands as she spoke, casually enough that they seemed almost accidental, but her touches were so rare that each one took on a particular significance.

When I displeased her, she banished me to the far end of the table and barely acknowledged me.

Between our meetings, there was nothing. No books, no television, no work— nothing at all to occupy my thoughts, except for the Contessa's face and the Contessa's words, fresh and vivid in my mind while everything else felt more distant every day.

She kept repeating those damned offers every goddamned day: I could go back to the Order, I could have my life back, I could have a goal and a purpose again.

But only through her. Only as long as I let her use me.

But could she really do that? It wasn't as though she could blackmail me with something worse than I'd already been accused of, and even her agents couldn't touch me once I was back within the safe confines of the Order. She planned to twist me around her claws until I bowed to her every whim, but I already knew that. I was intelligent, and strong-willed, and prepared for her psychological warfare. It couldn't possibly work on me.

Dragons are the children of lies, and so they are natural liars.

And once I was back in the Order's good graces, I could do so much good. Not just root out the corruption inside our ranks, but lead them against one of the most pervasive and ruthless dragons in modern history. Even the Archduchess hadn't managed that, and she'd built her reputation over a long career of dragon slaying.

I was playing into the Contessa's hands, and I knew it. She wanted me to analyze and deconstruct and second-guess my own thoughts until I was lost in my own confusion. I combated her efforts as best I could. I recited scripture and spells and prayers until the words came as naturally as breathing. I drilled what exercises and strength training I could in the small space, working myself into exhaustion just so I could sleep. I became meticulous about my hygiene, just to while away a few more minutes every day.

I did it all to preserve my slowly fraying sanity. Not to earn comments about how other clothes would better flatter my figure, or how another shade might better suit my hair.

"You have such lovely locks, *Häftling*," she told me one evening, carding her hand through my hair. It took effort not to lean into her touch. *She's a dragon,* I reminded myself. *The most ruthless and evil of all monsters. A daughter of lies.* "They've taken on such a pretty shine. Like spun gold."

"I need to get it cut," I muttered.

One eyebrow arched as she judged whether that had been defiance.

"I've got split ends," I added lamely.

"No matter." She patted my hand affectionately. "I know a lovely *friseur* who would be honored to assist."

The suggestion caught my attention. Another person meant a possible weakness in her cage. Someone who might help me escape, or at least someone I might possibly fight off long enough to do it on my own. I regarded the thought clinically, devoid of desperation or hope. It was merely a fact to be used. Nothing more.

"Did your old master enjoy your tresses?" she asked, going on before I could ask who she meant. "Did she have you long enough to make you cut that lovely hair, or did she encourage you to grow it out?"

Oh, I thought numbly. *She meant Arkay.*

"I… I don't know what she thought about my hair."

No. That was wrong. Arkay made a habit out of rubbing her hand along the very tips, back when it was still growing out of that old buzz cut. She'd commented on the color plenty of times, usually with mild curiosity.

"I think she liked it," I corrected.

"Of course she did, *Häftling*," the Contessa said fondly. "Even she wouldn't put so much effort into procuring a pet she didn't fully enjoy."

But that wasn't right.

"She didn't procure me." I wasn't some prizewinning Dalmatian, I was a stray she'd pulled out of a gutter. "We were only even together because she felt sorry for me."

"Is that really what she had you believing?" the Contessa asked, a note of sympathy in her voice. "Nonsense. Utter nonsense."

Dragons always lie.

"I've heard your story, *Häftling*. I've done my research. And it seems obvious to me that she took special pains to claim you for her own."

"But that's not what happened," I said. "My shooting Rosario was an accident."

"I never said it was extensively deliberated. But it was clearly deliberate."

That didn't make sense.

"Did you really believe she was feeling merciful when she saw you'd destroyed her favorite playmate? Did you think sparing your life was meant as an act of kindness?"

I shook my head. "She couldn't have known what the Order would do."

"All dragons know of the Order, what they think of our kind. Predicting their reactions would have been child's play."

"But she took me in—"

"She needed a new toy, and so she stole the weapon used against her and claimed it for herself. Didn't you tell me how much she enjoyed repaying attacks in kind? Turning a son of the Order against them would have been the most delicious irony."

"But we weren't fighting the Order. We were hunting child molesters and drug traffickers and serial killers."

"Was it really a hunt, though? Or was it a talent search? Didn't you tell me that killing your prey was only ever a contingency? First you gave them a choice."

"To do the right thing," I said frantically. "To turn their lives around."

"And who would decide what direction they would turn? Who decided what the right thing was to be?"

Arkay did. Because…

She's a dragon.

"Your prey was given the option to work for her. To submit their hearts and minds to her as you did. To join her own private army, or else be murdered by it. By you."

I felt sick.

"And you were a faithful hound to your master. Loyal enough in your duty to bring her a cavern full of minions in need of a dragon. And now that she's claimed ThreeClaw's Hoarde, she's more powerful than ever."

No no no. "She didn't. She wouldn't."

"Would you like me to call them up and see? You can speak to her yourself."

I clutched at the table to keep from sliding out of my chair.

Dragons always lie.

"I'm sure she would be delighted to hear from you. After all, she never could have found the Felldeep without your help."

The Contessa is a dragon. Most evil and ruthless of all monsters. A daughter of lies.

"We did it for Rosario. We needed to save Rosario."

"The girl was just a means to an end."

"No, she wasn't. You didn't know her like I did."

"Potnia Theron make lovely allies. They have a gift for bringing others into compliance, even after they're dead. How long did she hold the blame for the girl's death over your head? How long would you have had to grovel at Arkay's feet, murder in her name, to atone for that sin?"

Forever. I could never undo what I'd done. But that didn't mean—

"She's not like that," I repeated. "And Rosario isn't dead. She's comatose. Not dead. She can still get better. Arkay can find a way to save her."

"There's only one way to save a person who's suffered catastrophic brain damage," the Contessa said. "And I'm afraid it requires the services of a priest."

Arkay wouldn't let Rosario die. She wouldn't let that happen. She would fight to the death to save her.

And if she couldn't?

Arkay had gone near-feral for weeks after Rosario got shot. She'd nearly beaten me to death with her bare hands. What would she do if Rosario died? Did she finally have enough time and distance to process it? Or would Rosa's death send her over the edge?

Or was she already long gone? Had our time together really been nothing but a callous manipulation? Revenge for what I'd taken from her?

My head was spinning. A dull ache pounded behind my eyes. My thoughts ran in circles.

Every word out of her mouth is a lie.

She's a dragon. Most ruthless and evil of all monsters.

Dragons always lie.

Dragons always lie.

"Your confidence in this woman is truly inspiring," the Contessa said. "But it's time for you to admit the truth."

Dragons always lie.

Arkay

As soon as I slammed the door in Nadia's face, I scoured the walls, sending minute surges of electricity into every crack and crevice.

It was one thing to walk in on me while I was in bed. She was such a workaholic, maybe she forgot that other people actually slept. But now she was talking about phone calls I made and books I checked out, and suddenly I was asking myself how many times she'd let herself into my apartment. There was no telling what she could have done in that time, but I wouldn't put it past her to plant listening devices, or video cameras, or... or whatever.

It wouldn't be the first time I'd had my home bugged.

Fuck, as if I didn't feel caged enough already. Now she was tracking the queries I made at the archives. She didn't even try to hide the fact that she was watching me, lording it over me like fucking blackmail.

This complicated things.

I wasn't sure who she hated more, me or the Order. But either way, it would suit her perfectly to keep me locked up down here while Meph suffered. And thanks to her KGB-style surveillance system, she'd know all my plans the moment I made them, and she could block me at every turn.

Unless I didn't make any turns.

Right now she was angry, which meant she wouldn't be thinking clearly. Maybe she'd take some time to fume, maybe take a walk, kick a puppy or something. But that gave me an opening.

I grabbed my phone and as much cash as I could fit in my wallet, and I stepped into the bathroom.

Nadia had disabled most of the doors in my apartment, but one remained conspicuously open.

It was a small door, hidden behind the pipes of the bathroom sink, and it took some wiggling and contortion for even me to slip through. Getting someone Nadia's size through the narrow passageway would have been nearly impossible.

Maybe she thought I couldn't get through, either. Maybe that's why she didn't bother sealing it. Or maybe she assumed I was too stupid to find it. Most likely, though, Nadia didn't know it existed. I'd kept plenty of things from Rosa; I didn't put it past ThreeClaw to keep secrets of her own.

I'd used this door exactly twice: once out of curiosity, and then again to scurry back inside the second I realized where it led.

I took a breath, steadied myself, and unlatched the little door.

The space under my sink was cramped and dark on its own merit, but as soon as I crossed the threshold of the portal, the dark became absolute. I blinked a few times, but there was no acclimating to the inky blackness. I shivered as the comfortable apartment air was replaced by the icy chill of deep underground.

I'd barely wriggled myself through the door when I emerged from the hollow of an old oak. Not the big, wide cracks between roots, but the kind of hole a squirrel might disappear into, a good thirty feet up the trunk. I knew the distance almost exactly, because I hadn't expected to catch myself the first time I went through, and I wound up falling out of the damn tree. Sheer luck had kept me from breaking my neck on impact, which was probably the point. This time, I anchored myself against the branches, swallowed a few times to relieve a sudden pressure between my ears, and climbed down.

The Forest of the Damned had its redeeming qualities— a two-story-tall yggdradeer named Comet, for one— but I avoided coming here alone. Every aspect of the Forest of the Damned had been designed to instill its victims with paranoia and dread. The whole place was one great big act of psychological warfare.

A wet crack split the air. I turned on my phone, letting the screen illuminate the immediate area. Living shadows slithered past, snapping lazily at the light, but they kept their distance.

Another crack sounded, sharp as a gunshot, and another immediately afterward. They were getting closer.

I braced myself. Deep breath. Stay focused.

A shape emerged from between the trees. The dim light barely distinguished it from the shadows, but it gave me an impression of the thing. The creature was roughly the size of a lion, but without any distinguishable head. Instead it had seven canine-looking legs, and an odd radial symmetry, almost like a starfish. Its thick, leathery hide was dotted by dozens of eyes, the nearest of which swiveled to stare at me, and new welts started to rise along its side. I lowered my phone, partly to avoid shining a bright light directly into all those eyes, and partly to avoid a detailed visual of human teeth punching through flesh from the inside. The teeth rearranged themselves into two rows, and the central body folded in half with a snap of breaking bones.

"Hello there, Arkay," the groundskeeper of the Forest said through their newly formed mouth. "Fancy seeing you out here."

I waved my free hand. "Hi, Terry."

The spells that powered the Felldeep's doorways were recent inventions, commissioned specifically for ThreeClaw's personal labyrinth. The first few doors built into the Forest didn't go anywhere at all, and the next dozen or so didn't go anywhere most people would want to visit. At least, nobody who stepped through them had ever come back. The only living thing to ever emerge from those portals was Terry, and they had expressed no interest in going back the way they came.

"I'm afraid I've already fed Comet her breakfast," they continued. "But I'm sure she wouldn't mind if we snuck her a treat or two."

"I appreciate that." I flashed a smile that almost could have passed for sincere. "But I'd rather not get you in trouble with Nadia."

Terry blinked in interest, their dozens of eyes twinkling like stars as they caught the light of my phone. "Are you two fighting again? What happened?"

I waved my hand dismissively. "It's fine. But I was wondering, do you have a minute? I was supposed to go over which doors go where, but it's looking like Nadia won't be helping with that, and…"

"Something did happen!" Terry lowered their voice into an approximation of sympathy. "I've always got time for you, Arkay. You know that. Even just to talk, if, you know, you need to get something off your chest."

"Don't let Nadia hear you say that." I rolled my eyes. "I'm pretty sure she's one misunderstanding away from sticking me in a chastity belt."

Just like that, Terry was caught. All higher thought processes that would otherwise have been wondering why I needed to learn about the doors promptly disengaged, focusing instead on memorizing every juicy detail of my argument with Nadia. While I kept the conversation going, I steered us toward the patch of doors where Meph had disappeared.

"So you were—"

"Where does that one go?" I interrupted.

"Oh, that one's to the back room of a little bakery in Reykjavik. So you were a real live stripper?" Terry's voice squeaked. "Oh Arkay, that's *scandalous!*"

"It was just a job." I shrugged. "I climbed around on stage and people paid to watch me. It was kind of like being in a zoo, except I got to take home a cut."

"Were there drugs? Was it awful?"

"Not at the club I worked at. The owner had some bad experiences with people he knew, so he didn't put up with that shit in his place. He made sure to keep everything up to code. Though apparently nobody told some of our clients."

"Oh no!" Terry exclaimed eagerly.

"What about that one over there?" I asked.

"That one's to a mountainside in Bavaria." Terry waved one leg dismissively in the air. "So you were saying—"

"Is that the only door that goes to Germany?"

"It is. The closest door to it opens in a little village in Andalusia. You should see it sometime. It's absolutely delightful at night. But you were saying about the clients?"

While I regaled Terry with tales of beating the shit out of local assholes, I memorized the door and the mannequins that served as the nearest landmarks. Afterward, it was just a matter of chattering on until Terry tensed.

"Oh, dammit," the groundskeeper muttered. "Sorry, Arkay, but there's someone coming in from the rest stop entrance. Duty calls! But maybe we can continue this tour later…?" They bounced hopefully.

"Later," I said. "Thanks, Terry. You've been a real lifesaver."

"Always," they said, wagging one leg in a parting wave as they vanished into the darkness. "*Ta!*"

I waited until the sounds of Terry's passing faded into silence, then I rushed back. Left at the beech tree with a paratrooper in its branches, right at the stairwell in the ground, slight right at the Order uniform with a blood splatter that looked like a maple leaf. Finally I reached the door to Germany.

There was no keyhole, no latch, no lock whatsoever. If somebody took a wrong turn and wound up going through an unfamiliar door, they were probably someone the Hoarde didn't want here in the first place. That was the theory, anyway.

I turned the doorknob and pulled it open. The landscape on the other side was saturated by brilliant greens and browns and grays and a froth of purple flowers, all of them bright enough to hurt my eyes. But while the forest through the door was illuminated by an afternoon sun, no light diffused to the trees around me. I couldn't smell the trees on the other side, or feel the wind that rustled their branches. It looked more like a video than a doorway.

But when I reached through it, I felt the sun-warm air on my skin and the light drops of a recent rainfall filtering through the leaves.

It wouldn't be long before Nadia realized where I was going. I'd need to move quickly.

I crossed the threshold and, for the first time in four months, stepped into the sun.

Meph

I stared listlessly at the barred window. A stained-glass dragon glared back at me, like it held me responsible for the iron bars between itself and the open sky. I rolled over in bed and turned my back on it. I was tired. Tired of being used, tired of being manipulated, tired of being lied to. I was tired of dragons. And since escape looked impossible in the current conditions, I attempted to pass the time with sleep.

There was a time when I wouldn't have been able to sleep at all with that lead-lined monster staring down at me. When I was a child, I was secretly terrified of the beasts that inhabited the windows of our church. I hated the way they seemed to come alive every time something moved behind the stained glass. The archangel Michael seemed animated by the same trick of light, but he was only one soldier surrounded by so many monsters.

I'd admitted that fear to the Reverend Lieutenant once. I couldn't see his face through the grate of the confessional booth, but I could hear a smile in his voice. I was right to be afraid of them, he told me. Fear was what let recognize monsters for what they were. *Remember the creatures that frighten you, so you can learn to destroy them.*

Monsters were the work of the devil. In spite and jealousy, he ensnared man and bird and beast, corrupting them into twisted abominations. The most ruthless and evil among them were fashioned in his own image, and they were splashed across the windows and paintings of my childhood like carnage after a battle. They were the sons and daughters of the Father of Lies, who breathed lightning and hellfire, but took human form to better seduce God's chosen.

I remembered the old stories, even when I stopped believing them literally, even when I disregarded them as more superstition than fact. But somewhere along the way, the meaning had eroded away under the pressure of other philosophies.

I'd been in the focus of those influences for far too long. More than a year now, caught between the Contessa and Arkay.

Dragons were ruthless and evil. They corrupted and manipulated and lied, until everything under their influence was as twisted as they were.

I pushed the heels of my hands into my closed eyes. I needed to get out of this prison.

Nadia

"You did *what?*"

Terry's legs folded beneath them. Their many eyes flicked nervously around, like they hoped to find a timely distraction on the forest floor. "Well, she said she needed to learn about the doors, and she sounded upset, so— I mean, I figured, she's our dragon, right? She's supposed to know." The words came through a mouth so small it would have fit on an infant, and the voice that seeped between those narrow jaws was barely audible.

"She is in absolutely no condition to go gallivanting off across all corners of the earth!" I snapped. "Do you have any idea what you've done? What you could have caused?"

"No?"

I clamped my mouth shut before I made the situation worse. Bad enough I had half the security force scouring the Felldeep for Arkay. Feeding information to the biggest gossip in the Hoarde would only multiply the crisis.

"I didn't give her a very long tour," Terry said defensively. "Just a few doors. That's it."

"Which doors?" I demanded between clenched teeth.

Terry waved one leg at the dark. "The ones over there. Europe, mostly."

Oh.

Oh no.

"Does that include the passage to Germany?"

A cascade of confused blinks washed over Terry's many eyes. "Well, yeah. Germany is in Europe these days."

"I know where she's going." I turned away and broke into a sprint through the trees, ignoring Terry's call of "does that mean I'm not in trouble anymore?"

I raced through the door and into the hospital wing, tearing past nurses and gurneys until I all but dove inside the office of Doctor Quinque Magbantay.

"Quinn, I need a case of Styx."

The aswang looked up. "What happened?"

"She's going after the Contessa."

"God in heaven." He rose to his feet. "When?"

"Terry last saw her two hours ago, and she was heading through the door."

"Didn't they try to stop her? No, never mind." He started typing frantically at the keys while I hurried to open the safe that contained our supply of Styx. I grabbed two doses— one for her, and one for me. "Nadia, there's still time. She'll be another two hours in transit if she stole a car. Four, if she took the train. And that's assuming she didn't get lost—"

"Please don't try being optimistic right now," I snapped. "We can't afford to guess. See if Ivan can track her phone, and have her bring a car to the German door."

I wouldn't let this happen. I wouldn't let her run off and die.

Not again.

Arkay

The Contessa lived on a mountain.

I didn't anticipate that this would be a problem. I'd been to mountains before. Lots of them. Turns out mountains are a lot harder to scale when you're not in a car, and even harder when you've spent six hours going cross country by train. It was twilight by the time I reached what my map declared was the Contessa's mountain, and the light was fading fast.

The first stretch of the climb was steep enough that it was almost vertical, with thick layers of underbrush interrupted by naked limestone cliffs. Almost as soon as I crossed under the shelter of the trees, that all went away. The trees were impossibly tall, armed with the spiky remains of branches until they erupted into a canopy of needles high overhead. Those same needles formed a dense carpet underfoot, so thick and soft that my feet sank in with every step, until I learned to brace myself against rocks and exposed tree roots. Light, misty rain seeped through the pines overhead, leaving me cold and damp without the drama of a proper downpour. I grabbed at nearby trees for stability as I climbed, and too quickly learned that a population of fat orange slugs had decided to climb those same trees to get out of the rain. I wiped away the freshly squeezed goo onto my jeans and kept climbing, but more carefully this time.

By the time the waning moon made an appearance through the trees, I had every intention of turning around and coming back with the first motorized vehicle I could hotwire, except that would mean going back down and starting all over again. By midnight, I was second guessing that I'd even scaled the right mountain.

Then I climbed past a jutting cliff, and my doubts were laid to rest.

A huge house rose from among the trees, four stories tall under the blade of a steep roof. Overlapping slate shingles swept down the walls, looking impossibly like scales. It was a properly imposing house, perfectly befitting a dragon.

The building behind it, though, was even better. It was less of a house than a palace, huge and ornate. I spotted at least a dozen enormous windows from my vantage point, each one showing off a crimson stained-glass dragon. More dragon effigies served as water spouts and fountainheads and weather vanes. There was no lawn or garden to stand between the towering pines and the Roman columns that guarded the front door.

As I scaled the steep slope, I found a cobblestone road that twisted around to the other side of the mountain, probably taking a flatter path down the ridge. Some of the cobblestones carried ancient scorch marks, and patches of the rock were welded together with lines of rusted steel. The remains of a car, judging by the size. Maybe a truck. The damage to the road probably wouldn't have taken much effort to repair, but someone had taken care not to scrub away the scorch marks. They were trophies.

I started to wonder if setting unwanted houseguests on fire was her only major security measure. The trees grew close enough to the mansion that I would have no problem climbing up to one of the upper windows— and let's face it, nobody ever bothered locking those things anyway.

A light flashed in my direction. "Who's out there?"

The Contessa hired security guards. Good to know. I ducked into the shadows and flattened myself against the trunk of a tree.

More voices joined the first.

"Did you see something?"

"There's someone down there."

Footsteps clattered across the cobblestones toward me, accompanied by swinging flashlights. I froze, not even breathing until they passed my hiding spot.

I grabbed the first guard by the back of the neck and sent a surge of electricity down his spine. He dropped instantly, convulsing on the ground. The others turned their weapons on me. I dove for the closer of the two, ripping the rifle out of her hands and swinging it across her head. The third raised his rifle, took aim, and then collapsed in a heap on the ground.

I frowned, nudging him with my foot. What, did he faint or something? That seemed kind of unprofessional.

"Stop that," a familiar voice hissed. "You'll wake him up." Nadia stepped out of the shadows and yanked an assault rifle off one of the fallen guards. Her meticulous hair was disheveled and unkempt, and she looked like she could use a nap. Or a drink. Or both.

I took a step back. "What the hell are you doing here?"

She grunted. "There's a car down the road. We need to get out of here before the other guards notice they're gone."

Okay, fine. Don't answer my questions. "Sure thing. As soon as I grab Meph—"

"There's no time for that." She grabbed my wrist. "We need to go now."

I yanked my arm out of her grip. "Then make time. I'm not going back without Meph."

"There's no point! The Contessa has him now. She isn't going to just hand him over."

"Then I'll make her hand him over."

Nadia grabbed me again, her fingers clawing into my shoulders. "Think for once in your miserable life. She's bigger than you, and she's stronger than you, and she will kill you if you give her half a reason. You can't fight her, and I'm not going to let you throw your life away over some piece of shit Orderling."

I glared at her mouth to avoid looking at her ridiculously blue eyes. "I don't remember that being your decision."

"You made it my decision when you left me in charge of the Hoarde," she said. "You made it my decision when you walked away and got yourself killed by scum like him, and you left us alone to pick up the pieces. I'm not going to let you do this to us again. I am going to save you—"

"*Save me?*" I hacked out a laugh. "Is that what you call it? Shoving me into an oversized china cabinet and only ever letting me out when you want to impress company? Locking the doors into my room every time I talk to someone you don't approve of?" I twisted my arms, dislodging my hold and shoving her backward. "What the fuck makes you think I'm *ever* going back with you?"

Nadia froze like she'd been doused with ice water. "You aren't leaving."

"Look around you, Nadia. I'm already gone."

"You can't leave. We need you. You have a responsibility. A duty—"

"Yes, I do." A duty to Rosario, who I hadn't seen in months because Nadia kept me cloistered in the Felldeep. A responsibility to Meph, who was currently rotting in a cell because Nadia refused to help me look for him. "And I am done with you and the Hoarde trying to keep me from it."

"A duty to us!" Nadia reached out to me. "To me—"

"Fuck you," I snarled, snatching her hand out of the air. "I am done being used. I am done being locked up."

"No, wait—"

"And I am done with you."

I sank my teeth into her wrist and shot nine hundred thousand volts straight into her skin. Every muscle in her body contracted at once, but I held on until her eyes rolled back and she crumpled.

I turned away from her, ready to scale the trees to the windows, but something moved in the shadows. A change in the wind brought a new scent to my nose. Musk and ash and fire, accented tastefully with a flowery perfume. Deadly nightshade and dragon's blood. Subtle. The combination of odors was somehow not unpleasant, but instantly offensive. I coiled, my lips rising into a snarl.

"I'm sorry, was there something else you wanted to say? By all means, do continue. You've been so *very* entertaining."

A tall, broad-shouldered woman strode down the cobblestones with a confidence that shouldn't have been possible in those heels. The train of her off-the-shoulder gown pooled at her feet like fresh blood.

I straightened, narrowing my eyes. "The Contessa, I assume."

"I do hope that didn't take you too long to deduce." She flashed a coy smile. "You must forgive my eavesdropping—"

"No, I mustn't." I peered into the shadows. At least half a dozen men and women waited in the gloom, all of them heavily armed. They stood upwind, but I could barely register their scents over the Contessa's infuriating perfume.

"You picked such an interesting time for this meeting," she continued. "I hope you didn't get lost on your way up."

"I just thought I'd get you back for that phone call." I jutted out one hip, drawing undue attention to my muddy blue jeans. The Contessa and her guards all looked like they'd come from a night at the symphony. Elitist douchebags. "You have someone that belongs to me."

"You mean Mephistopheles?" She didn't pronounce his name quite right, and it grated my nerves. "Are you really sure the little pit bull is something you can handle? I find he has done far better in my care."

"And I find I'd feel a lot more *grateful* if you bothered asking me before you started babysitting him," I said. "You've held onto him long enough. Let him go."

She made a minute gesture, and I was staring down the barrels of half a dozen rifles.

"This doesn't have to turn violent," I said. "We're on the same side here."

She quirked an eyebrow. "Are we now?"

I'd read her files. I knew where she stood, at least on the major issues. "Hitler was bad, Stalin was bad, the Order is bad. That's a hell of a lot of common ground right there."

"You say you're an enemy of the Order, yet you make such a fuss about their chaff."

"He's my responsibility."

"He's an asset," she corrected.

No, he was desperate for positive attention and confused as fuck about how to go about getting it. He was the victim of a cult who was still trying to untangle himself from their twisted logic. He was a soldier who didn't grasp that life after combat was a thing that happened.

He was a frightened kid who needed help, and it was my job to help him find it.

"I can give you a bigger asset," I said. She raised her eyebrows. "The Hoarde. Hand it over and it's yours."

"Is it now?" She graced me with a dainty snort. "What makes you think I want it?"

I blinked. That's what I'd said, but my situation was different. She'd been trying to tempt away the Hoarde's key personnel with promises of better pay and a proper dragon. She'd been sending scouting parties into the Forest. The endless harassment had been one of Nadia's favorite things to complain about, second only to myself.

"You've been making offers," I said slowly. "For years. You flat-out said—"

"Posturing and politics," she said lightly, but her teeth flashed between her lips. "Do you really think I'm stupid enough to fight a war on two fronts? By all means, keep your little Hoarde, or let them find another dragonet to take your place. God knows there are enough ambitious neophytes looking for a stake of their own. Perhaps if they're all fighting over your Hoarde, then they're not trying to carve off pieces of my forest." She paused, tilting her head to one side. "I suppose keeping it for yourself really isn't an option. But I'm sure you take my meaning." She raised her hand in a wave goodbye. "Kill her."

"Why?" I said abruptly.

The gesture stopped before she could signal a fatal shot. "Hm?"

"Why kill me?" I asked. "I've never done anything to you. I don't even know you. The only reason I'm here in the first place is because you took Meph and then bragged about where you were keeping him. I mean, seriously. You practically invited me here just to murder me? What, did a magic mirror say I'm prettier than you or something?"

She didn't look amused, and she wasn't the kind of woman who would politely listen until I ran out of things to talk about. I needed an emotional response. Something to knock her off her train of thought.

"Because all this?" I gestured wildly at the firing squad. "This is petty. This is, like, *Mean Girls* levels of petty. And that kind of cattiness only shows up when somebody's feeling threatened. Seriously, what's got you so insecure?"

Her lips peeled back, baring teeth. "I am not threatened by the likes of you."

"Yeah, Voldemort said the same thing about a one-year-old baby. Seven books later…" I shrugged. "But you're totally right. I'm smaller than you, I'm younger than you, and I sure as hell don't want the Black Forest. So what exactly has you so scared that you have to kill me?"

I kept my eyes locked on the Contessa, but in my peripheral vision, I caught minute shifts in her guards as they exchanged glances.

The Contessa gave another short, sharp laugh. "What a nice little trap. Either I monologue like a cliché, or my darlings start filling the gaps with theories of their own. Very cute, Arkay."

I bobbed my head. "I aim to please."

"I could simply kill you now and divulge my plans later."

"I'm sure you could use a few more minutes to come up with a decent lie."

She scowled. "Try to swallow your delusions. You're a means to an end, not anything important."

I aimed a sympathetic cringe at the guards in the shadows. *Can you believe this lady? Talk about embarrassing.*

"Before Mephistopheles can return to the Order, they require him to kill a dragon. Namely yourself. It's nothing personal." Judging by the fire in her eyes, she was going to take a lot of satisfaction from butchering me.

I kept her talking. "But why? I mean, it's nice of you to help him out, I guess, but…"

"But what use could I possibly have for an Order war hero who's eternally indebted to me?"

Her words hung in the air for a few moments. I crouched low, checking on Nadia. "You want him as a double agent."

"I'm afraid my old one is getting on in years." She sniffed. "Tragic, really, how quickly humans break."

"Yeah. Tragic." I spared a glance behind me. I was caged in, with the house on one side and the cliff on the other. "Take it from me, you're gonna have an easier time picking someone else to be your spy. Meph got kicked out for a reason. It's gonna happen again, and you'll have nothing to show for it but his sad puppy face and a bunch of wasted time."

"You would be amazed what the Order is willing to put up with when they're presented with a dragon," the Contessa pointed out. "And there are so many dragons out to take my territory for their own."

I scooted back a few inches. "So that's how you held onto the Black Forest this long, huh? You had the Order kill off your rivals for you." I let out a low whistle. "That's fucked up."

"That's politics. I let my enemies destroy each other, and neither side ever lays a hand on what's mine."

"It's clever." I checked Nadia's pulse. She'd be waking soon. "Also cowardly as fuck, but definitely clever."

The Contessa's face twisted into a scowl. I'd hit a nerve. "Cowardly?"

"It's the adjective form of 'hiding behind a bunch of humans while they do your dirty work'. Killing me, killing other dragons, muzzling the Order… I'm seeing kind of a trend. But if it works for you, kudos." I held out my hands in a gesture of acceptance. "I mean, sure, the Order is murdering people by the truckload, but you personally aren't being affected, so I'm sure it's no big deal." I picked up Nadia and flashed a cheerful, toothy smile. Time to punch that last nerve. "I mean, that's how you got through World War Two, right?"

All grace and elegance drained away as she crossed the space between us. With every step she loomed larger, more predatory, more furious. I threw Nadia over my shoulder and backed away.

"Hey, it's not like there were, what, a dozen concentration camps right within your borders or anything. It's not like you had the badassery and sheer firepower to do something for all those people, right?" I narrowed my eyes. "Oh, wait. Yes, you did."

The guards lowered their weapons, watching their boss with abject fear. Had any of them ever seen a dragon rampage? Had any of them survived watching one up close?

The Contessa lunged at me and I jumped back, out of her reach and over the edge of the cliff.

There was no crystal moment of staring each other down, no Wile E. Coyote pause while I lingered in the empty air. The Contessa was gone and I was falling, twisting to glimpse something other than unforgiving stone. Inky shadows reached out for me, and I grabbed at them, catching a sap-covered branch in my hands. The rough bark carved into my palms and gouged my fingers. The force of my momentum nearly dislodged Nadia, and I scrambled to keep her from sliding the rest of the way down. Gunshots rang out behind me. The tree shuddered as it was stuck by a bullet.

I grabbed another branch and lunged at the next tree over, further away from the guards and their rifles, and then to the next. Flashlights swept over me, but their lights were weak and diluted.

Another round of fire perforated the trees before the Contessa silenced them.

"Save your bullets," she said, composed once more. "She'll come back soon enough. After all, we have what she wants."

Meph

The doors burst open and a pair of guards stormed into my room. Instantly, I started upright, jumping from the bed.

"What is it?" I asked, backing toward the wall. "What did I do?"

The nearest guard raised her rifle and I fell silent. "No questions." I nodded. "You're coming with us."

I moved passively as they marched me out the door and into the hallway. This was normal. They'd done this before.

But they'd never taken me in this direction before. I watched my surroundings carefully, peering at the hanging works of art that served to differentiate the halls from one another. We descended a staircase, and abruptly I recognized the paintings. I'd passed them exactly once before, when I was first taken from my cell to dine with the Contessa. The guards continued their march, taking me down increasingly familiar halls.

"I don't understand," I said. And again, louder. "I don't understand! Where are you taking me? What did I do—"

The butt of a rifle knocked the air out of my lungs.

"No questions," the guard repeated. She turned away from me and tapped a code into a keypad, yanking open a door. A row of fluorescent lights traced a staircase down to a long hallway. On either side of the hall were cells lined with bulletproof glass.

I staggered backward. *No.* No, they couldn't put me back. I'd cooperated. I'd done everything the Contessa asked of me. They couldn't put me back in that cell!

But that was just it: I'd been cooperating. They'd had no need to restrain me.

The female guard jerked her head at the stairwell. "Get inside."

I gave a shaky nod and obeyed. My heart pounded. Sweat beaded on my skin. Behind me, the guards packed in close to fit down the narrow stair.

I whirled, grabbing the female guard's leg and wrenching it out from under her. She fell backwards, crashing into the other guard and losing her grip on her rifle while she grabbed for the railing. I snatched the weapon out of her hand. The male guard moved to shoot me, but I was the quicker draw. He let out a howl of pain as a bullet tore into his arm. The rifle fell, and I kicked it off the stairs behind me.

"Next one hits your head." I jerked the gun again. "Back up slowly. Either of you try to run, and I kill you both." I marched them up the stairs and into the hallway, freeing a path for me to get out of that godforsaken dungeon. "Both of you down the stairs and into the cell."

I didn't wait for them to obey completely. As soon as they were in the stairwell, I slammed the door shut behind them and smashed the keypad with the butt of the rifle.

I'd fired a shot. Even if the dungeon was soundproofed, someone must have heard that. They'd be on their way any second. Now that I'd attacked my guards, there would be no mercy for me.

I had to get out of here fast.

I rushed down the hall, almost leaping toward what looked like a front entrance, then stopped short.

A cluster of guards waited at the front door. More surrounded a side entrance, and I spotted heads bobbing outside the first floor windows. No way of getting out that way. I needed to get somewhere else. Somewhere they wouldn't look.

I dove at the nearest staircase and rushed up, putting floor after floor between myself and the ground. Humans evolved from tree-dwellers, and it instilled us with an instinctive belief that no threat could possibly come at us from above. Consequently, humans rarely locked upper windows, and they never looked up when they were hunting for a threat.

It was an advantage I'd used plenty of times, hunting serial killers with—

I forced myself to focus on my surroundings. I reached the last landing, which let out into an enormous room. It was almost as broad as the entirety of the house, with high ceilings that sloped as they neared the walls, and wooden floors set into intricate patterns. A ballroom, most likely. The only things on the floor were a few chaises and armchairs, all of them covered in sheets to protect them from dust.

And a dragon.

She climbed in through the window, tracking mud and debris after her and pointedly grinding it into the floor under her feet. She could have been a hallucination, but I couldn't make up anything more at odds with her surroundings. Grass stains smeared her hands and knees. Pieces of a pine cone clung to her short, spiky hair. She wore mud-splattered jeans and an oversized blue hoodie, every thread at odds with the fiery elegance of the Contessa's manor.

"There you are," she said cheerfully. Like it hadn't been months. Like I hadn't been imprisoned and starved since she last saw me. "That was easier than I thought." She stepped into my personal space, looking me up and down and sniffing at me like I was a carton of old milk. "Are you good to climb? Because there's like a million guards down there, and they're armed like Rambo, but there are enough trees to get past their line of sight, and—"

It took too long before I could find my voice. "What are you doing here?"

Finally she stopped her incessant babble. "Isn't it obvious? I'm rescuing you."

I stared, incredulous. Now? After all this time? After everything that had happened to me? After I'd finally managed to escape?

She left me to rot, and now she wanted the credit for saving me?

I jerked away from her intrusion. "I don't need rescuing. Especially not from you."

"Meph?" She stiffened. She looked me over again, her stare lingering on my clothes and the rifle in my hand. "You're not... Meph, are you working for her?"

With the Contessa? Yes-maybe-no, no, she would kill me as soon as she found out what I'd done to the guards, as soon as she learned I escaped. She would hate me and she would find me and she would kill me.

Fear thrummed in my veins, cold and electric. I couldn't panic. If I panicked now, I'd be lost and she would catch me and—

I clung to anger like a shield. "I'm not working for anyone. I'm nobody's dog. Not hers, and not yours. Not anymore."

She reached for me. "Meph—"

"Get away from me!" I smacked her hand away with the barrel of the rifle. "Don't you dare play noble. I know what you did to me."

"Meph, we really don't have time for this." She grabbed at me again. "I know you've been through some shit, and we can get you a nice therapist once this is all over, but first—"

"So now you've got professionals to help you twist people's heads around?" I tried to dig my heels into the floor, but my soles slid across the polished wood. Her hands felt like iron around my wrists.

"We can talk about this later," she snapped. "Right now you need to just shut up and come with me already."

I managed to pull my hand back far enough to squeeze the trigger, and a spray of bullets arced across the ceiling. Arkay jumped back so abruptly, I thought she'd been caught in the fire.

I went rigid, frozen solid by horror and guilt and fear and—

And triumph.

"The fuck?" She stared at me, wide-eyed and confused, like she couldn't believe I'd just done that. Me. The man who'd been raised to exterminate her kind. The man who'd spent months watching her every move, waiting for the opportunity to take her down. The man who'd personally arranged to have her killed.

And she was *surprised* I pulled a gun on her?

Did she really think I was so completely under her control?

I leveled the gun on her again. "Get away from me."

Her eyes narrowed. "Meph, I'm trying to help."

My finger tightened on the trigger. "Yeah, that's what *she* said, too. Everyone's trying to help me, aren't they? How lucky that you're all feeling so *charitable*."

Arkay's help had gotten me nearly eviscerated by an unholy aberration. Her help had driven me into the Contessa's clutches. Her help had left me starved and alone in a dungeon cell.

"What the fuck's gotten into you?"

What had gotten into me? The enemy of all dragons: the truth.

"I know what you did to me," I said. "I know what you are. And I'm not going to let you use me anymore."

Arkay's expression turned stony and cold. "What the fuck did you do to him?"

She wasn't talking to me.

I turned to glance at the stairwell in the corner.

It wasn't empty anymore.

"Don't be so dramatic." The Contessa leaned against the railing, her gown as vibrant as spilt blood. "I merely pointed out the obvious." She pushed off, moving gracefully across the floor toward me.

My knees lost all substance, and I folded into a crouch. A bow. *Please, please forgive me, I didn't mean to—!*

Arkay lunged forward, her teeth bared at the other dragon. "Back off!"

"You forget yourself, *Schlängelchen*. This is *my* house."

Arkay started to circle the Contessa. The other dragon matched her strides.

"Don't you start on fucking courtesy," Arkay snarled. "You stole what was mine. Now back the fuck off so I can take him home."

"Home." The Contessa curled the word around her tongue as she drew nearer, and I shivered. "Don't you understand, you stupid child? That's exactly where I intend to bring him. Dear Adam belongs with his kind. With the Order."

Dragons always lie. Dragons always lie. The Order is broken and flawed and—

Merciful Jesus, I want to go home.

"The fuck he does." Arkay lunged sharply to the left, cutting off the Contessa before she could get close to me. "His name is Mephistopheles, and he belongs with me."

"Of course," the Contessa purred. "He's so much more useful to you when he's cut off from the rest of the world, isn't he? When you can forge him into your own little toy soldier."

"Shut the fuck up!" Their slow, distant dance had taken them across the ballroom, and now they stood at such an angle that both were framed in the window like stained-glass caricatures. The Contessa, close to the glass, tall and elegant. Arkay, nearer to me, nearly feral with rage. Pride and wrath incarnate. I could already imagine a banner spread across the bottom of the window, its lettering framed in lead: *The Queens of Hell fighting over a damned soul.*

I wrapped my shaking hands more tightly around the rifle.

One shot through the back of the head. That was all it would take. A single bullet through the brainstem, and she'd be gone forever.

Something in my mind screamed, but it blended seamlessly with panic and horror and rage until everything in my head cancelled itself out, leaving me with numb silence.

I took aim.

I breathed.

And I squeezed the trigger.

The shot was perfect. Or it would have been, if Arkay hadn't chosen that moment to leap at the Contessa. They fell back, both of them tumbling through the window in a shower of crimson glass.

Nadia

I knew the dream wasn't quite right, even as I was having it. The memory was off, distorted by recollections and lost details, but the scene remained vivid. Bright. The long table in the conference room was perhaps a bit more worn than it had once been, a bit more marked up by scratches and stray strokes of pen. For a moment, the chair at the table's head was an enormous pink monstrosity, but the moment passed and it was a stoic black office chair once more.

ThreeClaw perched in the seat, leaning over a binder of agendas and expense reports. A light fuzz had accumulated on her scalp, and I fought the temptation to see if it felt as soft as it looked. Her posture, normally as taut as the arc of a bow, was starting to flag. It had been a long day for her. For both of us. But she had to finish the day's paperwork, and I volunteered to assist for as long as it took to get it done. I did that often, in those days. I couldn't remember what it felt like to get enough sleep, but spending time with ThreeClaw was worth my fatigue. It wasn't like when we went on missions together, surrounded by the rest of the team. These moments were quiet. Intimate. They were just ours.

Or just mine. Generally, she seemed too engrossed in her work to indulge me with more than a few brief words. But that didn't bother me. It was enough that I could take a few moments between each page to bask in her presence.

She sighed, laying down her fountain pen to massage her forehead. I'd spent enough time with her to know the language of that sigh. She wanted a distraction.

I pounced on the opportunity. "Did you find anything interesting?" My words came through with difficulty, still heavy with a Russian accent.

"Not in this binder."

"Me neither." Pause. Allow for a natural transition. "I did read an interesting article the other day, though."

"Hm?"

"About... about *Beowulf.* The poem." *Хуй*, she was losing interest! I spoke faster. "The author refers to the dragon— and Grendel and his mother, really— with a word that doesn't quite fit into English. And— and many scholars want to translate it as 'wretched' and 'monstrous' and 'evil', because it describes creatures that aren't human, but the same word is applied equally to Beowulf. There is a debate about what it means. 'Monstrous' or 'supernatural' or 'warrior' or... or something else entirely." My voice trailed off. Why in the world had I picked that subject to ramble on about? It was stupid, and boring, and—

"Why not both?" ThreeClaw asked. "Heroes can be monstrous. Monsters can be heroic. We might as well have a word for the in-between." Ebony eyes flicked in my direction. "What did you say the word was?"

"Uh…" My heart stuttered more than my voice. "A-aglaeca."

She hummed again. "A lovely word for a brutal concept."

"Brutal things can be lovely."

It was meant to be a casual bit of philosophy, spouted offhand like I had insights to spare. Not blurted out while I stared like she was the summer sun. Maybe she wouldn't notice…

But her brow furrowed, and my stomach sank.

She knew. *Ой блять*, she knew. This wasn't supposed to happen. She wasn't supposed to find out. I knew my attentions were inappropriate— she was my dragon, my master, how could I even dare?— but I wouldn't ever ask anything of her. I was more than content to fight at her side, to serve her, to steal glimpses from across the conference table. I'd gladly stay this way forever.

But if she didn't believe that— if she thought my feelings would cause a problem— if she sent me away—

Panic and horror calcified into resignation, as solid and heavy as a stone in my chest.

If she sent me away, then I would accept her decision. I had never argued against her orders. Never disobeyed. If I started now, I would only prove that my feelings had made me a liability.

At least I could leave with dignity. I could walk out before desperation set in. "I should go."

She responded with a small twitch, almost a shrug. "If you want."

What did that even mean?

While I tried to work it out, she continued. "Do you read much old poetry, or is Beowulf the exception?"

I didn't know how to answer that, so I settled for the old fallback: "Ma'am?"

"*La Damnation de Faust* will be playing in Carnegie Hall next week. I find opera is much more enjoyable with company." The corner of her mouth lifted, just slightly, into the shadow of a smile. "You seem like you would get something out of the experience."

I swayed, lightheaded. Was she— was she really— "I— I would like that. Ma'am."

"You've been part of my team for months, Nadia. You don't have to call me that anymore."

"Yes, Aglaeca."

I don't know why I said it. Maybe giddiness left me bold. Maybe I wanted to act out, just once, and see if she would shut me down.

Instead she snorted, so short it could have passed for a gasp if it not for the quirk of her mouth, the shake of her shoulders, the sparkle in her eye.

It was the first time I'd ever heard ThreeClaw laugh.

I woke up with a headache and the taste of ozone between my teeth. It took a few more seconds before my eyes properly adjusted to the dark. I lay in the shelter of a fallen log. The air around me was thick with the scent of mushrooms and wet moss.

I crawled out, and found myself at the base of a sharp cliff, staring up at the Contessa's manor and her guardhouse. I swept my hand over the uneven rock and gingerly pulled myself from one handhold to the next. My muscles ached, still sore from electrocution. My hand buzzed with pins and needles where Arkay bit it. I was going to give her hell when I found her again.

If I found her again.

I quashed the thought and crawled over the last swell of stone and onto the wide ledge. Footsteps echoed through the dark, and I slunk into the darkest corners of the nearby house. Armed guards swarmed around the building, concentrating around windows and doors. They were looking for someone. For Arkay.

And all of them were looking in the wrong direction. I turned my gaze upward, squinting to make out the slightest movement among the wind-tossed trees. Within seconds I spotted her in the thick canopy, using the interlocking branches like a bridge to the highest levels of the house. I wanted to shout at her, to hiss, to throw something, but anything I could possibly do to get her attention would draw the guards right to her. I could only watch, powerless, as she lighted on the roof of the Contessa's manor and pried open the attic window.

Damn that idiot. She'd just trespassed into another dragon's house. If she got caught— I wouldn't let her get caught. Maybe I could cause a distraction. Something loud and flashy. Maybe I could go back and get the car and drive it through the crowd of guards. Dammit, why hadn't I thought to bring explosives?

I weighed my options for longer than I would have liked. Longer than I should have. I didn't get a chance to finish making a plan. A gunshot rang out. Two bodies burst through the attic window and fell, still grappling as they plunged six stories to the unforgiving ground.

Their trajectory changed mid-fall. The light of the house illuminated enormous crimson wings, ruby scales, a body that thickened and elongated into something that could no longer be mistaken for human. Those wings caught the night air and sent the two bodies arcing sharply upwards, snapping passing twigs as they broke through the canopy.

As the Contessa grew, so did Arkay, replacing hands with claws and wrapping the Contessa in her serpentine coils. Claws raked against scales. Fanged mouths closed around limbs. The sky was lit up with a jet of white-hot flame, and I caught the unmistakable odor of cooked meat. They were ferocious and indomitable, so enormous that their combat blotted out the moon and stars. And the grand scale of their battle made it obvious just how one-sided it was.

Arkay was giant, but the Contessa was titanic, at least ten feet longer, with more muscle and more mass. Arkay tried to crush the Contessa's lungs in her coils, but Arkay was too short, the Contessa too thick, for the river dragon to be more than an overly-tight belt. A small matter for a woman who had spent a quarter century in a corset. Splashes of blood rained over the trees as the Contessa's claws raked deep into Arkay's sides; meanwhile, her own scales were barely scored.

As the Contessa tilted her wings to spiral, Arkay lashed out and caught the Contessa's shoulder in her teeth. Lightning danced across crimson scales. The Contessa went rigid, and the two dragons dropped through the air, a meteorite of sparks and scales. They fell, and kept falling, and Arkay kept pouring electricity through the Contessa's veins.

They crashed back to earth, splitting apart in an eruption of shattered trees and burning pine. I took off running. I had to stop this. I didn't know what I could possibly do, but I couldn't just stand here, stunned into impotent silence like the wide-eyed guards who huddled in the light of the house.

I scrambled down the slope to the newly-made clearing, just in time to watch the winged beast sink her teeth into Arkay's shoulders. The Contessa's claw clamped over the smaller dragon's skull, grinding it into the dirt. Arkay thrashed and flailed, but she couldn't escape the Contessa's grip as the firebreather gave Arkay's shoulders one last wrenching twist.

The crash of debris almost drowned out the sound of snapping bone. There was no disguising the moment when Arkay's body went limp. Forty feet of dragon, no longer struggling to get free, became dead weight in the Contessa's teeth. The larger dragon opened her jaws, and Arkay slipped to the ground.

My mind went blank, frozen by horror. I didn't realize I'd started to howl until the sound shattered the sudden silence. I didn't realize I'd been running until I vaulted over the last pile of stones that separated me from the Contessa.

She was fifty feet long, and weighed at least ten tons. Her claws could rip me to shreds. Her teeth could snap me in half. A flare of her breath could leave me dying in agony.

I didn't care.

Because in her bloodlust and her fury, she'd forgotten who I was.

I was ThreeClaw's partner for thirteen years.

I was Nadezhda Ruslanova Alkaev, Fext of the Indomitable Hoarde.

I was a poludnica.

The Contessa turned to face me, flames gathering in her open maw, and her eyes fixed on mine. Just like that, a connection was made. I held her gaze, pulling her into my stare until she was transfixed, and then I snuffed the light in her eyes. The tension eased from her frame. Her mouth shut, and she staggered. Swayed. Her legs folded underneath her, and she collapsed like a burning building.

I could have killed her then. I could have gouged out her eyes. But she didn't matter. Not anymore.

I splashed through a pool of blood and knelt at Arkay's side. Her scales were blackened and twisted, the flesh underneath charred beyond recognition. Exposed ribs gleamed in the moonlight, gouged to the marrow by unforgiving claws. Her head hung at an unnatural angle, dangling from a broken neck.

I'd brought enough Styx for two people, but the dose was meant for someone my size. It would barely mend a scratch on a dragon in full scale.

My hand trembled as I reached for her face. A low, faint pulse pressed at my fingertips. Shallow breaths whistled through a crushed trachea.

Her pulse stuttered. Her eye twitched. Cracked. Slowly, wearily, it opened and tried to focus on me.

"It's alright," I whispered. My hand strayed close to her nose to let her smell me, so she'd know I was close and she was safe. "It's alright, Aglaeca. I'm here."

Her lid started to droop.

"Please, you have to stay awake just a little longer. I just need you to become small, that's all. It will be easy, I promise. Just become small again, and I can help you."

Her eye closed.

"Aglaeca, please." My voice cracked. "Please, this all I'm asking. Just this one thing. Please, just let me save you."

She let out a heavy, wheezing sigh, and went still.

"No, please no…" My hands fluttered over her, and I felt the soft warmth of breath against my palm. On her neck, a pulse. Faint and fading, but still there.

For now.

"It's alright." I swallowed a sob and stroked the concave of her cheek, the curve of her brow, the tender skin around her whiskers. "Everything is going to be alright. I'm going to take you to Quinn, and he will work one of his miracles. Just like he always does."

I didn't know if she could hear me, or if she was too far gone to take comfort in my lies. It didn't matter. At least she could feel a tender hand instead of the Contessa's jaws.

At least she didn't have to die alone.

Not this time.

I pressed a kiss to the ridge of her eye, but she pulled away from me. No, not pulled away. She shrank. With every heartbeat she became smaller, more compact, her excess length wicking away until she was small and fragile and so deceptively human.

I fumbled with my pockets, pulling the first case of Styx out of my vest so abruptly that I ripped my pocket. That didn't matter. None of it mattered. I could still save her. As long as she had an ounce of life left, I could still save her. I emptied a syringe into her fractured neck, her mangled chest, her charred sides.

Behind me, the Contessa groaned.

She was still alive, and still right here. If she woke up—no, she didn't even have to wake up. She had armed guards awaiting her return. If she didn't come back soon, they would come looking for her. We couldn't be here when that happened.

I stowed the rest of the Styx and scooped Arkay into my arms, carefully supporting her head. The Styx would mend any damage I inflicted by moving her, but I held her as tightly as I dared.

I couldn't stand the thought of hurting her any more.

Dawn came slowly that morning, caught in the passage of disconnected moments. I drove to the safe house outside Stuttgart. I laid Arkay across the clean white linens. I watched those linens bloom red as I cut away her clothes and filled her veins with new blood from cold storage. I cleaned her wounds. I vomited until I had nothing left in me. I emptied another syringe of Styx into her chest.

By now the Contessa would be wide awake and out for blood. I'd taken precautions to keep our German safe houses a secret from her, but she was resourceful in ways I couldn't imagine. There was no telling how long we could stay here before she brought the roof down over our heads. But we couldn't leave. Moving Arkay now would risk re-fracturing her spine and reopening her gaping wounds. It would be at least a day before she'd be up to travel.

Unless I changed the dose.

I had enough Styx for two people. Theoretically, if I flooded her system with the drug, it would speed up the healing process.

But pouring that much Styx into her system would rebuild her from scratch. There would barely be any original cells left in her body by the end of the week. It would be a complete *tabula rasa*.

Would that be so bad, though? Would it really be so awful to start with a clean slate? To wipe away everything crass and rude and flippant that she had picked up over the years, and let her be herself again? I could help her. I could teach her the things that made her ThreeClaw. I could shape her into the leader we needed. I could make her into the beautiful, perfect person I fell in love with.

I could call it an accident. As extreme as her injuries were, *tabula rasa* might even be unavoidable. I could take pictures if they didn't believe me. Show them what the Contessa had done to her, what I'd risked in coming after her.

Nobody would have to know. Not even her.

But I would.

And I would spend the rest of my life knowing I turned the woman I loved into a puppet.

I packed up the second dose and stuffed it into the upholstery of the car. It was too valuable for me to pour down the sink, but I didn't need to have the temptation right in front of me. Instead I pulled a chair beside Arkay's bed and took up watch.

ThreeClaw was my everything. She always had been. As a child, I'd been obsessed with stories of the one-armed warrior who saved our people from the wickedness of mankind. When I joined the Hoarde, I trained every spare moment, studied every strategy, took every risk I could, desperately hoping she'd notice me. I became her immortal Fext so I could always fight by her side. My whole life had been spent chasing after her. Even when she vanished, I had hired countless necromancers to find her spirit, just so I could see her one last time. But they failed. *I* failed. ThreeClaw was gone. No matter how hard I worked or how tenaciously I held onto her memory, I couldn't bring her back.

Maybe I had already lost the one piece of her I had left.

"Is watching people sleep a thing you do with everybody, or is it just me?"

I looked down.

Arkay's eyes were heavily hooded, open just barely enough to meet my stare. "Cause seriously, it's creepy." The muscles in her throat flexed in anticipation of motion as she tried to sit up.

"Don't move," I said. "The Contessa broke your neck. You're still healing."

Her sleepy haze dissolved and her eyes opened wide, her pupils dilating. "Wait. Wait, are we talking like a cracked vertebrae or something?" Her fingers and toes twitched clumsily. "It's not—she didn't—"

"Calm down. I already dosed you with Styx. You'll be fine in a few days, but only if you stop trying to move."

Her expression twisted into a glower, and then dissipated into mild annoyance. Apparently the prospect of paralysis outweighed her misgivings about Styx.

"Can I still talk?" she asked.

"Would you stop if I said no?"

That actually got a laugh out of her. Nothing strong enough to jostle her head, just an amused snort. The gesture was so familiar it hurt.

I deflected. "Perhaps you can begin by telling me what the hell you were thinking, going in there like that? You almost died."

Arkay quirked her eyebrows, almost like a nod. "That is what almost happened, yes." Her tone didn't betray surprise or fear. She said it with all the neutrality of obvious fact.

"You knew that going in." The realization curdled in my stomach. "That was a suicide mission."

"Spare me the freakout. I wasn't trying to get myself killed or anything. But it's not like I didn't know the odds, either. I read the Contessa's files. I know how much bigger she is than me."

"Then what was the point?" I demanded. "Why start a fight you know you're going to lose?"

Her lips curved into a sickle smile. "Because winning the fight wasn't the point."

I stared. She couldn't be serious. "A distraction."

"Two of them." She had no right to look so proud of herself. "One to goad the Contessa into moving him, and another to give him a chance to scram while everyone was looking elsewhere."

Ой блять. "You idiot."

"It worked. I saw him climb out the window during the fight. And everyone was so busy watching us, there's no way they were paying attention to him."

"You mean you were watching him?" I scrubbed my hand down my face. She couldn't give her undivided attention to the most vicious dragon in Europe in the middle of a fight? She almost *died.* "Why?"

"Well, it would have been a really shitty way to die if he didn't make it out. I figured I should at least check."

"Why did you do it at all?"

"Because Meph had to get out of there."

"But you didn't have to go alone!" I snapped.

Arkay stared at me like I was an idiot. It only took me a few seconds to realize my mistake.

Yes, she did have to go alone. I had made that abundantly clear.

"So," she said after a long silence. "Why are you here?" There was a forced lightness to the tone as she attempted to change the subject. I accepted it gratefully.

"Terry told me you were asking about the doors," I said. "It wasn't difficult to determine where you were going."

"Not what I meant." She looked me in the eyes, her gaze flickering between them to avoid getting caught in my stare. "The Contessa offered you a job. So why are you playing nurse instead of getting fitted for a cocktail dress?"

What kind of question was that? "You were hurt. You could have died."

"So? You hate me."

I winced.

It hurt that she could think that about me.

It hurt worse that she wasn't wrong.

"Do you want me to take her offer?" I asked.

"You're not happy here." She let the fact hang in the air between us. Not an accusation, but permission.

I could get up right now and leave. Arkay would be fine, given a few more days. She could go back to the Hoarde and do her work, and the world would continue turning without me. I could go back to the Contessa, or back to Russia. I could live out the rest of my life without having to see ThreeClaw in Arkay's face.

But I didn't want that.

I lowered my eyes. "I lost the love of my life. It's going to take a while before I'm happy anywhere."

"You mean ThreeClaw?"

It was supposed to be a secret. We'd always been so careful to keep it quiet. "Is it that obvious?"

"You tried to kiss me, and apparently you have a habit of watching me sleep. So yeah. Fairly obvious."

I attempted to smile, but it fell flat.

"I'm not her," she said softly.

"I know." I heaved a sigh, and she echoed it with one of her own.

"You want to talk about it?"

I hesitated, confused by the offer. "Do you?"

She twitched her eyebrows in something reminiscent of a nod. "It's not like I brought a book to read."

It felt absurd even to think about it. This was a private matter. ThreeClaw had only ever told Quinn about our relationship, and only because he was her doctor. I never spoke a word about it to another soul.

Maybe that was part of the problem.

"It's a long story," I said.

"I don't have anywhere to be."

I sighed. This was a mistake.

I let it out before I could change my mind.

"I was seventeen the first time an Orderling tried to kill me. I had heard of them before that, but I always thought they were another exaggerated horror story to warn us away from the west. 'Don't complain about waiting in lines, солнышко,' our elders would tell us. 'Because in America, they don't have such a luxury. Over there, if you stand still too long, the Order will catch you.' Nobody really believed it. But when the USSR began to collapse, our borders became porous. Members of the Order slipped through and arrived in our country. But so did she."

Arkay didn't mention the reason for her leaving for two full days after that. Not until she was well enough to travel, and we were already on the road.

"We still need to find him," she announced with no warning as I was pulling onto the autobahn.

I checked the mirrors. We had barely left the safe house. I didn't want to turn back now. "Who?"

"Meph. I'm guessing he's halfway to Spain by now. But we need to find him before he gets himself abducted by anyone else. Seriously, the guy has the instincts of a soggy cracker."

I tightened my grip on the steering wheel. "That isn't going to happen, Arkay." I took a deep, hissing breath. I had managed to make it this long without getting into another shouting match. "You helped him escape, and that's… that's fine. Congratulations. But whatever… relationship you two had? It doesn't change who he is. He belongs to the Order."

"I know," she said. "That's why he needs help."

"Can you hear yourself when you speak?"

"I'm serious. Between their indoctrination and whatever the fuck the Contessa did to him, I'm amazed Meph still has brains left to scramble. He's a victim twice over, and he's got literally nobody on this fucking planet who cares if he lives or dies. So that's my job."

I tried to keep my voice controlled. "Or you could admit that the rest of the world might have a point."

"No. There's still some good in him."

I kept my eyes on the road. "Do you actually believe that?"

She hesitated. "I have to."

"Why?"

"I just do."

"Why?"

"Because it's hard." Arkay adjusted her seatbelt over her chest. "He took everything from me, Nadia. Absolutely everything. If there's one person in the world I have a reason to hate, it's him." She sank lower in her seat. "If I can find good in him, then I can find it in anyone."

I had no answer for that, and she made no effort to continue. We sat in silence while the miles rushed past.

It took almost a quarter hour before I gathered the nerve to ask again: "Why?"

"Because that's what Rosa did," she said softly. "It's the one thing she ever asked of me, but I don't know how, and she's not around to explain it to me anymore." She curled close against the window. "She'd want me to help him."

I kept my eyes on the road to keep from staring. I had seen her unconscious, paralyzed, and near dead. In another life, I had seen her in the throes of passion.

But I had never seen her vulnerable.

I swallowed. "It isn't that simple."

Arkay sighed. "Nadia, are you really—"

"It may astound you to hear it, but I do have the discipline not to kill an enemy combatant, or a rogue agent, or whatever you want to call him." My fingers tightened around the steering wheel. "But I cannot promise the same of all my subordinates. People don't volunteer for the Hoarde's combat teams without a reason. Every single one of our soldiers has lost friends. Family. Some of them have lost everything to the Order. If they find out you want to bring him in alive, and it isn't to rip his beating heart out of his chest, someone is going to have a problem with that. There's no chance you will succeed in bringing him in alive."

"What do you want me to do? Send him to a civilian therapist?" Her tone lost its edge. She was angry, but not with me. "The minute he starts ranting about dragons, they're gonna have him sedated. Which really sucks, because he's got combat training."

And the Order was wiretapping police all over the country. One report, and they would descend to silence their apostate.

Arkay banged her head against the window, and immediately yelped in pain.

"Careful," I said. "You're still healing."

She growled. "Well, I'm not just going to sit around and do nothing."

"Give me a moment," I said. "I'm thinking." And I continued thinking, while mountains rolled into valleys and folded back into mountains again. And finally, after hours of deliberation, I came up with an answer.

"A nemesis."

She jerked awake from a fitful doze. "Huh?"

"Declare him your nemesis, and nobody else will have the right to hurt him. It's an ancient law, and relatively obscure, but you're a dragon. You can get away with it."

"And that'll work?" she asked, childlike.

"It should." Unless the Contessa had already thought of it. Unless other organizations decided not to respect Arkay's claim. "It isn't a perfect solution, but it may keep him alive long enough for us to come up with something better."

Arkay's shoulders lost a tension I didn't even realize they had been holding, and she nestled into her corner to rest properly. "Thanks."

I nodded in reply.

I shouldn't give a damn. And, truthfully, I didn't. I personally could not care less about what happened to the little lost Orderling.

But Arkay did. And that meant it mattered.

Arkay

I tried not to fidget as I crossed the lobby at the Rehabilitation Institute of Chicago. It was a nice lobby, all wide open space and organic curves and enormous windows. It was a place of light.

She'd like that. I hoped she'd like that. I wanted her to like it.

I swallowed and stepped through the glass doors into the garden. Bright trees and emerald lawns stretched to the edge of the building, then dropped off to reveal a serene view of downtown Chicago, high enough over the city streets to escape the worst of the noise. A few people meandered down the garden paths, some walking, some in wheelchairs, but my stare gravitated to the woman who sat at the edge of the garden.

Dark curls framed a warm, earthy complexion and a nervous smile. Her shoulders were broad, strong enough to hold the weight of the world, but still soft enough to give the best hugs. She leaned against the green on bare arms, idly threading one hand through the grass. There were no marks on her. No scars, no calluses, no crescent zombie bites.

I took a deep breath. "Is this seat taken?"

She looked up, startled. "No, no, go ahead. I was just waiting for…" She hesitated. "Are you Arkay?"

"The one and only." I flashed a smile.

She tried to mirror it, but the expression didn't quite reach her eyes. Her brows furrowed as she stared at my face.

"Do you know me?" I asked quietly.

"I…" She looked into my eyes. "You were at the hospital. When I woke up. Kindra told me a little bit about you." This time, when she smiled, it strained with frustrated sympathy. "I'm sorry."

I swallowed. "Don't be. You're up and moving. That's more than enough."

Her shoulders curled with the awkward need to comfort me. "Were we close?"

For five years we were inseparable. We were best friends. We fought and killed and nearly died for each other.

You were everything to me.

"We only knew each other for a short time," I said. "You made one hell of an impression, though."

"Oh." She paused. "Thank you, I think."

"It was a good impression."

She answered me with another half-finished smile.

"But that's not what you want to hear," I inferred.

"No, it's fine," she said. "I appreciate it. I do."

"But you get that a lot."

She bowed her head. "Kind of, yeah. Is that awful?"

"Not at all." I sat down beside her. "A bunch of complete strangers have all these expectations about who you are and what you'll do, and you don't know the first thing about them. That's a lot of pressure to put on anyone."

She sighed. "They're not strangers, though. They're friends. They love me, and I don't even know who I am. And the person they keep describing, the kinds of things they think I did or said, I don't think I can do that. I don't know if I want to."

I took her hand in mine. "That's okay. You don't have to be the person you used to be. Just try to figure out who you are now. Do what feels right to you. You've got good instincts."

"And what if I don't have good instincts anymore?" she asked with a sardonic smile, and I returned it with one of my own.

"Then I guess that's one more thing you know about yourself."

The Contessa

I reclined across the drawing room chaise while gentle hands worked ointment into my skin. Most of the injuries had healed rather nicely, leaving behind nothing but a faint lightness to show that the skin had ever been broken. I couldn't say as much about my shoulder. The little mud-crawler's fangs had penetrated deep, and the tissue closest to those teeth was ripped and burned beyond repair.

There were decisions to be made regarding my wardrobe, whether I would cover the scars or accentuate their asymmetry.

But later. For now, I had other business to attend.

My darling Safi waited on the other side of the drawing room door, his sultry voice turned coarse while he shouted on the phone. A few barks made it through the door: "For the last time, my name is Valentin Fabre. My ID number is R12-3477. My instructions were to report my findings directly to the Archduchess—no, it can't wait. This is a matter of utmost importance!"

My eyes fluttered shut as he continued fighting his battles, and I went back to enjoying the affections of my caretakers.

Finally the door opened and Safi stepped inside, sinking to his knees at my feet.

"She's ready for you, my lady." He bowed his head and extended the phone to me with both hands.

I leaned forward to cup his cheek, ignoring the ache of my broken ribs. "My darling Safi. Always so very clever."

He exhaled softly and shifted, daring to lean his lips closer to my hand.

He would be fully rewarded later. He'd risked so very much to catch me another Orderling so soon after I lost my last. And this one was still a full member of the Order.

Or at least, he was. Shortly, the remains of the real Valentin Fabre would be fertilizing the rose bushes.

I took the phone from him and brought it to my ear, dismissing Safi and the rest of my staff with a nod.

The phone clicked as the call was transferred.

"What do you have to report?" came a familiar voice, high and graveled from ages of use.

I smiled. "Only that you'll live to regret it if you hang up on me again."

She answered with a sharp intake of breath.

"Hello, Gianna," I purred. "I'm sure you're very busy. It's been so very difficult to get a hold of you lately."

She made a valiant effort at sounding courageous. "I've told you, we're finished. I don't want anything to do with you."

I feigned hurt. "My dear Gianna, you insult me—and after all we've shared."

"I said we're through." There was hesitation in her voice, and it brought a smile to my face. She never could resist my charms for long.

"But I've done you a favor. Call it a gift."

Her breath caught. "No. No, I don't want it."

"How unfortunate, then, that it's already done. Adam Preston is going to attempt to sneak into the United States. I want you to make sure he succeeds."

"Preston?" I could hear the frown in her voice. "Why?"

I lounged back, tracing a finger idly around the scar on my shoulder. "Because ThreeClaw's Hoarde has finally found itself a new dragon, my pet. And your lost lamb is going to kill her for me."

The Urban Dragon series will conclude in Volume 3

345

Acknowledgements

Tanya Poliakov, who gave me her passion, enthusiasm, and beautiful drawings.

Stacy Simpkins, who gifted me with encouragement and stories that were at times sweet, scary, sexy, and hilarious (and sometimes all of them at once).

Angie Sandro, who offered me invaluable advice.

EF Jace, who let me bounce my ridiculous ideas off her.

TJ Loveless, who gave me the push I needed.

Jackie Knake, who has a gift for inspiration and honesty.

Jishan Qiu, whose comments always made me smile.

And **Andrew Troemner**, who is my light in the dark.

Thank you so much. All of you mean the world to me.

About the Author

JW Troemner was born in Germany and immigrated to the United States, where she lives with her partner in a house full of pets. Most days she can be found gazing longingly at sinkholes and abandoned buildings.